To Damaris

Thanks for everything

Best wishes
Martin

Martin

THE CHRONICLES OF MARCO THE ZOMBIE: BOOK 1

BETTER OFF DEAD

A tale with heart!

(...and some other bits...)

MARTIN JOHN

First edition: February 2021

Published by Martin John.

ISBN: 978-1-8380471-2-2

Editor: Sophie Cole

Cover illustration: Yeysson Bellaiza

Cover design and interior formatting: Mark Thomas / Coverness.com

For Robin, the best brother a guy could have
and for Markus, my brother from another mother.
I love you both.

With special thanks to Donald,
who guided me throughout the entire process of writing this book.

Prologue

Better off Dead

I stared out of the window, watching the desolate landscape zip by in the darkness beneath us, and wondered how many people would try to kill me tonight.

To make matters worse, I wasn't entirely convinced that my travel companions wouldn't also take a crack at it. I caught a glimpse of my reflection in the glass and quickly turned away. Who could blame them if they tried. Not that I was looking forward to being killed, considering how crappy it had worked out for me the first time around. Quite the opposite – I was more scared than I'd ever been in my entire life. Scared without actually *feeling* scared, if you know what I mean.

You see, fear for me now was like a painting with all the color drained from it. My palms weren't clammy, my pulse wasn't racing, my mouth wasn't parched (or at least no more than normal), and my heart sure as hell wasn't racing. All the same, if you showed someone a black and white picture of the Mona Lisa, they'd still be able to recognize it for what it is. I didn't need my body's accompanying symptoms to confirm what my brain already knew - I was scared witless.

In less than thirty minutes, people were going to try and kill me. Sure, they may actually do me a favor by ending my miserable existence, but I wasn't pitching a tent to find out. There's a whole world of difference between knowing you'd be better off dead and jumping on board the train to Deadsville.

I glanced around, at the Marines sitting opposite and either side of me, for signs of fear. None! They were too relaxed, every last one of them. It was unnerving. Even Paxon Word, possibly the world's puniest Marine, was chewing on a Hershey bar as casually as if he was just sitting in a park.

The truth of the matter though, was that we were not in a park. No sir. We were in a modified Sikorsky Black Hawk Helicopter, explicitly designed for troops who, for whatever reason, needed to be transported behind enemy lines in the dead of night, as undetectable as ghosts.

This was not my idea of a fun time.

We had been running dark and hugging the ground for the last twenty minutes or so. Or, to put it more accurately, the rotor blades were making about as much noise as a mouse fart, and the only lights were in what we called the 'holding pen.' This was where those who were about to jump out of this perfectly safe helicopter, sat strapped to what must be the most uncomfortable seats in the world. Now, the term 'light' was a bit of an exaggeration, seeing as it was just a dull, red bulb that bathed the pen in a crimson glow. You could probably get more illumination from a clown's nose.

The helicopter banked unexpectedly, causing my head to flick sideways and my helmet to make a dull 'dong' sound against its hull. Sniggers and chuckles sounded in the obscurity. A few Marines shook their heads and looked away from me in disdain.

I tried to laugh it off with a smile but stopped when I realized how utterly ridiculous I must look. Smiling nowadays didn't do a lot to improve my appearance.

Word, sitting on my right, licked the last of the Hershey bar from his fingers. I found myself staring longingly. I couldn't even remember the taste of chocolate. Come to think of it; few flavors made sense to me anymore. I could, however, remember what it used to taste like if I bit my lip or sucked the blood from a cut on my finger. Compared to that salty, coppery tang, the distant memory of chocolate seemed pale and sad.

Why was blood the only thing I could remember the taste of? Oh, and on rare occasions, marshmallows.

What seemed like a million miles away, someone was asking, "What did you do before signing up for this?"

I tried to remember; how long had it been since I had eaten anything?

"Eh, Net-Head! I'm talking to you!"

I snapped back into reality, "Huh? Sorry. What?"

It was Jackson Cole who had rudely awoken me from my

day-dream. If Paxon Word was the smallest Marine in the world, then Jackson was most certainly the biggest. He stood just shy of seven-foot with muscles that looked like they had been produced in a nuclear power plant. Jackson had grown up on Detroit's rough streets and had managed to get a full football scholarship to Michigan State. He had been on his way to the big leagues until he threw his shoulder out his first season. His football career imploded and his face did little to hide the fact he had been pissed about it ever since.

He leaned towards me, his massive frame pushing against the safety harness holding him in his seat. "What… did… you… do… for… a… living?"

"I worked at Ed's Burger Bar." Even as the words came out of my mouth, the ghost of what used to be my dignity was trying to reel them back in. But it was too late.

This time, sniggers were promoted to full-blown laughs, and heads shook in disbelief. Even mine! I could have said something cool like Secret Agent, or Soccer Pro. But no! I had to confess to the most formidable bunch of SOB's I had ever met that the worst danger I'd faced before this was dodging hot burger fat.

I turned away and looked straight into the face of August Sanchez. He just shook his head in sympathy and said, "Man, it must just suck to be you."

But Jackson hadn't finished with me yet, "How many night drops have you done?"

Again, the words slipped out of my mouth without

consulting my brain, "This is my first."

The laughs that followed – they were with me, not *at* me, weren't they?

Welcome to the wonderful world of Denial, sir. If I could check your luggage for any sign of Dignity, Poise, or Pride before you continue?

Jackson pressed on. "So, how many actual combat situations have you been in?"

"None." Oh, somebody, please staple my mouth shut!

Thank you, sir; there seems to be no sign of that contraband in your luggage. Now, if you could just proceed through the door on your left. Yes, sir, the one which reads Looooserrr!

"What?" Jackson said. "Net-Head, are you tryin' to tell me that this is your first hostile mission?"

I clamped my mouth shut, determined not to let it embarrass me further. Unfortunately, this did not stop my head from nodding in the affirmative.

Jackson leaned closer to me, his safety harness creaking under the pressure. "Under normal circumstances, I'd tell you to keep your head down and follow our lead. But I guess that's not why you're here now, is it, Net-Head?" He grinned sardonically.

"No. No, it's not", I replied. Far from it, in fact.

The noise of the engine dropped by a couple of decibels, sounding less urgent. The helicopter was slowing down.

The co-pilot swiveled in his seat. "Approaching DZ alpha," he said.

Staff Sergeant Ballantine, directly behind the co-pilot, turned to address us. The Sarge was in his mid-fifties with skin that looked tough enough to make a decent canoe. He ran a hand through his short-cropped, bone-white hair and glared at us.

"Okay, Marines, we've got a job to do," he yelled. "After we drop the forward scout at Alpha, we'll fly half a click further on to DZ Beta and rendezvous with Phoenix White squad. From there, both squads will travel on foot to DZ Alpha and rendezvous with the forward scouts. Jackson will lead Red squad and Corporal Loomis will lead White squad. Any questions?"

"No, Sarge!" the Marines chanted in unison.

The helicopter came to a halt, hovering about four hundred feet off the ground. "DZ Alpha reached," the pilot said.

Sergeant Ballantine pointed a finger at me. "You're up."

Yes, I am. About four hundred feet up, to be precise.

Word reached over and unbuckled my belt, Jackson opened the chopper door and cool night air rushed in.

The Marines looked at me, eyeing the open door and making motioning gestures towards it with their heads.

Wait! What? Are you freaking kidding me? We're still in the air.

My hands were shaking as I frantically checked over my equipment again, looking for a parachute or maybe a rope that I could use to abseil safely to the ground - no such luck.

Sergeant Ballantine was glaring at me with eyes that could boil water at a distance of fifty feet.

"What the hell are you are doing?" he hollered over the rushing wind, so loud that, even if the enemies on the ground couldn't hear the helicopter, I was pretty sure they could hear *him*. I could imagine them looking up at the night sky and asking, "Did you hear that, José? Did God just ask me what the hell I was doing?"

"Er.. aren't you going to land first," I stammered.

"What the hell are you talking about? Why would we land?"

"I don't seem to have a parachute or rope to propel down with." I motioned towards my equipment to prove there was no such gear to be seen. I even offered an apologetic smile. "See?"

The Sarge thrust his face within two inches of mine and bellowed: "You don't need them, you pathetic worm. You're already dead!"

Oh yeah, thanks for reminding me.

"Now, get your zombie ass off my goddamned chopper!" Sergeant Ballantine motioned to Jackson, who, with one tree trunk sized arm, grabbed me and threw me out the door.

Suddenly I was sailing out into the empty air, freefalling, arms flailing, legs kicking, tumbling over and over. The chopper above me was getting smaller and smaller.

Eventually, I was able to right myself, arms and legs spread-eagled, hoping it would slow my descent. The air buffeted me as if it were traveling at a million miles per hour. Something was flapping in my face obscuring the vision of my left eye, and the wind rushing upwards was causing it to flick and snap uncontrollably.

I gripped the offending object between my thumb and forefinger and pulled it from my face. Whatever it was, it was stuck pretty tight as it took a solid tug to pry it free. Now that it was loose, I looked at the wildly flapping object in my hand. What was that? Paper? A piece of material? Leather...? Oh no! I got a sinking feeling and brought my other hand to my face to confirm my suspicion.

Yup, I was right. Clutched between my thumb and forefinger was the skin that seconds before had covered my left cheekbone. *Well, isn't that just terrific?*

I wondered how many other parts of me would drop off before I was no longer able to function. Would I have people running up to me saying: *"Sorry, buddy, but is that your hand on the ground?"* How much of me would be gone before the military decided I was no longer of use and tossed me into a furnace?

The reality of being undead finally hit home. This is what the future had in store for me. I would no longer heal cuts, breaks, bruises or bullet wounds. I would simply get more and more battered, decayed, and broken as the years went by. If I thought I looked terrible this morning, wait until tomorrow because today was the best I would ever look again.

I thought of August Sanchez looking at me in sympathy. *Man, it must just suck to be you.*

"Really? Ya think!" I yelled up at the helicopter he was still safely aboard, brandishing the strip of my cheek as if it were a train ticket.

But he was right. It truly did suck to be me. How had this happened? What was I thinking, signing over my body to Batoltech Global? I honestly had no idea it would be like this. Had I had an inkling, I would never have signed that stupid piece of paper. I would have let them bury me instead. I would have been better off dead.

Oh, and here comes the ground. Brilliant. Just brill...

FWUMP!!!

Bounce.

Thud, thud!

Sigh.

PART ONE

Book of the Dead

Zombies 101

You might be wondering how I got into this situation, so I will enlighten you. However, first, I should explain how Zombies came into being. Some of what I will tell you is general knowledge. Some of it is not. So much so that it is probably locked away in top-secret, classified files.

So how does a simple burger-flipper like me know it? Mr. Marshmallow, that's how. Most of the stuff he tells me would have been of zero interest to me when I was alive. To be honest, I'm no more interested in it now that I'm dead. I don't even know why he tells me this stuff. But he has made two things perfectly clear; first, somehow, this information is essential to my future survival. Second, if my creators discovered what I know, they'd destroy me.

Who is Mr. Marshmallow? Well, I'll get to that later. For now, let's talk zombies.

I will start with what we are not. Zombies are not the result of a voodoo curse, chemical spill, disease concocted in a super-secret lab, and hell did not become overcrowded and decide to send back all its dead – sorry, George Romero.

The truth is, teeny, tiny microscopic robots, also called nanobots, were to blame for the hell I was now in.

They were invented by Tiberius Farnsworth Bundy (TF Bundy to his pals). Now in TF's defense, he had no idea his little creations would result in flesh-hungry, mindless corpses coming back to life (or any of the other horrors these little suckers were responsible for). He was simply trying to help humankind live longer, healthier lives. D'you know how they say the road to hell is paved with good intentions? Well, TF Bundy must have had his very own super-highway, complete with gas stations, overpasses and highway patrol.

The nanobots originally had an extremely simple purpose – find and eliminate any virus or harmful bacteria within the human body. Their secondary function was to assist the healing process of any injury suffered by the host.

A small syringe full of nanobots (millions, to be precise) would be injected into the host. They would then be distributed via the bloodstream to every part of the body. Additionally, a tiny control center about the size of a pea (more commonly referred to as Neural Personal Control Pod – or NPC pod) would be surgically implanted into the back of the skull. It would receive medical data from the nanobots, such as the host's heart rate, blood pressure, cholesterol levels and what bacteria, viruses and other nasties were floating around. This NPC pod would then instruct the bots on how to respond – usually, "Locate and destroy! Right now!"

This NPC pod would send information about its host to a

central computer system based in TF Bundy's corporate labs, affectionately known as The Boris. The Boris would collect the data and relay it to a medical team. Additionally, if one NPC pod encountered something unusual, such as a parasitic insect or other foreign body, The Boris would research the anomalies. The best course of action would be transmitted to not only that NPC pod but to all of them, just in case they encountered a similar issue.

In short, anyone injected with nanobots would have their very own personal robotic army inside them, ready to kick the butt of anything trying to cause them harm. Orders on how to fight the battles would be received from their General (the NPC pod). Information on how well the battles went would be sent to the Commander in Chief (The Boris). Simple. However, as with all simple things, something is bound to go wrong sooner or later.

Original test trials showed that Bundy's nanobots worked exceptionally well. They improved healing rates by up to seventy-five percent and made the host virtually immune to all types of disease, including cancer.

After just six months of trials, TF's nanobots got the green light for sale to the public. In hindsight giving the trial another six months might not have been a bad idea.

Though TF Bundy's invention was eagerly awaited and well-received, it was not cheap. To be injected with Bundy's cure-all would cost about fifteen million dollars. Meaning only the super-rich could afford it. Those that could afford it were quick to hand over the cash.

Within one year, nanobots had been injected into over five hundred thousand pop stars, actors, oil tycoons, business moguls and Kardashians. Almost overnight, TF Bundy became one of the richest men on the planet and his company, NANOMED, was the number one company to invest in.

However, they say that all good things must come to an end. NANOMED and its meteoric success was no exception to this rule. And, just as David brought down Goliath with a simple stone, what brought down NANOMED was nothing more than an ingrown hair and a twisted toenail.

Sometime after being injected with the nanobots, Patient Zero, who was never identified, discovered an ingrown hair on the back of his leg. After some time of neglect and much scratching, the follicle became infected. Nothing serious as yet, and the nanobots were quickly able to sort the problem out. However, Patient Zero was also a chewer of fingernails and toenails. As often happens when you chew nails to the quick, infections occur. Again nothing that our little nanobots could not sort out.

After the second time that bots were sent to deal with an infection from a bitten nail and ingrown hair, the NPC pods concluded that the real enemy were hair and nails. After all, without them, the infections would not have occurred. They asked The Boris for advice, and it concurred, "To prevent further such infections, eliminate the cause – destroy all hair and nails." The Boris communicated the kill order to all NPC pods in every single host, and the nanobots were quick to carry out those orders.

Within hours of the download update, the hosts started losing clumps of hair. Nails came loose and fell off. Within twenty-four hours, no one injected with nanobots had a hair left on their body – including eyelashes and eyebrows. Even nostrils became bald.

The fun did not stop there. The Boris was smart enough to realize that, without hair, people had dangerously little protection from the sun, thus increasing the chance of sunstroke, sunburn, and melanoma. To counter this new set of base conditions, it told every NPC pod to assign a portion of their nanobots to stimulate the host's pain receptors whenever they went out in bright sunlight. Although no physical harm would come to the host, it would become excruciatingly painful for them to go out on a sunny day.

Just as things got about as bad as people thought they could, The Boris played its final ace. After researching high cholesterol and diabetes, it decided that obesity was just like any other disease that had to be fought. And so, it ordered the NPC pods to send their nanobots to work on fat cells. They ate virtually every single one until only the bare minimum were left, just enough to sustain a human body. No matter how much the host ate or sat around doing nothing, the pounds kept on shedding until they were skin and bones.

Overnight, every rich, powerful and influential person on the planet looked like a walking corpse, devoid of hair, nails, or color. It was not long until the media coined the name that would stick from that day onwards; Gaunts.

The Gaunts were less than amused at the predicament Bundy had put them in. When it was discovered that removal of the nanobots would not reverse the damage they had caused, outrage and lawsuits followed. Poor old TF Bundy and NANOMED were ruined. Everything TF had earned was paid out in damages to the victims and lawyers' fees, leaving him broke and facing a lengthy prison sentence.

But Bundy was not a callous or evil man, and he could see how many lives he had ruined. As far as he was concerned, prison was where he belonged.

However, prison was not to be his fate. At the final hour, he was reluctantly saved by one of the few wealthy and powerful businessmen who had not been injected with TF's nanobots. That man was Anton Batolgore, CEO of Batoltech Global, the largest independent supplier of military technology and weapons to most of the Western world. And, some speculated, to their enemies as well.

Anton saw potential in TF Bundy's invention and felt it needed additional exploitation. However, for that, he needed not only the invention but Bundy himself. So he used his political leverage and connections to save Bundy from prison and take control of NANOMED.

He gave Bundy unlimited funds to find a cure for the Gaunt condition and new ways the nanobots could be used. All the while, behind closed steel doors, Batolgore's researchers tinkered with Bundy's little creations with the aim of turning them into a weapon.

However, it was Bundy himself who would inadvertently hand them the weapon they were looking for.

Dawn of the Dead-Heads

Over the next three years, thousands of Gaunts elected to have their nanobots and NPC pods removed. Others held onto them, hoping that under new leadership, NANOMED would find a cure for their condition.

This left Batoltech Global with warehouses full of redundant NPC pods, trillions of nanobots, and under increasing pressure from shareholders to shift this stock.

Despite the hiring of the brightest in the field of nanotechnology, it was TF Bundy himself who discovered a new use for his nanobots. They could be used to help paralyzed people walk again.

The concept was fairly straightforward. When a person is paralyzed, their brain can only transmit signals down the spinal cord to the point where it had been damaged or severed. The nervous system on the other side of the break cannot receive those signals and cannot carry out the brain's orders, such as; stand, walk, pick up that book, scratch my nose, *for God's sake, please scratch my nose!*

Bundy's newly programmed nanobots would attach themselves to both sides of the damaged spinal cord. When the brain sent a message down the spine, the nanobots at the break would receive it and transmit it to the nanobots waiting on the other side, which would carry the signal to the rest of the body. In short, they would create a complete circuit allowing the victim to control their body normally as if their spine had never been broken.

Anton was reluctant to unleash the nanobots upon the public again (if not attached to the end of a missile, at least). However, since he had had little success weaponizing them and was eager to see some financial returns on his investment, he allowed Bundy to test his theory.

After a few successful experiments on lab rats, his theory proved to be sound. If the lab technicians had not incinerated the rats when their experiments were concluded, they may have discovered the nanobots could do more than just help paralyzed people walk again.

Eager not to make the same mistakes as last time, Anton and Bundy thought it best to ensure that the nanobots did not get too smart and start thinking for themselves. As such, the NPC pods, which were now surgically implanted at the base of the skull, were no longer uplinked to The Boris. It was believed that The Boris was destroyed, though rumors have persisted that it is hidden somewhere deep within Batoltech vaults.

Removing the uplinks meant that the NPC pods could

no longer receive harmful information or updates from an external source.

Lastly, the NPC pods were given a default, single offline command – keep signals from the brain running to the rest of the body regardless of the circumstances.

Nope, Bundy was not going to make the same mistakes again. Instead, he embarked on series of brand new ones.

*

Finally, the day came when NANOMED announced its new invention (or the same invention repackaged) to the world.

Understandibly, people were reluctant to get themselves injected with Bundy's bots. Independent medical research facilities and what was once known as FDA (US Food and Drug Administration) – but after Bundy's last fiasco changed their name to FD&NA (US Food, Drug, and Nanobot Administration) – scrutinized the nanobots themselves.

After hundreds of tests on living subjects, mostly rats, a few dogs and a monkey called Karl, they conceded that the new and improved nanobots did what Bundy said they would do. Again, if it were not for the protocol insisting that lab animals be incinerated on death, they would have discovered that the bots continued to function after their host's death. "Keep the signal going regardless of circumstances."

FD&NA approval was finally given for NANOMED to inject the first of its new batch of victims... umm, patients, with the nanobots.

However, this time the price tag was much lower, at around one and a half million dollars, because fewer nanobots were required and there being no need for constant updates. Moreover, NANOMED had a buttload of stock that needed to be utilized.

Initially, fewer clients were willing to try the 'new' nanobots. After the first year, only around ten thousand people had undergone the procedure and none appeared to suffer from side effects. That was until Arthur MacInley died, and then it all hit the fan.

*

After making a tidy fortune in small commodities trading, Arthur McInley retired when he hit forty to spend more time with his family and enjoy life. He was well respected in his neighborhood and known for his philanthropy.

When, in a car accident, he lost the use of his legs, the local community rallied around him. He was just the kind of guy you wanted to do things for. All-in-all, Arthur was a stand-up kind of guy. So, when he got injected with the nanobots, everyone was thrilled to see him actually stand up again. They were, however, less than happy to see him stand up after he died.

On a bright sunny day in July, Arthur died in his garden of a massive coronary. When his lifeless body collapsed to the ground, the nanobots inside him had no idea what had happened. All they knew was that the signals from the brain had stopped. This contravened their default order: Keep the signals from the brain going, regardless of the circumstances.

It took the NPC pod in Arthur's skull and the nanobots a little time to figure out what was going on, but it appeared to them that the signal had been cut off from the source – the brain. So nanobots moved to the brain and started firing off small electrical impulses trying to re-establish the signal. To some degree, it worked. The electrical impulses from the nanobots were able to get a portion of Arthur's brain working again. But it was the part that had the most basic of animal instincts – kill and eat.

And so it was that on this bright sunny day in July, the lifeless corpse of Arthur, the all-round nice guy, got back up off the ground and proceeded to eat his entire family.

Fortunately, the family cleaner, Betty, was able to make a panicked 911 before getting her throat torn out.

When the police cars screeched to a halt, sirens wailing and lights flashing, Arthur, covered in blood and gore, shambled towards the police (or food as I guess he would have referred to them), oblivious to their orders to 'halt and get down on the ground.' In the chaos and hail of bullets that followed, one caught Arthur in the brainpan and he collapsed, dead, for a second time.

At first, nobody knew what the hell had happened and what caused Arthur to go homicidal. The toxicology reports came back negative. Since the cause of death seemed obvious, the County Coroner's official statement said that Arthur died from multiple gunshot wounds.

It was TF Bundy who figured it out. Still paranoid after the previous disaster caused by the nanobots, he kept a close eye on all the patients injected with the new batch. When he heard about Arthur, he started to hypothesize what may have happened.

Not wanting to cause panic over his suspicions, he kept this information to himself. Only when the second of his patients died in a rock-climbing accident, then ate the paramedics called to the scene, were TF's suspicions confirmed.

Although terrified of Anton's response to the news, he was the first person Bundy told about nanobots bringing the dead back to life. Bundy laid out all the evidence and even admitted to conducting experiments on a couple of rats, with identical outcomes.

Oddly, Anton did not fly into a fit of rage or threaten to throw Bundy to the wolves. Instead, the ice-cold, usually scowling face of Anton Batolgore seemed to light up for the first time in the seven years that Bundy had known him.

He simply said: "Don't worry. Why don't you take a vacation. I'll take care of this."

And take care of it he did. The incidents were covered up. All existing patients were given a complimentary upgrade and asked to sign a new contract that had additional clauses hidden in the small print like; 'Nanobots may continue to function after your death' and 'NANOMED, a division of Batoltech Global, is not liable for any damages, injury or death caused by your reanimated remains.'

You would be amazed how few people read the small print.

In reality, the free upgrade was a chip that monitored the patient's vitals and sent a signal to a *special* division of NANOMED the moment they flatlined. This term was preferred since using words such as died, expired, or shuffled-off-this-mortal-coil gives one the impression that they were going to stay dead. The chip also acted as a GPS, so the whereabouts of the target was always known.

The moment a patient died, a specialist team was sent to the scene to 'retrieve company assets' before too much damage could be caused. Not surprisingly, any witnesses were bought off or threatened into silence. Those that could not also suffered 'tragic accidents' shortly afterward.

That is how it went for quite some time. Now and then a patient would die, the clean-up crew would be dispatched, and Joe Public was none the wiser.

All this time, Anton was receiving fresh corpses, mostly folk who had left their bodies to medical science, shipped to the deepest, most secret labs within his global organization.

When a body arrived at NANOMED it was retrofitted with an NPC pod, injected with Nanobots and then resurrected as a zombie. Each zombie was then classed as a 'Project' and given a number. For example, I am Project 2219. Each Project was assigned a list of experiments and modifications, all overseen by their assigned Project Leader.

Experiments on the undead went from the mundane to the outlandish. You see, the thing about being dead already is, you can take an awful lot of punishment. Some had blades grafted onto them to make them more efficient killers. Others had a form of resin injected into their bones to make them virtually indestructible. To name just some of the experiments dreamt up by Anton's very own team of Doctor Frankensteins.

However, one problem remained. Anton could see the benefit of dropping a box of unstoppable killing machines behind enemy lines. But zombies (the official term, he had been informed) were uncontrollable, mindless liabilities, incapable of reasoning or learning battle strategy, and devoid of even the most basic common sense. They were so stupid that the scientists working on them had started to refer to them as Dead-Heads – because the head seemed to be the only part not brought back to life.

Dead-Heads were probably how they would have remained if not for the death of Charles Simkins, who changed everything!

Day of the Living Net-Heads

Charles Simkins wasn't the most responsible of guys. Though well into his fifties, in his mind he was only thirty, so now that he had earned all the money he would ever need, he was going to enjoy life to the full.

He owned several companies but was more than happy to let other people run them for him. Sitting in stuffy boardrooms discussing business plans and financial budgets were never his idea of fun. He would much rather be sailing, or skiing somewhere on the Aspen slopes. It was one such fateful skiing vacation that resulted in Charles being injected with Bundy's nanobots.

Charles may have been a pretty proficient skier, but he was not the most observant individual. He frequently wandered off into his imagination instead of paying attention to what was going on around him. That, coupled with getting distracted by anything shinier than a bottle cap, meant that his fate was sealed. It also meant that when someone shouted, "Mind that tree!" all Charles managed to say before colliding with it at thirty-five-miles per hour was: "Huh? What tr...?" CRUNCH!

The accident not only left Charles paralyzed from the neck down, but it also caved in his skull so severely that part of it had to be replaced with a four-inch titanium plate.

However, thanks to NANOMED, it was not long before he was walking again.

He was so happy about the turn of events, he did not even stop to ask why he got a free upgrade four months later, nor why he had to sign a new contract absolving NANOMED of any liability *after* his death.

Now, at this point, I would love to tell you that Charles had learned from his mistake and became more observant. I would love to tell you he did not drift into his fantasy world when doing things like attaching Christmas lights to the roof of his house. I would like to say that he was more mindful of his surroundings as one usually would be at the top of an unsecured ladder. Lastly, I wish I could tell you that he no longer got easily distracted by things, such as a yoyo that had been thrown into his roof's guttering a few years previous by the neighbor's kid.

But I guess if I could tell you all these things, then Charles would not have completely forgotten he was twenty-five feet off the ground holding onto nothing but a roll of Christmas lights. He also would not have said, "Ooh, what a pretty yoyo," and overreached for it. He also would not have fallen to the ground, impaling himself on a 'Santa Stop Here' signpost he had hammered into his lawn just minutes before.

Alan Hooper was the *Specialist Unit Leader* when the signal from Charles's NPC pod was received to say he had flatlined. Hooper was a fifteen-year Navy Seal veteran and as hard as they come. Hardly an inch of his body did not have some sort of scar acquired over an illustrious career. When asked if he shaved his head to hide his grey hair, he replied: "Nope. I do it to show off my scars. I earned every last one of 'em!" With that, his steely blue eyes sparkled, and he flashed something that was more reminiscent of a snarl than a smile (but those who knew Hooper knew it was as close to a smile as his facial muscles could muster).

After a grenade blast took two fingers from his left hand, he was forced to retire, but not without a fight. His argument, that he did not need those fingers to kill a man, fell on deaf ears, and cold-cocking the Admiral presiding over the hearing didn't help his case. At this point he was left with a choice; retire with his honor intact or be court-martialed. Begrudgingly, Hooper accepted the honorable discharge.

Not long after this he found himself in the employ of Anton Batolgore. He was recruited to head up what everyone on the outside referred to as NANOMED's Specialist Unit but which members of the team, including Hooper himself, referred to as Undertakers.

During his time as an Undertaker, Hooper encountered just about everything he thought this job could throw at him. In the best-case scenario, he would arrive on the scene to find a single mindless, reanimated corpse lunging at him or his team, trying to eat their brains. These jobs he liked. They were quiet, quick, and easy to control.

The worst-case scenario, on the other hand, was a completely different story. This usually involved large quantities of blood and carnage, lots of eyewitnesses, cops, panic, and general mayhem. Hooper was no fan of these scenarios. But he was prepared for them. He thought he was prepared for everything. That was, until he met Charles Simkins.

Less than twenty minutes had passed between Hooper's team getting the call and arriving, armed and ready for action, on Charles's front doorstep.

Cautiously, Hooper tried the front door. It was locked. He glanced through the lounge window a little to his left and saw Charles's wife sitting on the couch with her arms protectively wrapped around her two children. They were all staring wide-eyed at something outside his view. Although unable see, Hooper had a pretty good idea what they were looking at: the undead Charles. But why hadn't he eaten them?

Hooper motioned to the four Undertakers behind him to get ready. They raised their guns and pointed them at the door.

Hooper knew noises distracted zombies. He rang the doorbell twice. If he heard pounding on the other side of the door, he and his team would open fire and obliterate the walking corpse formally known as Mr. Simkins.

The door opened. What stood there caused the usually unshakeable Hooper to stand stock still, his jaw open.

When you get to a scene of a zombie resurrection, you expect to see certain things: blood, dead bodies, some chaos, and possibly News vans. Hooper knew this all too well. However, when the door opened, the last thing he expected to see was Charles Simkins holding, squished between a hotdog bun, the family's now very dead miniature dachshund. He simply looked at Hooper and his team as if to say, "Can I help you?" before lifting the canine-filled bun to his mouth.

When Hooper finally grasped what he was looking at, he slowly motioned to his team not to shoot.

Being able to open a door, and having enough awareness to believe a sausage dog belonged in a hot dog bun, may not make you smart by human standards. However, this action made Charles Simkins the freaking Stephen Hawkins, Albert Einstein, and Steve Jobs of the Zombie world. When you add the fact that Charles had not eaten his family, Hooper knew he had something unusual which should not be eliminated.

Instead, he and his team restrained, secured, and bundled the now very annoyed Charles into their van and drove him straight to a NANOMED secret research facility to be studied.

Charles's family would later be told he had suffered a psychotic breakdown and had died later that day of a brain hemorrhage. I guess they bought it.

As it turned out, making pet sandwiches and opening doors were not Charles's only talents. After considerable testing, it appeared he was also able to operate light switches, turn on the TV and play Whack-A-Mole. Sadly, he still got distracted by shiny things and quickly lost interest, so testing was slow going.

While impressed by Charles's rudimentary reasoning, the boffins at NANOMED were stumped as to why he had retained some semblance of intelligence. Had the nanobots adapted? Had the NPC pod malfunctioned? Was there something unusual about Charles's genetic make-up or brain that caused it to function the way it did after death?

As it turned out, it was none of these things. After weeks of scans, probes, and blood tests, the scientists at NANOMED were no closer to an answer. So they decided the only option was to remove the brain and analyze it more closely. During this procedure they stumbled across the answer to their questions: the four-inch titanium plate in Charles's skull.

Charles had been strapped by his arms, legs, torso and head to a gurney when the scientists started to open up his skull. After all, it is not as if you can give a zombie a local anesthetic, so securing them is essential.

The moment the titanium plate was removed, Charles went crazy. He thrashed against his bindings and bit anyone who came near him. At this moment the scientists finally put the pieces of the puzzle together.

When Charles had died, the NPC pod had upped its electrical output, as had the nanobots trying to re-establish signals from the brain to the spinal column. The metal plate in his skull conducted the electrical pulse to other parts of his brain, thus amplifying the NPC pod's signal, making Charles smarter than your average Dead-Head.

Armed with this information, the scientists at NANOMED

were soon able to create a sophisticated metallic mesh that covered the subject's brain and fed impulses to every part of it from the NPC pod. With this, zombies were created that were *almost* as smart as when they were alive.

Thus were the born the Net-Heads.

Who Let the Dead Cat Out of the Bag?

Though Net-Heads were seen as the next step in zombie evolution, there is a lot to be said for the classic, mindless, flesh-eating zombie, or Dead-Head as they are affectionately known.

For example, after being brought back to life, a Dead-Head doesn't spend the vast majority of its waking day yelling about human rights. A Dead-Head doesn't accuse the employees of NANOMED of being soulless monsters, amongst other things. Nor do they know how to use guns, pick locks, over-ride computer safety protocols, disable security cameras, or steal cell phones so they can call home and tell Mom they are still alive. Wow, can you imagine getting *that* call?

Yup, NANOMED employees had learned what it meant to be on their toes every minute of every day since the birth of Net-Heads. But, despite some close calls and a few employee deaths, written up as 'Industrial Accidents,' not a single Net-Head managed to escape and alert the outside world as to what

NANOMED and Batoltech Global were up to.

As it turns out, they didn't need to. A Net-Head called Dr. Carsten Diederich found a much more eloquent way to let the cat out of the bag; get one of the living to do it.

In life, Carsten was a renowned, five-hundred dollar-per-hour psychiatrist. He finished in the top five at Harvard University, where he got his Ph.D. in psychology. In his spare time, he hosted a podcast about body language and deception. It can safely be said that this man knew how to get into people's heads. So, when NANOMED made the mistake of assigning a young, impressionable woman like Dr. Dana Rollins to be Carsten's Project Leader, it was only a matter of time before she was doing everything Carsten wanted her to do.

After just three weeks, the good doctor convinced Dana to secretly record, photograph and tape everything she could about NANOMED's activities and leak the information to the press and onto the Internet. She did such an excellent job of collecting evidence that, by the time it became public, Batoltech Global knew there was no way they could deny what they were doing. Anton also knew that someone would go to jail for this, and it was likely to be him, if not everyone else involved in the Project.

When the word got out about NANOMED's zombies, the world was in a unified uproar. Anton and the Company were universally condemned by everyone from religious groups and politicians to sociologists and even those guys who took years of grief for cloning Dolly, the Sheep. Actually, I believe they breathed a sigh of relief when NANOMEDs experiments hit the papers. *You have the audacity to call us mad scientists?*

In the meantime, the President was calling for all employees of NANOMED and key members of Batoltech Global to be indicted. The Geneva Convention was being amended on an almost daily basis to account for the existence of zombies, beings for whom they had never, in a million lifetimes, anticipated having to write protocols for.

The Vatican City was threatening to excommunicate the entirety of North America if something was not done about the problem, and quickly.

In short, TF Bundy, Anton Batolgore and all those involved in the creation of zombies, looked like they were facing the rest of their natural lives behind bars. However, it would appear that fate was not done with Zombies just yet and threw them an unexpected lifeline.

Your Country Needs YOU! When you're dead

Just as things started to look exceptionally grim for Anton, TF and the rest of the NANOMED's zombie division, two things happened that helped them turn things in their favor.

First was the worst terrorist attack on American soil since, well, the last one. The second was a good old country boy from Jefferson county Alabama called Ned Cunningham, or 'Ned the Undead' as he would be known by millions of his adoring fans.

On a cold November day in Washington DC, multiple explosions took the lives of over three hundred and forty American citizens. On the same sad day, seventy-nine American troops were killed in three separate attacks on military bases throughout the US. One of the soldiers killed was the eldest son of a powerful US Senator, Jerome Stockton.

A group calling themselves The Fundamentalists of Light took responsibility for the atrocities. Before this day, no one had even heard of them. The Fundamentalists were of no particular race, religion, or creed. Bottom line, nobody knew anything about these guys or what their agenda was. Some speculated they didn't know themselves. Some suspected they weren't even terrorists as their activities stretched way beyond regular terror attacks. Bank heists, drug trafficking, industrial espionage and arms dealing were all in a day's work for these guys.

The entire country, heck ⊠ most of the Western world, went through the stages typical of when one encounters tragedy on this level. First came disbelief: *surely this couldn't have happened again?* This was followed by grief: *our sympathies go out to the victim's families. Our thoughts and prayers are with you.* Finally came anger: *someone is going to pay!*

By the time the general populous was baying for blood in retaliation for these attacks, Anton and his highly paid team of PR spin-doctors were ready to launch a counter-attack of their own.

Anton went on national television to apologize for the distress his company's experiments had caused. However, in the next breath, he said they need never again know the pain of losing a loved one in battle if they backed his plan. His zombies could be used on the front lines and in hostile situations, rather than young soldiers with their whole lives ahead of them. His speech to the nation lasted about fifteen minutes and quickly became one of the most viewed videos in YouTube history.

To be honest, it was kind of emotional, filled with sorrow, regret but also hope, dignity, and resolve. At the end of the speech, the camera cut to a grieving Senator Jerome Stockton, who pledged his unwavering support to Anton. He vowed to get a bill passed that would allow Batoltech Global to produce zombies for military use.

Anton, however, had one more ace to play - Ned Cunningham. Ned was, and probably still is, one of the nicest people you could ever hope to meet - well-mannered, caring, thoughtful and warm (in the emotional sense of the word. On a physical level, Ned, like the rest of us zombies, is now just room temperature).

He grew up on a farm with four brothers and three sisters. Every day after school and on most weekends, he would help his father with chores around the farm. He never complained, never sought recognition, and never forgot how fortunate he was to live such a blessed life. Everyone who knew Ned loved him.

So when a tractor he was driving toppled over and broke his spine in two places, the local community raised the money to have NANOMED's bots injected into his body so he might walk again.

Ned learned a lot from that accident. He learned that you should always pay attention to your surroundings when driving a tractor, or any vehicle for that matter. He learned that you could never be too grateful for all the small blessings in life, such as being able to walk. He also learned that you could never work too hard for those that you love.

Sadly he did not learn that, in the event of a lightning storm, you should never, ever take shelter under the farm's water tower. A water tower that was not only made entirely from highly conductive metal but also served as the highest point of an otherwise flat piece of farmland.

Had Ned learned this final lesson, he would not have died at the tender age of twenty-two from a lightning bolt that sent enough electricity through his body to send a DeLorean back to the future.

However, Ned's death served as a vitally important lesson for NANOMED's zombie division. It taught them there was another way to put down a zombie.

When Alan Hooper and his Undertakers arrived on the scene and saw the motionless, and still slightly smoldering Ned Cunningham lying under the water tower, he initially thought they had found the wrong body.

Just to make sure, they did what any professionally-trained zombie killer would do in this situation - they prodded Ned with a stick.

No movement.

One of the Undertakers then seized the initiative, stepped forward, and tapped Ned's corpse with his shoe.

Still no movement.

When further experiments, which included a chorus of "Wake up!", a slap to the face and a swift kick to the testicles produced a similar lack of results, the Undertaker team conceded that Ned was well and truly dead.

They bundled his body into a van and took him back to the

labs for further study. Meanwhile, the company's PR people spun the Cunningham family a tale about what happened to their son.

At the labs, they discovered that the lightning strike and resulting electrical charge that passed through Ned's body had fried every single nanobot and blown the NPC pod in his brain. He was never coming back.

However, to avoid wasting a good corpse, Ned was fitted with a new NPC pod and Nanobots and was up and about in no time at all. After getting over the initial shock of being a zombie, which took Ned all of three minutes, he then spent the rest of the day thanking every single employee he met for giving him a second chance to do something useful with his life. It did not take long for Ned, who quickly became known as the most helpful zombie ever created, to endear himself to everyone who met him.

When Anton needed a zombie to be the face of his company, Ned was the obvious choice. The day after Anton's moving speech to the nation, Ned was thrown into the limelight with his very own ad campaign.

I remember his first television appearance as if it were yesterday. The camera focused on him as he strolled through the NANOMED labs, followed closely by white-coated lab technicians.

When not pretending to look busy analyzing computer screens, holding up test tubes, or reading clipboards that I suspect had nothing written on them, they were smiling at Ned as he walked by. In turn, he would smile and speak to them in his soothing Southern drawl. It almost made you forget that the person addressing you had been dead for six months and had to be injected with a special chemical to stop the entire lab from smelling like the Devil's anus.

"Hi," he said, the skin on his face cracking ever so slightly as he smiled. "My name is Ned. I died a while back, and I gotta tell you it weren't no fun. But these nice folk at NANOMED, well, they brought me back.

"My heart don't beat no more, but that don't mean it don't break when I heard about all those innocent people and brave soldiers who lost their lives a few days back. We don't ever want y'all to have to go through that again.

"Me and the other zombies want to help if you'll let us. Vote YES for Senator Stockton's Zombie Initiative, and we'll step into the line of fire so your children don't have to. I may not have been able to serve my country in life, but I am mighty proud to serve in death."

The advert then played out to the national anthem with an American flag waving gently on the screen. At the same time, information scrolled across telling people how to get behind Stockton's campaign.

Personally, I thought playing the anthem was a little cheesy but the general consensus at the time from all my family and friends was that it was better than playing out to Drowning Pool's 'Let the Bodies Hit the Floor.' But I still maintain that would have been pretty cool.

Putting Ned on TV had been nothing short of political genius. Public opinion of zombies swung in Anton's favor overnight.

Although it looked like the Stockon Bill allowing the production of zombies for military purposes would be passed by the senate, it was made very clear by the powers-that-be that someone still had to pay for the crimes committed.

Anton, who no longer had any real use for TF Bundy, used all of his considerable influence to ensure that the poor, aging scientist took the fall for everything. What was left of Bundy's reputation was ripped to shreds during a very public trial.

He was made out to be worse than Dr. Frankenstein, Dr. Jekyll, and Dr. Moreau combined. The guy couldn't even afford decent legal representation. By the time prosecutors were finished with him, TF Bundy was convicted of just about every crime against humanity you could think of. He was sentenced to a dozen life sentences back-to-back. On the bright side, I believe he is up for parole in about a hundred and seventy-seven years.

Shortly after Bundy's trial, Stockton's bill was passed, and Anton Batolgore's company was legally allowed to produce zombies for the military.

However, the bill was filled with stipulations and regulations that significantly restricted what NANOMED could and could not do.

One of the big ones was that no corpse could be used to make a zombie unless it was bequeathed to NANOMED by the owner of said corpse while he was still alive. That was to say that, for them to bring someone back to life, the person had to have legally left his body to NANOMED. Either in a will or in a personal visit to their offices when they were still alive, to fill out a mountain of paperwork.

Another requirement was that Zombies had absolutely no human rights. None whatsoever; they relinquished them the moment they died. Anton had no issues with this since he never planned on giving his creations any freedoms, but he was less than pleased when the requirement became very public knowledge.

Needless to say, this stipulation prompted few people to get in line to become zombified.

Realizing that his Project was going to be dead in the water unless he did something about it, Anton tried a different approach to get people to sign up. Cash.

Anton's company invested millions in a national ad campaign offering fifty thousand dollars in cash on the same day anyone donated their corpse to NANOMED (Batoltech Global) in the event of their death.

Before long, thousands were signing up to become zombies the moment their tickets got punched. It would appear that greed overcomes common sense, and any thought of this decision's long-term consequences.

Not that I can say much because I signed up the day after I saw the advert. At least I can say I did it for love... kinda.

How I became dead…and then not so much

Her name was Bethany Weaver. She was probably the most beautiful girl I had ever laid eyes on, or at least the most beautiful girl I had ever known who could eat a double cheeseburger every day for lunch and still look like she could grace the cover of Sports Illustrated. She said she got her freakishly fast metabolism from her dad, who was built like a chopstick.

I should say it took me six months to gain this little snippet of information. The first few weeks she started coming into the burger joint, I was so stunned by her beauty that I would lose the power of speech whenever she was within three feet of me. All I could do was nod, grunt or, on a good day, force out an 'uh-huh.'

Was it her long dark hair, or the cute smile that made the one side of her mouth curl up higher than the other, flashing perfect teeth? Or maybe it was her eyes, which seemed greener than the gherkins we put on the burgers. Looking back, it was the whole package.

Every day while I was fumbling for words, she was never short of things to say: "Hey..." (reading my name tag) "Marco. Are you gonna say something today or just continue with your goldfish routine?"

Was my mouth open? It must have been. It dawned on me that every time I tried to speak to her, my mouth would form a shape of an 'O', but then no words would come out. I blushed bright red, realizing how stupid I must have looked. Bethany simply smiled, grabbed her order, and said: "Maybe tomorrow, hey?"

From that day on, every day before she came in, I would boast to my workmates that today was the day I was going to flirt with her. Today was the day I would finally break the paralytic disease that seized my tongue the moment she arrived at my counter. I would rehearse well-practiced pick-up lines on my sympathetic but captive audience of co-workers:

"Hey, would you like a side of date with that burger?"

"Is that to eat here or at my place?"

"You're here every day. Is it for the smoothies or just the smoothie serving you?"

Most would shake their heads and walk away, but I would get the occasional word of encouragement. Not that it helped. The 'eyes greener-than gherkins' girl came in every day from Monday to Friday for the next two months but still not a word would pass my lips, even when she would lean forward a little, look at me thoughtfully and say, "Not today, huh?"

Even when, smiling that crooked little smile at me, she slid a book called *English For Beginners* over the counter, I remained dumbstruck. Only when she started to walk away did I manage, with what seemed like superhuman effort, to hold up the book and say: "Funny."

She half-turned and smiled the broadest smile I had ever seen. "Maybe tomorrow I'll get a full sentence out of you, Marco."

Inspired, I practiced my pick-up lines that night, over and over again in the mirror. I watched Rocky One through Four to gain courage and motivation to conquer my fears, and when Beth arrived the next day, I was ready for her.

"Can I get just a thick shake, please?"

WHAT? She had never asked for that before. All my lines and witty comebacks were based on what she had ordered religiously for months. This was a disaster! What was I going to do? What could I say? *Think, Marco, think!* I must have been standing stone-still for ages with a look of panic written on my gormless mug because Beth furrowed her eyebrows and asked, "You okay?"

It was now or never. Trying to muster up the calm, confident, and sophisticated personality in the mirror the night before, I replied: "Sure. Of course I am. Hey, you know what else is thick here - me."

A slightly befuddled look crossed Beth's face, and she scrunched it up a little. "Really?"

Oh crap! "I mean... I'm not thick... I meant; I mean, it's not a smoothie, like me. Not that you don't look smooth, oh nuts. Erm, would you like a shake with that side of date?" *And the nominations for the Worst Epic Fail while trying to pick up a girl are...*

Beth laughed so hard everyone stopped eating to stare at her. I could have slid behind the counter and just died at that moment. But then the strangest thing happened. Instead of running in the opposite direction, Beth put her hand on my arm, making my heart skip a dozen beats, and said, "Well, that's an interesting first sentence. But how about next time you just be yourself?" She frowned. "That *wasn't* your normal self, was it?" I shook my head. "Okay, phew! But just a hint; lines don't work on girls anyway, even when they aren't screwed up as badly as that."

And that was that. The curse was lifted, and we chatted every day from then on. Sometimes it was just small talk or as much as I could get in when I had a line of customers waiting to be served. But occasionally, when it was quiet, we would talk a little longer. That's how it went until the day Beth dropped the bombshell to end all bombshells.

"This is the last time you are going to see me in here for a while," she chirped, brimming with excitement, not realizing that I felt like someone had ripped my heart from my chest and slung it on the griddle to be served with a side of fries. "I'm leaving this weekend to tour Europe for six months."

"Six months? Really? Wow, that sounds... fun," I managed,

all the while imagining my heart getting slapped between a burger patty.

"Yeah. I've been planning it for years. I'm going with some friends from college and my ex-boyfriend."

Ex-Boyfriend? On went the lettuce, pickles, and tomatoes.

"Er, ex....ex....ex-boyfriend?"

Beth looked a little guilty. "Yeah, we arranged this before we split. He's really sweet, but I'm not sure I want to get back together with him, even though I think he wants to?" *Well, he's got six freaking months to try and convince you, hasn't he?* And finally, on goes the mayo and cheese, and voila, your Marco Heart Burger is ready.

"You know," she continued, "I would have invited you, but I figured working here you'd... at such short notice... find it difficult to come up with the money."

"Are you kidding?" I exclaimed. "I've got the money. I could jump on the plane tomorrow if I wanted." *If it would stop your Ex from making moves on you, I'd swim to Europe.*

Beth smiled, hopefully, "Really?"

No! I flip burgers for a living! I share an apartment with my cousin in the worst part of town, and at the end of the month, I can hardly afford toothpaste. Of course, I don't have the money.

"Yes, of course, I have the money."

"Well, do you want to come? I'd like it if you said yes and you'd love my friends. I even think you'd get on with Chad. Say you'll come?"

Chad! Your ex is called Chad? Oh, I'm going alright! "You

bet." How was another matter.

"Yay!" Beth gave a little jump and quickly scribbled her number on a napkin. "Phone me tonight, and we'll go over the plan."

"Okay," I said, although I suspected her plan was far removed from the one formulating in my head to rob a bank, kidnap an heiress or win the lottery in less than seventy-two hours.

I spent the rest of the day imagining what this Chad guy looked like. I imagined he played varsity football. Probably a quarterback and built like a Marvel superhero. What was I thinking? I couldn't compete with that. The last time I went to the gym was, erm, never. I should just back out now while I still had some dignity. Beth was too good for me, anyway. But then I pictured *him* sweeping her into his arms, this guy who, in my mind, was stronger than Hulk and better looking than Captain America. At that moment, I wanted to punch him and scream, "She's mine!"

Somehow, I needed to come up with the cash and quick. I must have stood under that massive Batoltech Global poster for ten minutes wracking my brain for a solution before turning around and reading, in big, bold letters:

$50,000!

Why not spend the money now?

Because you can't spend it when you're dead.

By five PM that same day, I had quit my job and signed my un-life over to Batoltech and NANOMED and was sitting with more money than I ever imagined in my bank account. I had not even considered what this would mean to me in the long run. After all, at the time, I figured I had years and years of life ahead of me. Instead, all I could think of was Beth and how I couldn't wait to call her that night. We spent three hours talking about everything we were going to do on our trip.

The next morning, I bought my ticket, new clothes, a backpack, and a brand-new phone. I kept imagining the smug look on imaginary-Chad's chiseled face when he sees me at the airport - dweeby, pathetic, little me…um. Maybe Beth is attracted more to personality than looks. *Yup, I'm still in trouble.*

I never did get to see what Chad looked like. I never got to see Europe and spend the next six months falling head over heels in love with Beth. I never got to wake up next to her or hear her whisper, "I love you, Marco."

Instead, I died before I even made it to the airport.

Even with everything I've been through, I regret the timing of my death more than I ever regretted coming back from the dead. And I started regretting that pretty damn quick, I can tell you.

Rise and Shine! Today Is the First Day of the Rest of Your Unlife

The first couple of weeks of being a zombie are, by far and away, the toughest. I mean, let's be honest, you have an awful lot to deal with. The fact that you died to begin with! Trust me, that takes some getting used to.

When I woke up or, more accurately, was rebooted like a computer, I knew something was seriously wrong, but the idea I was a zombie was the last thing from my mind. For the first half an hour or so after coming back up, nothing worked. My eyes could not focus. Everything was a hazy blur, like looking at the world through bubble wrap. I could not speak because my mouth was drier than a mummy's butt crack, and my tongue felt like someone had replaced it with beef jerky.

All I could manage was "Uuuurgghh! Arrrr, ughaaarrr",

which was fairly impressive when you consider the parchment-dry throat and lungs that no longer pumped air past the vocal cords.

Fortunately, I was strapped to an operating bed when I came to, or else I might have flopped to the floor like a wet fish. That being said, only my legs, waist, and upper arms were strapped in. So, I was able to move my arms from the elbow down, and that itself was an entirely new adventure.

Like pretty much everyone on the planet, I am sure at some point, probably more than once, you have woken up to discover that you've slept awkwardly on one of your hands. The prolonged pressure causes it to be starved of blood and oxygen, resulting in the hand losing all sensation for a few minutes until the blood flow resumes, followed by painful pins and needles.

Like me, you have probably waved it around in amusement like a limp glove, while waiting for the feeling to come back. Now imagine that sensation over your entire body. It's not quite like being paralyzed because there are the vaguest remnants of feeling, and also, you can move your limbs. However, your body feels alien, like it is not your own to control.

You have to learn how to operate it on memory and sheer willpower rather than the sensation of touch or feeling. It gets easier with use, but that's if you are a Net-Head with the ability to learn, practice, and more importantly, remember. Dead-Heads, though, have the memory of a goldfish and the learning capacity of a burrito. It's no wonder they can only shuffle and stagger along like the zombies from 80's horror movies.

So there I was, flailing my arms around from the elbow down, like a demented seal learning to clap. Spluttering, gurgling, and trying desperately to focus on the seemingly indifferent shapes walking around me. I thought, *Mmm. I might be in trouble here.*

Gradually my vision returned in part, followed by some control over my tongue.

Through blurry eyes, I made out the figures walking around the lab; two men and a woman with fiery red hair that hung halfway down her back. She approached my bed and touched a button that caused it to slowly fold into a chair until I was sitting in a slightly reclined position. She dragged a metal chair, which scraped along the floor, and sat down facing me.

By now, I could make out the freckles on her face and the fact that her gums seemed a little too big for her teeth when she smiled at me. The smile was filled with sympathy, the kind you give someone just before you give them some bad news. However, something about it seemed forced, rather than genuine compassion.

"Hello, Marco," she said. "I am Emily Aiken. I am your Project Leader."

"Ham hi sthick?" I managed to ask, with a serious amount of concern.

"No, no, no. You're not sick," she said with a reassuring smile.

Phew!

"You're dead."

"WHUH THUH THUCK?"

Here's the thing, though, about waking up on a slab in NANOMED's labs; your first thoughts are not: "Oh my God, I'm dead!" No, no. It's: "Hey I'm alive!" So it comes as quite a shock when someone in a lab coat tells you otherwise.

"I know this must come as a bit of a shock to you," she continued.

Really? You think? Instinctively I struggled against my restraints as if breaking them would allow me to escape the reality of this situation. There is no way I could be dead!

"There muth be some mithtake!" I pleaded and thrust my tongue in and out, trying to get the damn thing to work properly.

"There is no mistake," she said, and proceeded to tell me how I died.

As was consistent with the kind of luck, or lack thereof, that I had grown accustomed to over my life, I just happened to be at the wrong place at the wrong time.

The official police report said that a couple of crooks had stolen a car no more than three blocks away from where I was living. They were speeding away from the scene of the crime just as I was crossing the street to grab a taxi to take me to the airport.

She continued. "We have brought you back to life, well sort of, not exactly life - you're a zombie."

"That can't be," I protested. *Oh, thank God.* My tongue is working again. "But I don't remember dying."

"You won't. None of you do. The last twelve hours of your

life doesn't come back with you. The phenomenon is called Dead Air.

She was right about that. I honestly couldn't remember how I died, and neither could any Net-Head I've met.

Nobody truly knows why. Some have speculated it has something to do with the brain not having time to convert the day's events from short-term memory to long-term memory. The fact remains, every person brought back to life by NANOMED draws a complete blank when trying to recall the day they died.

Most would say this is a blessing in disguise. After all, who wants to remember how they died? *Hey, did I ever tell you about the time I stepped out of my car at the Drive-Through Safari Park and got mauled to death by two brown bears? Boy, that was a good day.*

I say *most* people would not want to remember their own death, because I did meet one Net-Head who desperately wanted to remember. His name was Eduardo Flores. He was a hotshot lawyer from San Diego who had spent the last six months of his life trying to bed his exceptionally attractive, young, blonde secretary. He died of a heart attack on the same day he succeeded, while making love to her - for the third time. Now and then, I can still hear him weeping at night when he thinks no one is listening.

"Even though you cannot remember," Emily said, all pretense of sympathy gone, "you are dead; take it from me."

"Are you sure?" I asked.

"Your internal organs are sitting in a plastic bag on that table over there. So yes, I am sure."

I looked over at the table in the corner of the lab. True enough, there was the transparent plastic bag filled with red and grey meaty objects.

"Anything vital?" I was clutching at straws now.

"Pretty much everything in the bag," Emily said. "You are dead, Marco. Accept it." As she spoke, I could see the color draining from her freckled face and the clenching of her jaw.

"Yeah," I said, "but is it possible I can live without all that stuff?"

"Without intestines, stomach, liver, kidneys, and a heart?" She raised an eyebrow, "No, Marco, it is not possible to live without that stuff!"

"Then why did you take them out then if I need all that stuff to live?" I shouted.

Slamming her clipboard on the floor, she yelled: "Because you are not freaking alive! You are dead, D-E-A-D... Dead. Get it?"

"Yeah, I get it," I mumbled meekly, now a little scared of the red-headed tyrant in front of me.

Emily huffed, stood up, and bent down to pick up her clipboard.

"But… how can you be really certain I'm dead?" I asked.

"Oh, for the love of - !" Emily threw her hands in the air. Then, in one fluid motion, she removed a pen that was tucked into her pocket and plunged it straight into my chest.

"Aaargh!" I screamed, though I did not feel a thing. "What the hell are you trying to do? *Kill* me?"

Emily shrieked and shook her fists in front of my face in pure rage. She spun around twice, still waving her fists in the air, and then grabbed me roughly by the shoulders.

She leaned in close, just inches from my face and glared at me with murderous intensity. Then, mustering all the skills I figured she had learned through years of anger management classes, she said through gritted teeth, "I...am not....trying....to kill you...because....you are already... DEAD!"

She breathed out and loosened her grip a little, then nodded toward the pen sticking out of my chest.

"Do you feel that?" she asked.

"No. No, I don't." I replied, which was true enough apart from a slight sensation of pressure.

"Well, that is where your heart used to be. Had you have been alive, then you would be dead right now."

Not wanting to incur more of her wrath, I quietly replied, "But you said I'm already dead."

"Yes... but... no... what I meant...you are, but... aargh!" Emily buried her head in her hands, and I heard her repeating, over and over, "Control, control, control!"

Finally, she removed her hands from her face, sat down and forced a smile.

"Okay," she said, "Let's try this again. Yes, you are dead. That is why my stabbing you in the chest with a pen, and I am sorry for that, by the way, had no effect on you. The reason why you are able to talk to me and function, to some level of normality, is because you have been brought back, through the power of medical science, as a zombie. Do you know what a zombie is?"

"Yes." I figured short answers were my safest option as it dawned on me that, even though she was sorry for stabbing me with a pen, she still had not bothered to remove it.

"Ok. Good. We are getting somewhere," she said. "Now, I am going to get a coffee, and when I come back, we are going to discuss what this means to you and what work I've done to you. Understand?"

Keep it simple, Marco. "Yes"

Emily stood up, took a step away, then turned around and tugged the pen free of my ribcage before heading toward the door.

Coffee, hmmm.

I was craving something, although I was not sure what. A quick image flashed through my mind of my teeth sinking into Emily's arm, but I shook my head in horror to dislodge the thought. It vanished, but I still needed something to quench my thirst for…for blood?

"Er...Emily?" I called after her before she reached the door.

She turned, exasperated. "Yes?"

"May I have a cup of coffee too, please?"

"No, Marco. You may not."

"Why not?"

"Because you do not need one."

A little confused at this point, I asked, "Why don't I need a coffee?"

Almost faster than the eye could see, Emily's metal clipboard came spinning towards my head like a ninja's throwing star, missing my skull by millimeters. The ensuing scream was so shrill I was surprised it didn't shatter all the glass in the lab.

"BECAUSE YOU ARE FRIGGING DEAD!"

*

Returning with a piping hot coffee in a cardboard cup, she sat down, placing the cup and her clipboard on a table in front of her chair.

She smiled at me. Then, in a tone of forced serenity, she said, "Marco, I am now going to talk to you about your condition and the next steps. Before I do, I need to make sure you and I are on the same page. So, I am going to ask you a few questions. Okay?"

"Sure," I replied, feeling a sense of dread as she pulled out half a dozen pens from her lab coat pocket. She placed each pen on the metal table until they formed a neat little row. After she had positioned the last pen, she looked at me and smiled, which made me feel even more uneasy. My granddad always used to say, "An alligator smiles broadest just as it's about to bite your butt off." I never understood what he meant until this moment.

"Good," she said, tapping the desk with both hands. "Marco, are you dead?"

I knew what she wanted to hear, but hesitated anyway, if only to make sure I would answer correctly. The last thing I wanted was for this crazy lady to use my body as a pencil case.

"Yes," I replied.

"Excellent. How would you describe your current condition, considering that you're able to talk and move, even though you are clinically dead?"

Tough one. My initial reaction was to describe my current condition as 'less than desirable,' but I figured that would only result in another pen thrust into my body.

"A zombie?" I winced, half expecting another assault.

"Correct," Emily said approvingly. *Phew!*

She continued, "Now that I am sure we understand each other, I will try to explain your situation in a manner that your pea-size brain will comprehend." *Ouch!*

"Before your death, you signed your body over to Batoltech Global. NANOMED is a division of that company. You were sent to us so that we could repair, modify and reanimate your corpse. We have done this in a fashion that allows you to maintain your higher functions, such as reasoning, logic, emotions, and intellect...or at least to the rudimentary level you had in life" *Thanks for the confidence boost!*

She carried on, "I would describe the intricacies of how we achieved this, but I fear it would be like explaining the renaissance to a possum."

I was about to fiercely object to her blatant insult but stopped when I realized I had no idea what the renaissance was. Maybe it was a new type of hybrid car. If so, I wouldn't understand it if she explained it to me either. I'm not great with cars.

Emily took a sip of her coffee but then obviously realized she needed to give me something, "In short, a neural net, nanobots and NPC pod have been inserted into your skull."

"Cool," I said. "What are those?"

She looked at me, expressionlessly for a moment. "A type of hokery-pokery magic you could never understand. However, without these, you would be nothing more than a mindless zombie, capable of only one thought. The cravings you are currently experiencing are for flesh and blood." *Hmmm, I could really go for some of that right now.* "You will receive both of these in due course, but in the meantime, you must resist all murderous thoughts you may have." *You ain't making it easy, lady!*

She raised an eyebrow as if she had read my thoughts, but continued nonetheless. "In addition to the devices in your head, your entire skeletal structure has been reinforced with a resin, which makes your bones tougher than steel. This will make it pretty difficult for you to be destroyed" *Sweet!* "But not impossible" *Awww!* "Destruction of your brain or removal of your head will terminate your un-life. Likewise, if the Nanos or NPC pod are shut down or destroyed, such as with a strong electric current, you will also cease to function. Understood?"

I nodded.

"Now," she said, taking another sip of coffee, "Although it is difficult to destroy you, remember that you are dead. Ergo, you will no longer heal. We can repair some damage caused to you, but we cannot heal injuries."

"My name is Marco, not Ergo," I reminded her.

Emily gritted her teeth. "Ergo means 'therefore.' I was not calling you Ergo, you cretin."

"Sorry," I said. "I don't always understand big words."

"Ergo is *four* letters long…" She stopped herself mid-flow, took a deep breath, and with a strained smile said, "Did you understand what I was trying to tell you, and may we continue?"

"Yes. And I understand that I no longer heal… wait a second!" I said, looking down at my chest. "You mean I am stuck with that puncture wound you gave me?"

"Yes," she said. "Is that an issue?"

"Oh no," I yelled back, hardly able to contain my rage. "By all means, stick some more pens into me. I relish the idea of looking like Swiss cheese with a mouth!" Another flash leaped into my mind, of Emily's blood and sinking my teeth into her.

"Do not tempt me, Marco," Emily said with the cool calm of a serial killer. "I have bigger things than pens in this lab, with more interesting places to stick them than in your chest."

I didn't imagine, for an instant, she was bluffing. I clamped my mouth shut.

After some moments of uncomfortable silence and several more sips of coffee, she continued, "From here, you will be handed over for indentured service to the military. Batoltech has contracts with the US military to supply them with weapons, vehicles, and zombies. Are you still with me, Marco?"

she asked casually, running a finger down one of her pens.

"Yeah, I think so."

"Excellent," she said. "Now listen very carefully to what I am about to tell you because, during your induction, it will not be explained again in a manner as nicely as I am about to. Any freedoms or rights you once had, died with you. Even your name died. From now on, you will simply be referred to as Project 2219. You are no longer considered human. You are a product, owned by Batoltech Global and leased to the military, no different from any other piece of equipment they own. You are completely, totally, and utterly expendable. You will do as they say when they say, without argument, or you will be destroyed or worse."

Give the woman her due; she knew how to hammer a point home.

"The sooner you accept this fact, Project 2219," she said, "the happier you will be."

Happy? I am not sure I would ever be happy again. The fifty thousand they paid for my afterlife wasn't looking like such a great deal now.

When the realization of what happened finally came home, I was less upset about being dead than I was about missing Beth. She would not have heard that I died. She would have got on that plane thinking I'd let her down. What would she think of me now? She would never know how I felt about her or how badly I wanted to spend those six months with her. Instead, she probably turned to the only guy she thought wanted to be with her, Chad. Oh, how I hated him and how it broke my heart every time I thought of my beautiful, perfect Beth.

"Now, are you ready to look at yourself?" Emily asked.

Fifty Shades of Decay

The most nerve-wracking experience for most Zombies is getting that first look at themself in the mirror. How one dies plays a big factor in this. A person who dies of a heart attack is likely to be a lot prettier than one who died trying to wrestle a chew toy off their neighbor's Rottweiler.

Take, for example, my best zombie pal, Ash. Before zombiedom, Ash had been a professional wrestler but was forced to retire after a bad knee injury. Being skilled at little else, he scraped a living by being a bouncer at a local club.

He had been spending the evening with his family on the night of his death. It was their first evening in their refurbished home, paid for courtesy of NANOMED's fifty thousand dollars. No expense had been spared - new carpets, new fireplace, new furniture, and a new TV with a surround sound system. However, because no expense had been spared on everything else, Ash could afford only the cheapest electrician to rewire the house. Had he thought to save a little more for a more qualified electrician, the wiring might not have fused and caught fire in the middle of the night.

Fortunately, some of the money had been used on a state-of-the-art fire alarm, which woke Ash's family and enabled them to evacuate the burning building before tragedy could strike. Unfortunately, Ash's wife convinced him to run back in to save their pet goldfish. Needless to say, neither Ash nor the goldfish made it back out.

When the coroner handed his body over to NANOMED it was covered, head to foot, in third-degree burns. For a while, Ash's Project Leader was not even sure Ash could be brought back due to the damage caused to his body. As it turned out, the nanobots were even able to work their magic on him. I mean, he's mostly blind in the one eye, mute because his vocal cords were burnt out, and now looks like Freddy Krueger's uglier brother, so it's a miracle they were prepared to reanimate him at all.

Amazingly, a short time after meeting him, I discovered that Ash was not the nickname given to him after being burnt to a crisp but the name he was born with - Ashley King.

So, as you can probably imagine, when handed the mirror, I was expecting to look like every zombie you had ever seen in a movie, full of blood, gore, gaping wounds and rotting flesh.

Even though I had been hit by a car, most of my injuries were internal, along with a few broken bones. I also had a nasty scar running across the back of my head where it hit the pavement. Still, because it was covered mostly by my hair and stapled together, it did not look too bad. Also, the fact that I could not see it helped.

Admiring myself in the mirror, I had to confess I had expected worse. Sure, my skin was pale with hints of purple and some yellowing from all the embalming fluids they pumped into me. Also, my cheekbones stuck out a little more, but probably because the skin around my eye sockets and jaw was starting to sink inwards. And sure, my hair was looking dead and lifeless, but still as unruly as it was when I was alive.

All things considered, I was a pretty good-looking zombie! I didn't even look dead that first couple of weeks. At best, I looked ill; at worst, I looked like an Emo.

Sadly, that condition was not to last. After the first couple of weeks, the wheels start to come off pretty fast for zombies.

By week three, the delicate hints of yellow and purple deepen, and what skin is left takes on a variety of different tones of grey.

As it turns out, discoloration is the least of a zombie's worries because, by week four, the real fun starts to happen. The skin around your face and skull sinks and contracts to the point where it is no longer possible to pass for one of the living. It also gets so dry and leathery that it starts to crack along the joints and other areas where the skin is forced to move, like the face, especially around the mouth whenever you eat, speak, smile, etc.

At this point you have to be real careful about how you treat your body because it is not uncommon for noses, ears and other extremities to fall off because you have been too reckless with them. No zombie knows this better than Andrew 'The Action Man' Johnson. His story has been a cautionary tale for every zombie ever created.

When I first met Andrew Johnson and learned that his nickname was 'The Action Man,' I thought, *Wow, this guy must have done something outstanding to have earned that name*. Maybe he took out a bunch of terrorists single-handed or jumped onto the hood of a speeding car to stop criminals fleeing the scene of a heist.

The real origins of his nickname are a much grimmer story, and one that does not have a happy ending. You have been warned.

Andrew was a pool cleaner before he died at the age of twenty-four, after slipping and drowning in one of the pools he was cleaning. He would tell people that he was six-foot-tall, but he was more like five-eight at a stretch. He liked to dress well, or as well as his meager budget could afford, and would spend ages making sure not a single hair was out of place on his blonde head.

It's safe to say that Andrew loved the ladies almost as much as he loved himself, and he was confident they loved him back. He would often refer to himself as the Don Juan of Poughkeepsie.

However, it's a sad fact that when you are brought back, not everything about you returns to life. More specifically, the parts just south of your belt remain well and truly dead. A zombie's heart no longer pumps blood, and if it doesn't pump blood, it can no longer send it rushing to your man-junk when required. That's not to say you can't be attracted to someone or mesmerized by their beauty. It just means that the bits that allow you to act on such attraction are on permanent vacation.

This realization is difficult for some zombies to accept. In particular, Andrew Johnson found the idea of never feeling arousal again, hard to swallow. So adamant was he to not accept a life, albeit an undead life, of celibacy that he decided to take matters into his own hands… literally.

One night he snuck into the crawlspace above the female military personnel's locker room. He gently moved a tile so he could look down into the room below and waited for them to arrive for their evening shower. When they finally did, Andrew set about trying to resuscitate the one part of his body that had, up to that point, refused to come back to life.

As mentioned earlier, a couple of things happen when you become a zombie. First, things start to become a little more brittle, like skin and other bits that require a steady flow of blood to keep them supple. Secondly, because your sense of touch is virtually non-existent, it becomes difficult to gauge how much pressure and strength you are applying when gripping or pulling something.

Tragically, when you combine these two facts while performing certain actions, especially one that you might be getting carried away with, there can only be one inevitable outcome.

Andrew pulled a little too hard, heard a sickening tear, and briefly stared in stunned horror at the member now lying detached in his hand. Those who heard the scream that followed say it still keeps them awake at night.

Panicked and still wailing like a banshee, Andrew lost his footing in the crawlspace and came crashing down into the locker room below, causing mass hysteria amongst the mostly naked occupants. He ran screaming from the locker room, holding his manhood above his head as if it were the Olympic Torch.

Fortunately for Andrew, in the chaos that followed his fall into the locker room, no one noticed what he was holding in his hand. If they had, he would have earned his nickname earlier. In the havoc caused by his abrupt entrance and hasty exit, no one had been able to identify him as the intruder.

However, for every Ying, there is a Yang. Whereas Andrew may have considered himself lucky to escape with his anonymity intact, it turned out to be very unlucky for another poor Marine, Private Julia Hancock, the following day.

After escaping into the night, a desperate Andrew had sought out his Project Leader to convince him to reattach his junk. It was not a long conversation. Though, it took a good forty minutes for the Project Leader to stop laughing before Andrew could plead his case

After the point-blank refusal, Andrew spent the rest of the night begging him not to tell a soul about what had happened. He may as well have been asking the Hunchback of Notre Dame to stand up straight; with fingers crossed behind his back, his Project Leader promised not to tell.

Andrew was not prepared to give up there, though. The idea of walking around with a part missing, especially his favorite part, was just too much for him to bear. So, on his way out of the labs, he stole a stapler from one of the scientist's desks and sought out a quiet spot to do some amateur surgery.

Several minutes and a dozen staples later, he decided he had done just about the best job he could. An A+ for effort but, as it turned out, an E- for execution.

The next day he, like the rest of our zombie unit and a squad of fresh-faced Marines, tackled the assault course behind the army barracks. We had to navigate through seventeen physically demanding obstacles, each designed to make us or break us.

The course included a barbed wire low-crawl lane, a rope climb, a log jump, a beam balance (with the muddiest of mud underneath, so if you fell, your boots got sucked right off your feet the moment you tried a pull them out), a twelve-foot wall and, the one that no zombie ever seems to get right, the tire-hop.

While Andrew was busting his butt on the course to impress everyone watching, his staples were breaking free of their charge. He had spotted Private Julia Hancock at the very start of the course. Although dead, decaying, and now having the kind of smile that could crack mirrors, Andrew was not about to stop doing what came naturally to him.

"Hey, that uniform looks good on you," he told the pretty

young Marine, as they lined up for the low-crawl. "This course is tricky, but I'll help you get through it, sweetheart," he said, pursuing her to the beam balance. "It was fated, our meeting like this."

If you had to say one thing about Andrew, say that he was no quitter. No matter how many times Julia said: "Get lost, creep!" or "Ugh, you're disgusting," or "Never in a million years," did he stop trying.

Instead, he stayed right behind her on each obstacle and took every opportunity to say: "Hey, nice butt!" And so, by the time they got to the rope net, Julia had taken just about as much as she was going to take.

She spun around, grabbed Andrew by the collar, and yelled right in his face, "I am not interested! You repulse me, as do all of your kind! Do not talk to me again; do not even look in my direction again! And if I so much as see you glance at my backside again, I will make you dead-dead! Do you hear me?"

Dead-dead was a term used by both us zombies and the living Marines. It meant killing us for a second time in such a way that there would be no coming back.

Our Project Leaders were more polite. When they spoke about ending our un-life, they would use the term 'dismantle.' I found that even more unnerving than 'dead-dead.'

Andrew stood there, open-mouthed, looking crestfallen. Julia was not going to back down until she knew he got the message, loud and clear. After a few agonizing seconds, Andrew nodded his head.

She shoved him away and said, "Now get up there," pointing to the rope net, "and stay in front where I can keep an eye on you."

This turned out to be the worst order Private Hancock had given during her brief military career. As Andrew was halfway up the net, with Julia right behind him, the last of the staples worked their way free. The first he knew anything was wrong was when he felt something slide down the inside of his army fatigues.

"Huh?" *What was that?* he thought and looked down, only to see Julia glaring up at him. He quickly looked back up again and continued to climb. The moment he took his next step up the rope net, the penny finally dropped, as did the mystery item - right out the bottom of his trousers. He spun around and tried to grab it with one hand while still clinging to the net with the other, but it was too late.

He saw it tumble downward in slow motion, like a starving man might watch his hotdog slip out of the bun and fall to the ground.

Over and over it spun, getting further and further away from his grasp, until it fell into the outstretched hand of Private Julia Hancock. Months of military training had honed her reflexes and reactions to the point where she acted on instinct. She could duck for cover without thinking, draw her gun as if it were a part of her, or snatch a falling object out of the air in the blink of an eye, even before taking a moment to see what it was.

However, now that she had caught it, she had all the time

in the world to see what it was. Her eyes slowly widened as the realization of what lay in the palm of her hand started to dawn.

She looked up at Andrew with an expression that could only be described as somewhere between horrified and nauseated. All he could do was look shamefaced and mutter, "Sorry!"

Suddenly the reality of Julia's world snapped back into place. She hurled the last remaining piece of Andrew's pride away from her as if it were a tiny cobra and leaped off the rope net, landing badly on her ankle. Screaming and crying, she hobbled from the course, leaving the rest of the befuddled Marines looking down at what she had thrown to the ground.

It did not take long for them to put all the pieces together, so to speak, and the obstacle course erupted in laughter. Every living Marine, and even some of the zombies, were pointing at Andrew and laughing so hard they were unable to formulate the words to mock him properly. But when the words did finally come, his nickname was born. Because, just like The Action Man, Andrew now had nothing left below the belt but a trademark for Batoltech Global.

Regrettably, he was not the only one to gain a nickname that day. It would seem that fate had Julia's card marked the moment her father signed his surname on her birth certificate. Despite two weeks' of counseling, the kind the military offers to personnel who have PTSD, Julia Hancock left the army and was never seen or heard from again.

Although rumors would surface on occasion, like she had joined a convent, had gone bankrupt paying for hypnotherapy, or gone insane and tried to blow up an Oscar Mayer factory.

Week five of the zombie transformation is the kicker. Hair starts to fall out in clumps. Lips contract, so most of us, when we are not talking, look like we have a constant sneer. Bones begin to poke through on the tips of your fingers, especially the index fingers, as they get the most use.

To make matters worse, because every zombie has a limited sense of touch, pain, or sensation of almost any kind, we tend to be pretty clumsy at first, or at least until we get used to our 'new' body. This, coupled with the fact that we go through rigorous and punishing training to become zombie soldiers, we all end up damaging our already battered bodies.

Remember that a zombie does not heal. Ever! So, every scratch, nick, scrape, cut, bullet wound, burn, you name it, is there for good. To put this into perspective, imagine every single injury you've had since childhood. Every scraped knee, every bloody hole where you've squeezed a zit, every cut, every broken bone. Tally up all those wounds, big and small, and then imagine waking up tomorrow with every last one of them as fresh as the day they happened. Now imagine them there every day for the rest of your life, and instead of healing, growing gradually worse. Welcome to the wonderful world of Zombidom!

By week six, the decay rate has started to slow down a little. But that doesn't mean you no longer have the daily adventure of exploring your body for injuries that were not there the day before. Cuts widen, holes deepen, and just a little more flesh drops off every day.

As Andrew the Action Man can testify, if your injury doesn't hamper your ability to do your work, the Project Leaders simply do not care. So, you will often find a zombie trying to stitch itself back up or using duct tape, staples or band-aids to patch up fresh wounds.

Naturally, prevention is better than cure. Since embalmed skin tends to turn leathery, there are ways to ensure it stays supple and doesn't crack as easily. The best solution is the wax leather protector Marines use on their boots. You can always tell when a zombie has managed to get their hands on some because, after a while, their skin acquires an orange tan. Understandably, even zombies are reluctant to walk around with orange skin, but some felt it preferable to the alternative.

If falling apart were not enough, zombies have even bigger issues to contend with. First is an ever-growing hunger for flesh and blood that never truly goes away, even after you've fed. If left long enough, this hunger can turn even the most placid of Net-Heads into a homicidal savage to rival the ferocity of any Dead-Head, or even surpass them, because Net-Heads' higher reasoning makes them more efficient hunters.

NANOMED was quick to recognize this fact, so each zombie is fed fresh meat every day, mixed with one-quart of human blood, which for some unknown reason, improves the taste. It is like chocolate sprinkles on vanilla ice-cream. And Friday is raw steak day. Nom nom nom.

At first, eating created its own issues. Zombies are no longer capable of digesting food. So everything they eat just sits in their stomachs, decaying and putrefying quicker than the zombie itself. Because the meat goes nowhere, it just piles up, causing the stomach to swell up until it either bursts, or until the zombie is no longer capable of swallowing anything else because the food is backed all the way up to its throat.

Then there is the smell like a Hades' toilet. It is a well-known fact that after a person dies, the bacteria in their stomachs continue to produce gases causing their abdomens to swell as those gasses fill the intestinal tract. It is not uncommon for a dead person to burp or break wind hours after they have died. Press them hard enough in the gut, and it is like playing a human bagpipe, except you're not sure which end the tune is going to come out of.

This biological fact means that every zombie still in possession of a stomach, will break wind and burp regularly with absolutely no control over it. And we are not talking about the usual kind of gas your grandmother passes at the dinner table. These farts come from the bodies of things decaying from the inside out. The smell has been known to make hardened Marines vomit, stun police dogs and cause bumper stickers to peel off cars.

NANOMED was aware this was going to be a serious issue. It just won't do to have zombie soldiers that can be smelt by the enemy a mile away and was causing his living comrades to pass out. So, NANOMED techs came up with a simple but ingenious solution to the problem.

They removed the intestinal organs from the zombie before

bringing them back online. Stomach, small intestines, large intestines, the whole lot are scooped out. They also do away with the liver, kidney, spleen, and bladder. Once this is done, they fit a connection to the bottom of the food pipe that feeds into a bag that can be easily unclipped and replaced when it becomes full.

To gain access to this bag, each subject has a zip sewn into their body, stretching from the sternum to navel. It can be unzipped and zipped back up whenever the zombie needs to reach inside and replace his artificial stomach. The removal of all those organs creates a nice empty space inside the zombie, more than is necessary for the bag. Fortunately, this additional space inside the abdomen and chest area can be used to store small firearms, ammunition, explosives and all manner of useful items you would typically carry in a backpack. However, if ever you are called into the lab to be packed with C4 just before you go out onto a mission, buckle up because the chances are they're not planning on you coming back!

Lastly, there is the issue of sleep or, more precisely, the lack thereof. When the nanobots bring you back to life, the biological and chemical reaction in your brain that makes you sleep, no longer works. Never feeling fatigued or needing to sleep may sound cool, to begin with, but there is a reason why your brain shuts down and forces you to sleep; it stops you from going bat-crap crazy.

Deprive a living person of sleep for forty-eight hours and see what happens. A single all-nighter is likely to result in mere grogginess, grumpiness, and an all-round intolerance of others. However, by night two, the subject loses the ability to make rational judgments, suffers increased forgetfulness, hampered ability to speak and severely affected reflexes. Trying to function after extended periods without sleep is like drinking a barrel of beer and then attempting to play Sudoku while River Dancing.

Even longer periods without sleep can cause hallucinations, depression, memory loss, stress and temper tantrums. And guess what, kids? All of the above affect the undead as much as the living. Ever wonder why zombies in the movies look angry, clumsy, and ready to tear anyone's throat out? They've spent months without a single night's shuteye.

Having an entire population of zombies going slowly crazy through lack of sleep is never a good idea. The only way to shut down a zombie's brain would be to turn off the nanobots, but this would not solve the problem.

Firstly, shutting off the brain is vastly different from natural sleep. It is like blinking and finding eight hours have passed in that instant. The time may have elapsed, but your brain has not benefited from the downtime. Secondly, 'rebooting' a zombie that has had its NPC pod and all of its nanobots shut down, comes with a risk. The zombie may not come back, or even if it does, brain damage and decay caused by the shutdown process could cause it to come back no smarter than a Dead-Head.

Without shutting down the nanobots, there is no way of shutting down the zombie's brain. However, there is a way of slowing down the bots. Through this process, it is possible to put a zombie into an artificial sleep.

When it is time for zombies to sleep, they go to the 'Blue Room.' This room is essentially a large barrack filled with bunk beds, which are uncomfortable even by zombie standards.

Unlike regular beds with a nice soft mattress, zombie beds are simply foam wrapped in plastic, thrown upon metal and wire bunk-frames. We get no blankets, no sheets and no pillows, although the top end of the foam mattress is shaped into a small mound to support the head.

Why are we subjected to this? Simple. No one wants to wash a zombie's bedding. As far as the military, our owners, are concerned, we don't need the luxury of a blanket because we don't get cold. We don't need proper pillows or sheets for similar reasons. You can easily sponge down a plastic cover after eight hours of a decaying corpse lying on it. However, a sheet requires a lot more time, effort and washing powder to clean after a week of zombie snuggles.

Horrible bunks aside, the Blue Room is not too bad. It is painted a lovely serene blue, which is meant to be the most calming color. Tucked away in the corners of the room are small speakers that play gentle new-age music or sounds of crashing ocean waves, gentle breezes, or the soothing crackle of log fires, designed to relax even the most stressed of brainpans.

Although, whenever crackling log fire sounds are played in the middle of the night, Ash jumps out of bed and dives out of the nearest window.

Lights-out in the Blue Room does not mean complete darkness. Instead, the lights are dimmed and gently change hues of blue, giving the impression of moonlight shimmering off a pool of water in an almost hypnotic dance of light.

A signal transmitted from within the Blue Room to all of the zombies' NPC pods, gives the order to slow down the nanobots' productivity. This, combined with all the room's calming elements, allows the zombie to enter an almost meditative state. It's not quite the same quality of sleep, but it's close enough to help us recharge.

But we do not dream.

Personally, I miss dreaming. I miss those little nonsensical movies that my brain made when I slept. I miss the faces of friends and family that are recreated with complete accuracy in my dreams, unlike the hazy, out-of-focus blurs when I try and picture them during waking hours.

In your dreams, your brain analyses, organizes, and files away your thoughts and experiences from the day and prepares you for the new morning. Losing the ability to dream does not seem like a big deal until you can no longer do it. Then it is like losing an old friend and a safe haven that was yours and yours alone.

The closest I get to dreaming now is the rare times Mr. Marshmallow visits me. But that feels less like dreaming and more like voluntary abduction.

The Thin Undead Line

Keeping a zombie in line is a challenge. After all, if someone believes they have nothing left to live for and hates every day of their life, one cannot simply threaten them with death. Although it works for most, some might think you're doing them a favor by releasing them from their pitiful existence.

Batoltech very much favors the carrot and stick approach to keeping their zombies in check.

The stick is reserved for any zombie who disobeys an order or oversteps their mark. If they are guilty of either, the usual punishment is confinement in a small room we fearfully refer to as The Cupboard. The inside is brightly lit and painted stark white, a far cry from the serenity of the Blue Room.

The offender is then forced to listen to Miley Cyrus, Justin Bieber, or Baby Shark, over and over and over again until driven to the brink of madness. Additionally, they are deprived of meat and blood during their entire stay.

The length of punishment in The Cupboard depends on the offense, but it is usually long enough to ensure the zombie in question has remembered its place in the world - at the very bottom of the ladder. Or, more accurately, the dirt upon which the ladder is propped.

After a week of such torture, most zombies are half-mad, half-starved, and broken to the point where they would do almost anything to avoid going back in there.

Less common punishments involve orders being relayed to the zombie's NPC pod to get the nanos to seize control of their body. Nothing quite like seeing a fellow undead slapping himself in the face continually for two hours because he spoke out of line to his drill sergeant.

But the punishment that filled us all with the most terror was not a spell in The Cupboard, nor losing control of our bodies or listening to Baby Shark. It was what the living jokingly referred to as 'the Top-Popper.' It was so terrifying to us that we dared not speak of it, and when we did, it was with a justifiable amount of dread.

At the base of the zombie's skull, attached to the NPC pod, is a small explosive. Not big, probably only the size of a bean, but powerful. Powerful enough to obliterate the NPC pod and the zombie's head at the same time. Hence the nickname. And no zombie, however grim his life, wanted to have his top popped.

The punishment served several purposes, each one as nefarious as the next. Each zombie base has a kind of radio beacon that sends and receives signals from the NPC pod. If a zombie tries to run away, or moves out of range of the beacon… Boom!

Naturally, this could be over-ridden when we were on a mission. But if the enemy caught us? Batoltech made it clear they would not let their technology fall into hostile hands, so… Boom!

There were rumors that Dead-Heads were occasionally dropped into situations so dangerous that even hardened Marines or Net-Heads would be unable to keep their cool. When the screaming had stopped, and the Dead-Heads had done their work…Boom!

Lastly, the 'Top-Popper' was used to terrify us into submission. It was the most effective way to demonstrate how little our lives - our un-lives - meant. The military could do with us as they wished. And they would.

On my first day of boot camp, Ash, myself and about two dozen other zombies, were made to stand to attention in a straight line for three hours. The zombie standing to my right was Russel Finkle.

When he was alive, Russell had been an accountant for a small but well-respected firm in Tulsa. He was short, podgy around the middle, and still lived with his mother. He'd had fewer girlfriends in his entire life than the number of wieners he was born with. So, when a tall, gorgeous lady he met online promised to be the former and play with the latter, he was instantly smitten. It took her less than two weeks to clear out his bank account, convince him to take a second mortgage on his house and max out his credit cards. The moment he had nothing left to give, she left without giving him so much as a peck on the cheek.

Not wanting to see his dear old mom out on the streets, Russell signed up to the Batoltech program so he could save the house, at least. It seemed that the stress of it all put too much strain on Russell's heart and he died less than a month later.

We stood stock-still in line, murmuring out of the corners of our mouths to avoid attracting attention. I was scared, but Russell was petrified.

Zombies cannot cry, but he was going through the motions nonetheless.

"Oh, Jesus. We are going to die… we are going to die," he whimpered.

"I've been reliably informed that we have already," I muttered through closed lips, looking straight ahead, "and I have a pen-shaped hole in my chest to prove it."

"Oh, no. Oh no, oh no," Russell wailed. "I want to go home. I don't want to die - again."

"Relax," I hissed, trying to calm him. "How bad could it be? Look," I continued, "we're as tough as nuts now. It'll be virtually impossible to kill us. The resin they injected into our bones makes them tougher than steel. We're like Wolverine without the claws…or rugged looks…or muscles…or retro-hair."

"I wasn't injected with resin," Russell said, his voice a little too loud and a little too high pitched.

"Shhh!" I said. The last thing we needed right now was to

get caught talking by one of the Marines keeping an eye on us. Then, "Are you sure?"

"Yes," Russell replied, barely moving his lips. "I didn't get nothing."

As I was trying to figure out why I'd got the resin upgrade and Russell hadn't, our Drill Sergeant, Wallace Hauser, strode out of his portacabin office and right up to us. Two serious-looking Marines flanked him but neither appeared more menacing than Hauser himself. No smile lines framed his mouth, no wrinkles spread from his cold, pale blue eyes. No, no tears for Bambi from this man, no Charlie Chaplin laughs, and Love most certainly was not 'All-Around.' When Hauser did display emotions of any kind, they seemed mimicked and forced, which in turn made him even creepier.

"I bet right now, most of you are wondering why the hell you didn't let The Reaper keep your sorry asses," he bellowed, straightening the cap on his head. "Well, so am I. Because now you belong to me. And when I'm done with you, you'll belong to whoever takes command of you next. End of story."

He marched up and down the line of zombies with his hands clasped behind his back. "No doubt your Project Leaders explained to you how you're now the property of the US Army. They would have explained how you have no rights and no freedom. You are now nothing more than a military asset. But I bet some of you are thinking this cannot be true, this cannot be fair." He placed the palm of a hand on his chest, faking campness. "Surely, when they get to know what a wonderful human being I am, they'll treat me with a little more kindness and respect?"

Hauser stopped right in front of me and glared into my face, "Let me assure you this will *not* happen. Allow me to demonstrate."

He turned to Russell. "What's your name, son?" he said, his icy tone softening a little.

"R…Russell, sir. Russell Finkle."

"Russell. Well, that's a fine name you have there, Russell. Where are you from, Russell?" Hauser asked with a smile.

"Tulsa, s…sir."

"Well, that's twice you've called me Sir now, instead of Sergeant," Hauser said, gently tapping Russell on the chest with a finger, "but you know what? I'm going to let that slide. You got family in Tulsa, Russell?"

"Just my mom, sir...Sergeant."

"What made you sign up, Russell?" Hauser said, putting a hand on his shoulder.

"I…I ran into some money issues, and I wanted to make sure my mother didn't lose her home," Russell said, looking ashamed but slightly more relaxed.

"Wanted to make sure your mother didn't lose her home. Well, isn't that nice?" He glanced at his entourage and us and mouthed, "Aah." He squeezed Russel's shoulder a little. "I bet she is mighty proud of you, Russell. I bet she thought you were a good son."

Russell smiled a little. "Yes, I think so. I hope so, Sergeant."

"I'm sure she did," Hauser said in a fatherly way. He patted Russell's arm then took a few steps back.

"Now, you see that?" he said to all of us. "Russell and I just shared a moment. I got to know him. I bet you're thinking we bonded a little there. That maybe I warmed to him a bit?"

Hauser pushed a button on a small black box he was holding.

Boom!

Russell's head exploded, showering those of us close to him with grey matter and bone.

"Wrong," Hauser said coldly. "I have no more compassion for you than I have for the metal trays in the mess hall or the laces in my boots. None of us do. We all *hate* your sorry asses. You repulse us. The only reason we tolerate you is because one of these days, you may actually end up saving the life of someone worth a damn. That is the *only* reason we don't terminate each and every one of you right now!"

We stood there in utter shock. I tried not to think of the bits of Russell's head sliding down my face. I wanted to cry but was glad that was something I could no longer do.

And that was how it went with every new batch of zombie recruits. From inside our bunks we would hear Sergeant Hauser give The Speech, and then Boom!

We could hear the Marines laughing and joking as the new zombie recruits arrived. They would all watch in eager anticipation from their windows, taking bets on which one would bite the bullet and serve as an example to the others.

We could not bear to watch. We would sit in silence, waiting for the whole grotesque display of power to be over. Each day, the stick used to keep us in line seemed to get longer and longer. Only the carrot at the end of that stick kept us going, for that carrot promised the one thing that every zombie desires: Freedom.

The carrot, in this context, is a place where every zombie is free to do as he or she wishes. It's called The Pastures.

Every evening, just before retiring to the Blue Room, all the zombies are required to watch a short documentary about this little slice of paradise reserved exclusively for the walking dead. For most of us, this glimpse of our future is the highlight of our day.

The documentary is shown in a prefabricated building situated near the Blue Room. The seats are arranged, so it becomes like our very own cinema. Sometimes we even get to watch a movie beforehand. Though, these are carefully selected and usually carry the themes of heroism, honor, and duty. A subtle bit of mental conditioning to ensure we continue to put the greater good above ourselves.

Old war movies, such as Bridge Over the River Kwai, Saving Private Ryan, and Kelly's Heroes, are the regulars, but now and then Forrest Gump will find its way into the mix, for reasons that are beyond me. But after the movie comes the moment we have all been waiting for, The Pastures!

We all sit in silence in the dark; it's dead quiet (excuse the pun). Then brightness fills the room once more as we are treated to a lush green field on the screen. Above is a sky of the palest blue, so bright that it's as if the sun itself is shining out of the screen. The camera pans across to show forests beyond the fields, and further still to reveal that one edge of the field ends in a sandy beach with gentle waves lapping against it in a hypnotic, rhythmic motion. By this point, every single one of us is hooked. We may have seen this scene a hundred times, but each time is like the first.

When the camera stops panning, it has done a full 360-degrees and is back where it started. But this time, standing there waiting to greet us is every zombies' favorite walking corpse, Ned the Undead. A spontaneous cheer goes out amongst us. I have no idea why; I guess we just love this guy. Ned seems like the only zombie to have truly found happiness in his condition. Maybe that in itself gives the rest of us hope.

"Hi, y'all. I am Ned Cunningham. But my friends, well, they just go right ahead and call me Ned the Undead. I don't mind because, after all, that's what I am, just like you good folk. Now I know that, up to now, you've been havin' a helluva rough time and at the moment, things look pretty bleak. But I am here to tell you there is hope." Ned then flashes the warmest, sincerest of smiles, and all at once we know that this guy has our backs. Ned, the brother we all wish we had.

The scene cuts, and Ned is walking through a quaint village filled with log cabins that, even from the outside, looked safe, warm and inviting. Live chickens run between the buildings, chased by carefree zombies, and every time at least one of us will yell, "Catch it! Catch it!" and lick our lips.

The camera soon zooms in on Ned, who has taken up position on a wooden swing bench outside one of the cabins.

"Like you, I once thought there was gonna be no end in sight to the hardships I would have to endure. But then I realized that, with loyalty, hard work and devotion to my duty, a reward was waitin'. And this, my friends, is it," spreading his arms wide, "the Pastures."

The scene cuts, and Ned is once again walking through the peaceful village. Now and then, the shot will cut to a zombie on his porch or working in a small garden outside the front of their cabin. They smile and wave at the camera or to Ned as he strolls past.

"Look around, y'all. No one barkin' orders, no bullets, no electricity to accidentally fry our brains. Heck, not a single livin' soul on the entire island. Just zombies. Now, doesn't that sound nice?" *It sure does.*

Ned is back on the beach, walking on the sand with the waves gently lapping against his bare feet. He continues his pitch to the captivated audience: "This could be your home too. All ya do is serve your country with honor, listen to your superiors and do as they tells ya. Do that and you could be here in just four years.

"With exceptional service, you could be walking along this very beach in as little as three, you betcha. However, failure to follow orders, insubordination and general misbehavin', well, they add on time for that. It sure would be a shame to be servin' longer than ya'all have to, especially see'n as we ain't getting any prettier."

With that, Ned stops, flashes one more honest smile at the camera, waves goodbye and says, "Take care y'all. Look forward to seein' ya'all here real soon".

To which, every last one of us would reply in chorus, "See you soon, Ned."

I may not be the best zombie soldier ever created; actually, most days I would settle for just competent, but I was determined to make it to The Pastures. Looking around the room, I could see my fellow zombies were thinking the very same thing.

Secretly I would smile to myself, hoping they would all make it, and imagine the day when we would all sit around a campfire reminiscing about our time in the military. But sadly, in my heart of hearts (metaphorically speaking), I knew that few, if any, of us would make it.

PART TWO

Book of the (Almost) Living

Undead on Arrival

Where was I?

Oh yeah, I was bouncing unceremoniously off the hard, dirty, arid terrain in some godforsaken area in Mexico.

I lay face down in the dirt for a moment, somewhat disappointed that the fall and subsequent landing hadn't cracked my skull open like a watermelon and spilled my brains, neural net, Nanos and all, across the ground.

I knew I wasn't meant to just lie here. I had to be up and mobile before the other Marines arrived. I had to run ahead and scout for enemies. If they were present, I had to lay down cover fire if required or charge headlong in and act as a decoy if necessary.

I knew I was meant to do this, but I just needed a moment. A few scant seconds, with no one barking orders at me. No one trying to kill me (again!) and no constant reminder that I was a zombie. Just a moment.

Suddenly, one very large and angry-looking scorpion a little to my right, flipped itself back onto its stomach, scurried over to my face and stung me twice on the lip. *Well, isn't that nice.*

It backed off a little and then prepared to make a second assault.

"Ok, ok!" I yelled at it. "I'm getting up."

As I sprang up from the ground, it lunged at my boot, repeatedly jabbing its stinger into it. I flicked it away with the toe of my boot; it landed about four feet away and charged at me again.

"Geez, what's your problem?" I said, backing away a little. I looked down and to my left saw a human-sized crater about two-feet deep where my body had initially impacted with the ground. It was smooth like a bowl; all the small rocks and rubble had been jettisoned away when I smashed into them at near terminal velocity.

By this time, the scorpion had found its way onto my boot and was making the climb towards a softer target.

I was about to bat it away when I noticed something in the center of the bowl-shaped indentation in the ground. It was small and black and surrounded by yellowish goo that had been squished out of it. I squinted and realized what I was looking at – a squashed scorpion.

My attention returned to the scorpion making its way up my leg and I was filled with overwhelming guilt. *Oh, my God! Had I just killed this thing's brother, mother, father, or WORSE… date?*

I plucked it up by the tail and whispered, "I am so, so sorry. It wasn't my fault. You see, I was pushed out of a helicopter because there are these bad guys here…"

Oh, crap. I remembered what I was supposed to be doing. I gently dropped the scorpion, grabbed the automatic rifle that was slung over my back and raced up the ridge a little further ahead.

The moment I reached the top, I dropped flat onto my stomach and aimed my rifle down into the valley below. In the distance, probably half a mile away, I could see dim lights glowing from within a walled encampment. Apart from that, I could make out nothing.

I pulled up my camo shirt, reached under my bullet-proof tactical vest and grabbed the zip sewn into my stomach. Unzipping it felt just wrong. Oh, so wrong. Reaching inside, I grimaced and fumbled around for the little plastic bag that had been shoved in there earlier. My fingers found it and pulled it out. I then quickly zipped up my stomach. "Ugh!" I shivered.

Inside, surrounded by a thick layer of bubble-wrap type lining built into the packet, was a pair of sleek night vision goggles. I slapped them on and looked once more into the darkness that now glowed green. The camp's stone wall was clearly visible and, by the wooden gated entrance, two armed guards paced back and forth. Apart from them, I saw no one.

I looked up at the night sky through the green hue of the googles, but then I removed them to get a better look. Millions of stars twinkled above me in the cloudless sky, and for a moment I felt like I was lost in the vastness of the cosmos. I could no longer feel the hard ground beneath me. There was nothing but me and a sea of beautiful shining stars - all alone and peaceful.

I sighed. All good things must come to an end. I turned my head and put the night vision goggles back on and saw, making their way towards me through the darkness like little, florescent green bowling pins, were the rest of my squad. I reckoned it would be about another sixty seconds before they reached my location.

Suddenly, something slammed into the ground next to me at hundred miles per hour. There was a loud, sickening thud. I was showered by dust and rubble and nearly jumped out of my rotting skin with fright.

I leaped to my feet and took a couple of hasty and awkward steps backward. I leveled my rifle at whatever had hit the ground. Millions of dust particles, luminous green, completely obscured my vision through the goggles. I swiped them off my face as I tried to steady my shaking rifle. As the dust settled, I noticed a large body lying face-down on the ground, dressed in the same military garb as me. The back of its head was black and charred, but it took me a little while to realize I was looking at Ash.

He moved, and I could hear his bones and joints creak as he did so. He pushed himself up a little off the ground, looked up and gave me a big ol' thumbs up. I bent down and helped the mammoth of a man to his feet. He brushed the dust off his vest and shot me a wide toothy grin that sparkled brightly in contrast to his black-as-burnt-toast face.

He looked so happy to see me that I didn't have the heart to tell him that all the skin from his forehead was now lying in the dirt. The once blackened flesh was no more and in its place, smooth pearl-white bone (glossy-looking, thanks to the resin injected into it) stretched the width of his forehead. The poor guy looked like a double-thick Oreo cookie.

Ash rolled his shoulders and I heard more bones clicking back into place. I was contemplating giving him the bad news when another body slammed into the ground at meteoric speed. Within the dust cloud, Andrew 'The Action Man' Johnson cried, "Jesus, why? Why would they do that?" His fist shot out of the dust and shook wildly at the night sky. "Sadists!"

FWUMP! Another body slammed into the ground as I was about to help Andrew up. However, this time, even before the dust cloud could fully rise, a female zombie stepped out of it. She did so as casually as if she had just jumped off a step, not plummeted half a mile to earth without a parachute.

She glared down at Andrew, who was still lying prone, and hissed, "Shut up! You could be heard from a mile away."

We recognized her immediately. This was Angelique Ortiz – Tizzy to her friends. Or so we had heard, we sure as hell weren't allowed to call her that. We just adressed her as Ma'am or Yes Ma'am when the occasion called for it. Once a zombie even called her 'Sir' when she caught him off guard. That did not go down well. Rumour has it that his lower jaw is tucked away somewhere within her abdomen of goodies. It was the last time he or any zombie had called her that.

In life, Angelique was an enforcer for one of the toughest street gangs in LA. She had been running with them since she was twelve and had spent half of that time in jail. However, when her brother was killed in a drive-by leaving their mother to raise his infant son, Angelique decided enough was enough. She signed her body over to Batoltech and used the money to get her family out of LA and away from the gang lifestyle. She was gunned down as they were loading up the car.

Most greenhorn zombies walk into Bootcamp looking like scared (albeit dead) lambs. But not Angelique. The moment she stepped off the van you could tell she meant business. She intended to own that yard and every zombie in it.

Although there was no way it could have actually happened like this, my recollection of her walking into the yard was like a John Woo movie. And Andrew said he remembered it the same way too. All in slow-mo. Helicopters kicking up dust behind her, doves flying out of her way and, from out of nowhere, someone shooting a flame-thrower. She was covered head to toe in tattoos. The right side of her head was shaved and the long, dark brown hair on the other side was braided. It seemed that she had also 'convinced' her Project Leader to let her keep the piercings in her nose, ears and lower lip and, I'm guessing, wherever else she may have them.

I had asked Andrew at the time if he thought she was as tough as she looked. He said, "If such a thing were real, she would be tougher than piranha nipples." I laughed so hard the skin to the left of my mouth split open. Nothing a little thread couldn't fix.

He was right, though. Not even Ash, who was easily a foot taller and a hundred and fifty pounds heavier, would mess with her.

"Get up," she growled. "We've got work to do."

Andrew leaped off the ground. I'd never seen him move so fast.

Tizzy (don't tell anyone I called her that) reached into her gut, pulled out her night vision goggles and, without even bothering to zip back up, took a knee on the ridge. She put on the goggles and surveyed the valley.

"The only people outside the encampment are standing by the front gate," I said quietly.

Tizzy removed her goggles and motioned for me to come close. I leaned in. When I was close enough, she reached up and grabbed my bottom lip between her thumb and forefinger.

"Aurgh!" was all I could say.

She put her goggles up against my eyes. Then using my lip as a rudder, steered my head in the direction of a rocky hill, off to the right of the encampment. About halfway up was a small cave entrance. Without the goggles it would be impossible to see inside, but with them on I could just about make out two figures sitting near the entrance.

"Oh," I drooled.

Tizzy let go of my lip and removed her goggles from my eyes. "Nice going, moron,' she said. 'Down to you, they'd have radioed their pals before we got halfway there, and we'd have been gunned down." Then she looked down and inspected her thumb and forefinger in disgust. They were covered in a goopy liquid that she rubbed between the two. "What the hell is this?"

"Scorpion venom?' I said, not totally sure. "One stung my lip a couple of times when I landed."

She wiped the sticky residue on my fatigues. "Gross."

By now, the other Marines had started to make their way up the ridge. The first one to reach where we were squatting was Jackson Cole. Even in a crouched position, he was taller than your average man.

When he got close to us, he said, "Ok, Net-Heads, what have we got?"

"There are two guards stationed by the front gate," I said.

And before Tizzy could say anything, Andrew jumped in with, "And there are two more lookouts in a cave in that hill over there."

Jackson took Tizzy's night-vision goggles, looked in the direction Andrew had pointed, then dropped the goggles back in Tizzy's hand. Looking somewhat impressed, he said to Andrew, "Nice spot, Net-Head. Maybe there's hope for you yet."

Andrew's smile vanished the moment he saw Tizzy glaring at him, her jaw clenched tight enough to crack a billiard ball.

In under a minute, we were joined by Pheonix Red, the squad from my helicopter, and Phoenix White squad, from

Tizzy, Andrew and Ash's helicopter. All told, four zombies and twenty-six Marines.

Jackson motioned for August to join him. "Sanchez," he said, pointing to the hills, "Take six men and that Net-Head," pointing to Ash, "and take out those lookouts and clear that cave. Don't forget to send the Net-Head in first. Wait..." Jackson took a step closer to Ash. He pulled the huge zombie towards him with a single tug of his tactical vest. "What the hell happened to your head?"

Ash looked at him, confused for a moment. Then he raised his hand to his forehead and felt smooth bone beneath his fingers. His jaw dropped open and he looked at me in horror.

"Sorry, buddy," I said.

"Dammit," Jackson said. "Your head looks like the tip of a Converse boot."

Ash put his hand to his forehead again, looking utterly forlorn.

"C'mon, big guy," August said to Ash, and they and the squad headed out into the night. As Ash disappeared into the darkness, I could not help but feel incredibly worried for my friend. I had completely forgotten that, in all likelihood, I would be in more peril than him in a short while. The idea of him being forced to go first into that pitch-black tunnel filled me with dread, and anger for our 'masters.'

At least when his skin had been charred, Ash might have been able to blend into the shadows, but now that his forehead looked like a hi-viz reflector, he was an easy target. Not, of course, that the living heading out there with him cared, so long as their sorry-butts made it home in one piece.

Jackson made the signal for everyone to hold the position until they got the all-clear. I knelt close to him and looked in the direction of the cave through the night vision goggles. Occasionally I would see Ash and his squad clamber over a rise or small outcrop of rocks before disappearing over the other side and out of view. The closer they got to the cave entrance, the less often I caught sight of them, and when I did, they vanished as quickly as they appeared. Then they were gone from sight.

Through the goggles' green haze, I saw three quick flashes of light coming from within the cave entrance. Then I could just about make out Ash's hulking frame heading cautiously into the darkness. After about a minute, the radio attached to Jackson's shoulder crackled to life.

"Pheonix Red Six? Over." August's hushed voice came over the radio.

"Red Twelve, this is Red Six. Over," Jackson responded.

"Red Twelve confirming target has been neutralized. All clear. Over," August confirmed. He did not mention if they had taken any casualties so I presumed they had not. But I also knew he may not have bothered if Ash was the only casualty. I wanted to ask Jackson to confirm if Ash was okay, but he continued to give orders to August before I could.

"Copy that, Red Twelve. Hold position and be our eyes."

"Affirmative, Red Six. Want us to send down the Kentucky

Fried Net-Head?" August replied, and I, metaphorically, breathed a huge sigh of relief.

"Negative," Jackson said and then looked directly at me. "You may still need a meatshield."

"Roger that, Red Six. Over and out," August replied, and the radio went silent.

Jackson ordered, "Net-Heads, get over here."

"I'm already here," I said.

He glared at me, "I know that, numbnuts. I was talking to them."

Tizzy and Andrew scurried over, keeping low to the ground. When they got with a few feet of Jackson, he said, "Right, you see that big rock, dead ahead, about a hundred yards away from the base? I want you to head for it in a straight line. Keep low and make sure you have a three-foot spread; I don't want you going single file. Hold position, if you get there."

"If?" Andrew asked, sounding worried.

"Mines," Tizzy said flatly and unafraid. "That's why we're going first."

Andrew's eyes grew so wide I thought one might pop out of the dry eyelids keeping them in place.

If I remembered how to gulp, I would have. "And if we step on a mine? Then what?"

Before Jackson could answer, Tizzy said, "If any of us are still standing, we charge straight in. We create as much commotion as possible to draw enemy fire and give the squad a chance to get into position." Then to Jackson, as if remembering her place, "Correct, Sir?"

Jackson looked at her with a modicum of respect and nodded. "Affirmative. You two, are you clear?"

Andrew and I nodded.

"Let's go," Tizzy said and headed straight down the steep, rocky embankment into the valley below. We followed but with less grace. She made it to the bottom, quickly, quietly, and with the agility of a mountain lion. The same could not be said for Andrew or me. I got no more than ten steps down the embankment before a stone shot out from underneath my foot and I slid the next ten yards, creating a small rock avalanche in my wake. As I was getting to my feet, Andrew slid past me on the flat of his stomach. This made me lose my footing again and skid another five yards until my foot snagged a jagged rock sticking out of the ground, and I was catapulted upwards. Fortunately, I landed on my feet, but nothing could stop my downward trajectory, and I ended up careening past Tizzy like an ungainly giraffe on ice.

Both Andrew and I managed to come to a complete halt at the bottom of the incline.

"Thanks, buddy," Andrew said as I helped him up off the ground. "Do you think Jackson saw that?"

A stone flew out of the darkness from high up on the ridge and smacked me square on the forehead. I stumbled back a little and said, "I think so."

"I'm surprised the enemy didn't see that," Tizzy jeered. She shoved past us and we hurried to keep up. "Do anything to give away our position again and I'll kick both of your asses," she fumed.

Andrew smirked, "You can kick mine if I can feel yours."

Tizzy stopped dead in her tracks.

Andrew looked at me with wide-eyed terror.

"What the hell made you say that?" I whispered.

"I have no idea!" he said, his bottom lip already starting to tremble.

Tizzy spun around and marched right up to him. She drew a savage-looking knife with a twelve-inch blade from her belt and, in one fluid movement, grabbed his right ear and sliced it clean off. She inspected it for a second and slammed it into his hand.

It took Andrew a moment to realize what he was looking at. But when he did, he raised his hand to the gaping wound on the right side of his head and cried out, "Oh my God. Why did you do that?"

"Because you disrespected me. Do it again," she pointed the knife down towards his neither region, "and you know what'll be next to go."

Andrew took a step back in horror but then retorted, "Ha! The joke's on you because it's already missing."

Tizzy tilted her head and gave Andrew an evil smile. "I know the meat is gone. Everyone knows. I was planning on cutting the veg off too."

Andrew gasped. Gawping first at me and then at her. "You're the meanest lady I have ever met."

"Better believe it, bitch. Now move!" Tizzy, crouched and with her automatic rifle at the ready, hurried towards the rock with us in tow.

Andrew held his weapon in one hand and his severed ear in the other, whimpering all the way. I guess he could sew or staple it back onto his head, but I doubted it would stay put any longer than his Johnson had. I hate to admit, as sorry as I felt for Andrew, I was just glad it wasn't me who had annoyed Tizzy. At that moment, she scared me more than the hostiles we were about to face. She had done such an excellent job of terrifying us, I only remembered about potential mines when we were just yards away from the massive rock.

I tip-toed the rest of the way to the truck-size boulder and was thankful to be enveloped in its shadow, still in one piece, unlike poor Andrew, who was still cradling his severed ear in his hand.

"Drop it or I'll make you eat it," Tizzy warned between gritted teeth. Andrew defiantly shoved the ear into a pocket on his tactical vest.

Tizzy slowly poked her head around the corner of the boulder. Instinctively I did the same thing. Andrew followed suit. Less than a hundred yards away, the two armed guards chatted quietly by the closed wooden gate of the compound, utterly oblivious to the zombie versions of Mo, Larry, and Curly peering at them from behind a rock.

Tizzy moved back, shoving us in the process. She took a pencil-sized infrared light and clicked it twice in the squad's direction to signal that we were in position. I half expected to see, and was disappointed when I didn't, a red beam of light shooting from the Tizzy's hand and into the night.

Jackson and the rest of the squad had not waited on the ridge for us to arrive at our destination. By the time we were halfway to the massive rock, they were already catching us up. So when Tizzy sent the signal, it took them less than a minute to reach us.

"Report," Jackson said to Tizzy, completely ignoring Andrew and me.

"Two by the gate,' Tizzy said, "but I also saw a head pop up over the wall, just once."

How the hell did I miss that? The wall was easily twenty-foot high. Either there was a walkway on the other side, or they had the BFG in there (and I don't mean *'friendly')*.

"It could be someone hunkered down, or a guard patrolling the wall," she continued. "Won't know for sure until we see him again."

Jackson nodded. "Well done. Keep this up, and it won't be long before The Morgue Horde snatches you up."

"Thank you," said Tizzy, genuinely smiling for the first time since I met her.

But Andrew and I were not smiling. The Morgue Horde were legend amongst zombies, spoken of only in hushed whispers. They are elite of the elite. Most were killers and military veterans before they died, and they excelled at it. The Morgue Horde were used for the most dangerous and secretive of missions. They had fearsome callsigns like Rigor Mortis, Cold Grave, General Demise, Bone-Yard, and Mr. Squeezy. It was also rumored they were the zombies they sent to kill other zombies if the Undertakers failed. I could see Tizzy taking no small amount of pleasure in doing just that.

Jackson thought for a moment. “We can’t afford to wait.” He motioned for Paxon Word to move up next to him. He pointed up at the wall and whispered, “Hold position here until we are inside. You see a head pop up over that wall, you blow it off.”

Word nodded, lay prone on the ground and aimed up at the wall with his scoped rifle.

Jackson backed off towards the other men. We followed without being asked, and all crouched down behind the rock.

Jackson whispered, “When Alverez and Hill take out the guards, we’ll approach the gate. Once we’re inside, Loomis, take your squad and clear left. We’ll clear right. Take these two Net-Heads with you,” he said, motioning to Andrew and me, “and I’ll take this one.” He jerked a thumb towards Tizzy, who beamed broadly.

Loomis shook her head. “Not a chance. Paper beats rock, remember?”

Wait. Had they played rock, paper, scissors to see who would be stuck with us? Well, that’s just charming, that is.

Jackson gritted his teeth. “Fine, you take her, but you take The Action Man as well. I’ll take burger-boy.” *God, I hope that nickname doesn’t stick.*

Andrew had once said that Adelle Loomis was way too

pretty to be a Marine, let alone a Corporal. Sometimes he would refer to her as Marine Barbie. But since he had already lost one body part, I doubted he was going to say anything else stupid tonight. But when it came to Andrew being around attractive women, or women of any kind for that matter, you never could tell. I said a silent prayer just in case.

Loomis nodded, and everyone sprung into action. Alverez and Hill rounded the rock and, with two shots from their silenced rifles, took out the guards by the gate. The rest of us double-timed it towards the gates with our weapons at the ready.

We silently lined up against the wall. Jackson motioned to another Marine who gave the sturdy wooden doors leading into the compound a careful push. They did not budge. He shook his head. Jackson gave another signal to the Marine. I had no idea what the gesture meant. We were taught about thirty hand-signals in basic training, and I remembered about four. However, the Marine seemed to understand what Jackson meant. He removed a small brick of C4 from his backpack and started attaching it to the doors.

I looked down at the two dead guards. This will sound like the dumbest thing ever, but I'd never seen a dead person before that wasn't, well, already dead and walking around and stuff. Apart from poor old Russell, but when he 'died' I just felt terror and pity. Now I wasn't sure if I felt repulsed or hungry. I looked across at Tizzy. She was gazing at the corpses and licking her lips. Andrew was looking at her, licking *her* lips.

Jackson shoved me roughly and I hit the wall, almost dropping my gun. "Snap out of it, Net-Head. You can eat when they're all dead. It'll be a regular buffet. Intel says there's about fifty of them in there."

Fifty! There were twenty-four of us. I did the math in my head. *Damn, they outnumber us six to one.*

I tapped Jackson on the shoulder just as he was about to signal the Marine to blow the entrance. He glowered at me. I whispered, "I may have missed this in the briefing, but why aren't we just torpedoing this base from the sky. Like, boom!"

Jackson gave the signal for everyone to hold position. That one I did know. He then grabbed me by the collar of my body armor and lifted me off the ground with one hand. He grimaced as he brought his face close to my rotting one, but his obvious repulsion didn't stop him. He seethed, breathing hot air onto my face. "Two reasons. First, there's intel in that base we need, so we can't go blowing it up. Second, and most important reason why we can't do that is because… *torpedoes are used underwate*r, you freaking moron!"

Jackson let go abruptly, and I fell to the ground. He gave the signal for the doors to be blown and we all pressed ourselves against the wall.

There was a click of a button. A hole the size of a basketball was blown out of the wooden doors and they swung inwards. All of a sudden, everyone was charging forward and all hell broke loose.

We're Gonna Need a Bigger Fan

Jackson grabbed me by the shoulder and shoved me forward before I even had a chance to think about what was going on.

I ran inside the compound to a cacophony of screams, shouts and gunfire. A siren began to blare out in the night. Red hot streaks zipped through the darkness from both enemy and friendly fire.

Tizzy, Andrew, Loomis and her squad, peeled off to the left the moment they entered the compound. Tizzy was the first in and immediately started shooting at bad guys. Andrew was right behind her. He was screaming and shooting at what appeared to be the stars in the night sky. Loomis, using Andrew as cover, took considered aimed shots at anything that moved. I saw her bag a man armed with an AK-47 within a couple of seconds of entering the compound.

Were we meant to be going right or straight ahead? Inside the compound were about a dozen self-contained buildings and a large one of three stories in the center. Directly right of the entrance to the compound, another building stood close to the wall forming a narrow, two-foot gap between them. If I turned immediately right, I'd be heading straight down the space between the wall and building, which did not seem correct, but I didn't want to vex Jackson any further. *Oh well, here goes.* I charged down the narrow gap, rifle in hand.

I got about half a dozen paces down when I heard Jackson yell, "Moron, where the hell are you going?"

I made to turn, but as I did, my rifle got stuck between the outer wall and the wall of the building. I tried again to turn, but the rifle was just too long and prevented me from doing so. Do I drop it? *Oh, hell, no!* Jackson would skin me alive, er, dead... you know what I mean.

My only option was to carry on running forward, which I did as fast as I could. It was only as I got closed to the far end that it dawned on me that if I held my rifle straight up instead of horizontally, I wouldn't have had a problem turning around. *Idiot. I'm sure I wasn't this stupid when I was alive.*

I rounded the building into an open area, flanked by yet more buildings and the outer wall. About a dozen men armed with automatic rifles and shotguns were charging in the direction of Jackson and his squad, who were rounding the building from the other side.

None of them had seen me. I had a clear line of fire on all of them. If I could take down at least half of these guys, I would be a hero. The problem is, I'd never shot anyone before.

I had never caused injury of any kind to anyone.

I did not relish the idea of shooting these people, *riddling them with bullets...watching the blood gush from their open wounds...fresh, warm blood...then they'd fall to the ground like sacks of juicy, succulent meat... yummy.*

I have no idea what came over me. All I could see was red, the crimson kind, and I turned into freaking Rambo.

"Aargh!" I charged forward, unleashing a storm of bullets. Caught off-guard, they darted for cover, returning panicked fire as they did so. I didn't care; I was invincible. I was death incarnate. I was freaking *starving!*

Unfortunately, but unsurprisingly, I didn't hit with a single bullet. The same, however, could not be said for the opposing team.

I imagine, having never experienced the sensation myself, that getting shot when you are alive hurts. Hurts a lot! At which point, one would probably fall to the ground, either dead or dying, writhing in agony and wondering if it was too late to find religion. However, getting shot when you're dead is a weird sensation, to say the least. Although we don't feel the pain, which is kinda an upside to being dead, a bullet still hits with the same force it would a living person and, to that end, has the same effects. In most cases, it will hit you hard enough to knock you down, or at the very least stop you in your tracks for a second or two. It is a bit like being slammed into by an invisible quarterback.

This is how I knew I was getting shot - a lot! Slam! A bullet hit me in the hip, causing me to stumble. Slam. Another in the shoulder almost spinning me like a top. Slam, slam! Two in the chest forced me backward. This was followed by a third hit that completely took me off my feet, and I landed in a heap on the ground. No sooner did I get back on my feet, when two more bullets hit me high in the chest, almost causing me to lose my footing again.

Fortunately, I was wearing a bulletproof tactical vest so at least the body shots were not turning me into a walking version of Connect Four. However, I should point out that the bulletproof vest is not supplied for my protection but rather to protect the cargo I was carrying inside the empty cavity in my rib-cage. Heaven forbid military equipment should get damaged unnecessarily.

Another bullet zinged past the right side of my head, too close for comfort. A lot closer than I initially thought, I would later realize, at the discovery - much to my dismay - of a perfectly round chunk missing from the top of my ear.

My rifle was out of ammo and I was in serious trouble. I heard one of my attackers yell, “It’s a zombie. Aim for the head.”

“Or not,” I yelled back, fumbling frantically for a spare clip from my ammo belt.

They were within ten feet of me now, with weapons aimed at my head. Just as I thought I was about to die for real this time, Jackson and the squad rounded the corner and opened fire. Within seconds, all of the enemies trying to gun me down were dead.

Unable to breathe a sigh of relief, I faked it. "Phew!" I said as Jackson approached me, crouching low with his rifle at the ready.

"What the hell were you doing, Net-Head?" he barked. Elsewhere, all around the compound, gunfire was exploding.

"You said go right," I answered, really wishing his rifle was not pointed at my head. "Besides, I caught them totally off-guard. You should have seen me. I fired an entire clip before they even realized I was there."

"Did you hit any of them?" he challenged me.

"No," I answered meekly. "But I came, like, real close."

He lowered his gun. "Close only counts if you're throwing a grenade. It don't mean squat with a bullet."

He had a point. Trying to regain some credibility, I said, "Yeah, but I did draw their attention, allowing you guys to shoot them."

Bullets ricocheted off the wall near our heads. "Move it!" Jackson grabbed me and pulled me in front of him, so hard that he nearly took me off my feet.

I ran forward and over one of the enemy corpses. The smell of fresh blood and flesh hit my nostrils. I longed to stop for a little snack, but Jackson was shoving me forward. I felt like a dog on a lead, yanked away from a tasty treat he found on the sidewalk. Crazy to think that of all the senses you lose as a zombie, the sense of smell is the one that gets heightened.

More bullets smashed into the wall next to us, and Jackson continued to push me forward. It was only when we rounded the corner of the building and two more bullets slammed into my chest that I realized he wasn't trying to get me out of harm's way, but using me as a human shield.

Around the corner, gunfire erupted from every window of the building opposite, accompanied by an adrenaline-fueled battle cry from the people firing on us. A couple of them, I was sure, sounded American.

The squad darted for cover, returning fire as best as they could. Three of our team made it to a stationary beige-brown pick-up truck, parked by the building that shielded us. By the time they reached it, the vehicle was riddled with bullets.

Jackson yanked me closer to his chest, pulling me straight off my feet, and we were once more against the corner of the building we had just rounded. Two more of the squad followed us, frantically firing at the single-story building no more than twenty yards from us, as at least three gunmen retaliated. The wall was peppered with bullets, exploding in shards of brick and concrete that pierced our skin and bounced off our clothing. Jackson, hunkered down by the corner of the wall, was trying to shoot anything that moved in either direction.

I crouched behind him, not entirely sure what to do. We were well and truly pinned down. We couldn't stay here for long, and we couldn't go back around the corner without being gunned down. I could only hope that Andrew and his squad were fairing better. I was sure they were. They had a Tizzy.

As he shot a controlled burst around the corner and another at the building facing us, Jackson yelled at me, "Fire, dammit!"

The order snapped me out of my stupor. I saw a man aiming at us from a window of the single-story building and I pulled the trigger of my rifle. My bullets tore holes around the edge of the window, but again it was close but no cigar. However, it did cause the man to duck for cover, giving us a couple of seconds reprieve.

Jackson grabbed the top of my bullet-proof vest and shoved me violently away from the wall. "Get in there and take them out, Net-Head, or we're all dead."

I knew he was right, and I knew I was their best hope, but I was terrified. Still, I did as he ordered and ran towards the building. But then I saw them.

Two of our squad had not been as lucky as the rest of us to make it to cover before bullets rained from all directions. A Marine I did not recognize was lying dead in a heap, his rifle still clutched in his hand. The other was Alverez. He had taken a bullet to the shoulder and another to the thigh of his right leg. He rolled on the ground, crying in agony. He clutched the wound on his leg with his good hand. Blood oozed from between his fingers, seeping onto the ground and creating a delicious crimson puddle.

I couldn't help myself. I dropped my gun and charged towards him, teeth bared. All thoughts of the people trying to kill us were forgotten. I didn't even notice the bullets that hit the ground by my feet or zipped past, mere inches away from my head, or the two or three that grazed my undead flesh. All that mattered was food.

Jackson was bellowing behind me to get back, but I didn't care. Alverez was within my grasp. I launched myself at him. His eyes filled with dread and he screamed, "No!"

I grabbed his shoulders and pinned him to the ground. I opened my mouth wide to take a huge chunk out of his neck. He screamed again. "No, please!"

I stopped myself just inches from his flesh. I looked into his eyes and realized I was the cause of his terror. It made my stomach churn, and I was hungry no more.

I pushed myself off Alverez, grabbed him by his shirt and dragged him with all my might towards the sanctuary of the pick-up truck. It was no haven, but a helluva lot safer than being out in the open. Bullets slammed into my back, my jacket absorbing most, but one tore a hole in my side and came straight out of my belly.

I screamed as a dragged Alverez. All fear had gone. Now I was angry. Correction, I was *hangry.*

I dropped him behind the truck and ran back towards my rifle, barely giving him time to say, "Thank you."

I picked up my weapon without breaking stride. Dozens of bullets flew past me, but I paid them no nevermind. I was a zombie on a mission. I charged at the single-story building, roaring the first word that came into my mind: "Freedom!"

I busted through the wooden door. It tore free of its hinges, and I landed heavily on top of it. Both I and the door slid across the ground. The man standing in the room opened fire as I came crashing through, but I guess he wasn't expecting me to slide along the floor as he shot wild, missing me by a mile.

I fired back, while still in transit, also missing by a mile. The man screamed in horror. I suspected this was his first encounter with a zombie. He turned and bolted for the door to his left. He threw it open, greeted by panicked yells on the other side. Gunfire exploded in the room beyond, riddling the man with friendly fire. He was dead before he hit the ground.

More frantic yells from the other room.

"Surrender now or I'll eat your freaking faces off," I yelled, getting up from the floor.

The yells dropped to a quick, hushed exchange. *Oh, screw this.* I ran towards the door, just as a thrown object landed at my feet. Before I could see what it was, my boot connected with it and kicked it straight back in the direction from whence it came. It was only when it reached the arc of its return to the room beyond that I realized what it was.

In chorus with the two gunmen in the other room, I yelled, "Oh crap!"

BOOM! The explosion was deafening. I was thrown by the force of it but was shielded by the walls separating the two rooms. A dust cloud billowed out from the room beyond, along with flying chunks of rubble and furniture.

As I lay on my back, covered in dust, something fell onto my chest from a fluorescent light that swung back and forth from the ceiling; a hand, separated from its owner, midway down the forearm. I will neither confirm nor deny that I took a quick bite before charging onward.

It was carnage in the other room. Smashed furniture and pieces of food, um, I mean bodies, were strewn about the floor and the walls were splattered cherry-red.

There was another door on the opposite side of this room. The firing had stopped from this building, but I needed to make sure that room was clear. I threw open the door, preparing for the worst. Nothing happened.

The room was empty save for a single wooden table in the very center. Preciously placed in the middle of it, lay what I was sure was a bazooka. *Ooh, that could come in handy.* Confident that the building was now clear of enemies, I grabbed the bazooka and ran outside.

I could tell the moment I exited the building that things had not really improved for my fellow Marines.

Jackson and the two Marines by his side were still pinned down by enemies firing from the three-story building opposite. The pickup truck sheltering the other three was smoking badly, and I thought it wouldn't be long before it burst into flames. To make matters worse, I could see at least three hostiles had taken up position on the roof and were preparing to fire down on them with belt-fed heavy assault rifles. The kind that would rip through a pick-up truck like it was a cornflake box.

I have to say I was a little surprised, in the midst of all the chaos, Jackson still found the time to give me a look so thunderous it would have made Thor quake.

I genuinely didn't know what the problem was. I'd taken out

the bad guys as he asked. Well, sort of. Sure, I took a quick detour to eat Alverez, but I didn't do it. I saved him. That, surely, had to count for something? Maybe he'd be happy that I found a bazooka?

I made to run towards him but tripped over a chunk of rubble and landed flat on my stomach. The bazooka hit the ground hard, and I think… I can't say for certain… there was the teeniest, weeniest chance that my finger might have pulled the trigger.

WHOOSH! A missile shot from the bazooka. It Catherine-wheeled several times and spun wildly through the air and straight through an open window of the three-story building filled with gunmen.

There was an almighty explosion. Fire and debris erupted from every window. Brief screams were cut short instantly, and the shooters taking up position on the roof barely had time to react before it collapsed in on itself.

The Marines, taking refuge behind the pick-up truck, all looked at me in stunned disbelief, as did Jackson and the Marines by his side. Still lying flat on my chest, I gave them a big toothy grin and thumbs up. *Yeah, I meant to do that. Call me, Rambone.*

Dust clouds billowed out of all sides of the destroyed building, completely obscuring the line of sight for anyone close to it. A firefight was still raging on the other side of the compound, but Jackson used this temporary wall of fog as cover and charged over to me. He hauled me off the ground with one powerful arm and screamed in my face, "You idiot, you could have killed us all!"

"But I didn't," I protested. "No, I took out the bad guys and *saved* all of you."

"You got lucky," he yelled. "And 'bad guys?' Are you a kid? Do you think this is a game? There are no good guys or bad guys - just people trying to kill other people. Now, thanks to your stupidity, we have to run blindly through that," he pointed to the dust cloud, "to reach our team before those people kill them."

"Fine," I grumbled.

Jackson thrust me forward toward the wall of dust and said, "You first Net-Head."

Looking back on it now, I must have seemed like a sulking child.

"Whatever," I griped, as I walked away from him. I kicked an errant stone and shook my gun in frustration. *Who does he think he is? I just saved a whole bunch of people, and he is making me out to be some kind of idiot. He should be thanking me.*

"Oh, and Net-Head," Jackson called after me.

I spun around and instantly regretted yelling, "It's Marco!"

"Net-Head," Jackson repeated with menace in his voice. "You ignore an order of mine again and you're a deadman. Clear?"

I just looked at him. Did he really just threaten to turn a zombie into a dead man?

What's next? You gonna threaten to rip the legs off a snake.

I turned back towards the dust cloud. "You should write a book," I muttered under my breath. "The Idiots Guide to Redundant Threats." I half-hoped Jackson wouldn't hear me because, well, quite frankly, he scared the crap out of me. *Hey, that's weird; I've just thought of something else I haven't done since I died.*

Although, when I tell this story later, I will say, "Yeah, I was like all up in Jackson's face, and I said, *'Hey you dumb ox, why don't you write a book and call it an Idiots Guide to Stupid Insults because you're stu...'*

SLAP! Jackson's hand collided with the side of my head like a one-ton buffalo.

"Ow!" I yelled instinctively. I didn't feel any pain, but I knew he hit me because my head shot to one side, my eyes rolled around in my skull like billiard balls, and the cup of his hand, which had suctioned itself to my ear, made a satisfying 'Pop!' sound as he pulled it away, like a plunger being removed from a sink's drain.

"What did you say?" He growled.

Oh damn....

"Nothing. I said 'clear,'" I mumbled meekly. But later, when Jackson was safely out of earshot, it would be, "And then I was like, *'You heard me! Now get outta my face before I go all Zombie on your ass!'*" Boy, they'll be impressed. I bet even Tizzy will be.

Behind me, Jackson angrily barked at the remaining squad, "Weis, stay with Alverez, the rest of you with me."

I headed into the veil of dust, a good ten paces ahead of the others. I couldn't see more than three yards ahead of me. On the other side I heard an explosion and a bright light illuminated the dust, which glowed orange for a second. More screams, more sounds of automatic gunfire.

Then there was another sound like an engine firing up. A gale came from nowhere, blowing dust straight into my face.

I shielded my eyes with my forearm while trying to maintain a reasonable grip on my rifle.

The good news was that the strong wind cleared away the worst of the dust cloud within seconds. The bad news was, once it was gone, I could see what had caused it to be blown away – a black attack helicopter not more than ten yards from my position. It was stationary on the ground, but its main rotor was picking up speed as it prepared to take off.

Sitting in the cockpit, I saw baddies…sigh, I mean two people who wanted to kill us, and when they spotted me they seemed quite prepared to do so. The gunner's lips curled into an evil grin. He gripped the control lever and twin Gatling guns, mounted to the front of the helicopter, raised a little.

Oh, this isn't good. I heard Jackson scream, "Take cover!"

The only problem was, I couldn't see any cover. Or at least none close by. While the Marines to my rear ducked this way and that, I stood there, rooted to the spot by indecision.

The Gatling guns spun and burst into life, unleashing a storm of bullets. Some slammed into the ground by my feet and others whizzed past me, creating a path of destruction in their wake. By fluke, I was directly in the space between both waves of bullets, and unscathed. I knew I wouldn't be for long. I had to move. But I could not move right without being obliterated and moving left would result in the same fate. I had no choice. I charged towards the helicopter.

Both the gunner and pilot's expressions changed from sadistic satisfaction to shock as I ran headlong at them. The gunner tried to turn the guns on me, but it was too late. I was already mere feet away from them. I dropped to the ground and let my momentum propel me forward. I slid directly under the front of the helicopter. *Haha! Can't get me now!* Surely this had to be the safest place to be.

The pilot pulled back on the control stick, and the helicopter lifted off the ground. And to my horror, so did I. I looked down and saw the landing skid had slipped through my tactical vest, effectively hooking me to the helicopter.

I was hoisted into the air and twenty feet off the ground before I could even react.

"Help. Jackson help!" I screamed. It was no use. Over the roar of the helicopter blades, he wouldn't be able to hear me, or even give a damn if he could.

I knew I was in all kinds of serious trouble here. If this helicopter were blown out of the sky, it would not end well for me. If they managed to get away, my fate would be worse. Without doubt, the moment they noticed I was outside the mission zone, the explosive in my skull would be detonated to prevent the precious technology in my head falling into enemy hands. My only option was to take this bird out of the sky myself. But how?

I fumbled for the grenades hanging from my tactical vest. I had three. I threw the first, just as the helicopter banked. By some miracle, it flew into the open door on the side of the helicopter. I squeezed my eyes shut and braced myself for the explosion. If I managed to get out of this, I wouldn't be pretty, that's for sure. After five seconds, I cautiously opened one eye. Nothing happened. After two seconds more, I opened the other. Still nothing. *Oh, you schmuck, Marco. The pin. You were meant to pull the pin before throwing the grenade. Never mind, take a mulligan.*

By this time the helicopter was circling the compound, shooting at anything in an American uniform. Marines returned fire and bullets clattered off the underside of the helicopter, narrowly missing me.

"Hey, I'm still under here, dammit," I yelled down at them.

Okay, here goes. I grabbed another grenade, pulling the pin this time with my teeth, and tossed it upwards. It went wide and bounced off the side window screen. It tumbled to the ground below and exploded.

Andrew would tell me later that the grenade took out four of the enemy who had him and Loomis pinned down.

I raised my rifle and was about to shoot into the undercarriage but noticed the indentations made from my fellows' bullets. If theirs couldn't penetrate the metal, mine certainly wouldn't. Then I had a thought. If I could not take down the chopper, maybe I could take out the Gatling guns. They were secured to the underneath by metal brackets that could pivot. They looked sturdy but not indestructible.

I struggled to aim my rifle at the furthest Gatling gun as I swung back and forth as the helicopter banked from side to side. *Here goes nothing.* I emptied the entire clip at the gun. Sparks flew everywhere as the bullets smashed into the brackets. Just as the last shot left my rifle, the brackets snapped. However, the cables were still attached to the gun and the underneath of the helicopter. As the bracket fell it pulled the gun down, but the cable pulled its muzzle upwards. Hundred of bullets from the Gatling gun's red hot and smoking barrels tore through the helicopter's rotor blades and underbelly, directly below where the pilot was sitting.

Without warning, the helicopter tilted and spun wildly as it started to plunge towards the ground. I was flung loose of the landing skid. My initial thought of, *Yay, I'm free!* was quickly followed by, *Oh, nuts!* as I found myself, for the second time this night, plummeting from a great height. Only this time it didn't look like I was going to smash into the ground but instead, onto the flat roof of a double-story building.

As the roof rushed towards me, I saw two gunmen standing by its edge, shooting down at the rest of my squad. Also, the way I had been propelled off the helicopter meant that I was coming in at a forty-five-degree angle instead of straight down.

I don't know why, but I yelled, "Lookout," as I pinwheeled towards the gunmen. Both turned and gaped, but it was too late for any of us to act. The impact as I slammed into them, catapulted them both off the roof. One of them, I swear, let out a Wilhelm scream as he plunged to the ground.

"Sorry," I called after them instinctively.

I lay on the roof for a moment, wondering how much more of this I would need to endure. I also wondered if the guys I had just knocked off the roof had survived. The out-of-control helicopter spinning directly overhead and crashing to the ground below in a fiery explosion kinda answered that question.

As I lay there, gazing up at the stars and basking in the warm glow of the flames that licked up the side of the building, I wondered if it would be acceptable for me to take a time-out right now. Hadn't I done enough for one evening? I was sure the rest of my team could handle it from here. Would they even notice if I just lay here? Just as I started to sing, "would you lie with me and just forget the world," my awful rendition of Snow Patrol's song was interrupted by the sound of Andrew screaming. The scream seemed to come from directly below me.

I jumped to my feet and scanned the rooftop. Roughly in the center was an open trapdoor. I sprinted toward it. A ladder lead straight down into the room below. I didn't bother with it, but leaped down, feet first.

I landed hard in the large room below. The moment my feet hit the floor, I noticed half a dozen automatic rifles pointed directly at my face. I closed my eyes and prepared for the inevitable, but then heard Loomis shout out, "Hold your fire!"

When I opened my eyes, she and another five Marines were lowering their guns.

"Jesus, you Net-Heads are going to be the death of me," she said.

Standing just behind her and to her right was Andrew, looking pitiful. His trembling bottom lip was sticking out and his gaze was purposefully averted from Loomis. There was something different about him I could not quite put my finger on.

Tizzy was standing to the left of Loomis, looking equally unimpressed by my entrance.

Maps and floorplans covered the walls in this room. Three desktop computers and a laptop lay on a long table against one wall.

A large table in the middle of the room was strewn with papers and files. Now the Marines knew I was not a threat, they turned from me and started to scour the room. Tizzy resumed position by the door, pointing her rifle down the corridor.

Loomis's fingers were closed around something in her right hand. Whatever it was must have been small as she was still able to point a finger at me without revealing what it was. "Where's the rest of your squad, Net-Head?"

'Erm, I dunno," I said. "I just fell from a helicopter."

Loomis looked at me in exasperated confusion and shook her head.

One of the Marines, who was tapping away at the laptop,

said, "I think this is the intel we're looking for."

Another Marine, rifling through the papers on the table, said, "This is definitely what we were looking for."

I glanced down at the table. Among transcripts and official-looking documents, were blueprints of buildings. One, I read, was for a Hospital in San Diego, another looked like the floorplan for a bank. Yet another was a detailed layout of the Chinese Embassy in Washington.

"Excellent," Loomis said. "Livingstone, take the laptop as well as those hard-drives. Brennan, put what you can of that lot in your backpack. When you're done, torch what's left. The rest of you come with me."

Loomis nodded toward me. "You come with us. Let's find the rest of your squad."

Brennan and Livingston set about scooping up papers and breaking open the desktop computers.

Loomis tapped Tizzy's thigh with her boot and said, "Move out."

Tizzy, without turning round, nodded and took off down the corridor.

Loomis then turned and slammed her closed hand into Andrew's chest. She uncurled her fingers and whatever she was clutching fell out. Andrew caught it mid-fall. He looked down at it mournfully. She hissed at him, "Stay here and watch their backs - and your mouth." Then she shoulder barged past him and out of the door.

When she had left, followed by the Marines, I trotted up to

Andrew. When I got close, I realized why he looked different. On his open palm lay his left ear.

"Oh, you didn't?" I said.

Andrew looked at me with big doe eyes. "I couldn't help myself. I really do think I have a problem."

"Well, it's one you'd better get a handle on. If you keep losing bits like this, you'll be just a head by the time we make it to The Pastures."

Andrew nodded. He slipped the ear into a pouch on his tactical vest, where its partner was residing.

"Net-Head, get your butt here," Loomis yelled.

"I'd better go, pal. Stay safe," I patted Andrew on the shoulder.

"You too," he replied.

By the time we got out of the building, I had been pushed to the front once more with Tizzy.

We advanced into the night, weapons at the ready. Floodlights illuminated this area of the compound and cover was scarce. Fortunately, it seemed like the majority of the fighting was over. Only the occasional shot rang out in the darkness.

"Head right," Loomis whispered. We complied, but I gave Tizzy a sideways look and noticed red around her mouth. She smiled a mouthful of bloodstained teeth at me.

"You've eaten?" I mouthed.

Tizzy nodded. "Reward for taking out three HoMS."

I had heard this term before. It stood for Hostile Mercenaries. However, when a Zombie says HoMS, they mean Human Occupied Meat Snacks.

"Mercenaries?" I said quietly, not wanting to be heard by Loomis. "I thought these were terrorists?"

Tizzy shook her head. "Not a chance. These guys are ex-military – US, I'm betting. At least the three I bagged were. How many did you kill?"

"Deliberately?" I asked.

Tizzy scrunched up her face. "Huh?"

Before I could answer, a stone hit me on the side of my head. Again, I have no idea why I said "Ow!" Maybe it was out of habit, learned from a time when things like this actually used to hurt.

I turned to see where the stone had come from. Ahead of me, at the far end of the compound, was a double-story building, which seemed the only one without combat damage. A little way in front of it, and to my right, was a broken wall. Crouched behind it was Jackson with the two of his squad and Paxon Word.

It was Jackson who had thrown the stone.

He beckoned us urgently. Tizzy gave Loomis and her cohorts the rally point signal. Keeping low, we all crept to Jackson's position.

Loomis moved to the right beside Jackson, who was having difficulties keeping his massive frame concealed by the wall. He shifted a little from side to side, trying to peek out at the building in front of us, then quickly ducking his head back behind the highest point of the stonework

"Report," he whispered to Loomis.

"All buildings cleared on our side. Intel retrieved. One KIA - Dever. And you?"

"Left flank cleared. Two casualties. One WIA and one KIA – Alverez and Hobart," Jackson replied, through gritted teeth. "This is the last building. We saw three running in. Word bagged a fourth."

I peered over the wall and saw a sprawled body, about five yards away from the building entrance.

"Call for choppers and order a tactical retrograde?" Loomis asked, which was military slang for 'get the hell outta here.'"

Jackson shook his head. "Not before we bag those last HoMS."

Loomis nodded. Jackson hissed to the two Marines from her squad. "You two circle left, keep low, make sure no one bugs out of the building from that side. You two," he told a pair from his own squad, "flank right, cover that side and the rear. Got it?"

They nodded, grunted, and sped off with heads low.

Jackson tapped Word on the shoulder. "Cover the front. Net-Heads...," he pointed to us, "you charge in first."

Charge in? How about, cautiously approach within the safety of a tank?

"Shake the nest and we'll follow," Jackson finished.

While I had reservations, Tizzy seemed more than up for this suicide mission. She nodded eagerly. Probably keen to munch down on another kill.

"Ready? Go!" Jackson ordered. Tizzy leaped the short

wall, landed gracefully on the other side and charged towards the entrance. I did the same, but less gracefully. I stumbled, regained my footing and resisted the urge to scream, "Leee-roooy Jenkins!" as I charged forward.

We got about halfway when bullets began to rain down on us from the roof of the building. The three mercs had decided to take the fight to us instead and were now firing down on us from behind the small perimeter wall.

Tizzy rolled to her left but not before two bullets had ripped through her leg. She seemed not to notice. Jackson, Loomis and Word returned fire as best they could, but were forced to take cover as bullets tore up the wall they were hiding behind.

As for me, I took a couple of steps right. Nope, no cover in that direction. I then darted a little to the left. Nope, no cover there either. Fortunately, my little dance meant that the guy shooting at me was hitting nothing more than dirt.

Tizzy yelled, "Fire in the hole!" and hurled a grenade high into the air and onto the roof.

I suddenly remembered I had one grenade left. I grabbed it from my tactical vest, tugged out the pin, and tossed it towards the roof.

I yelled, "Fire in the…oops!"

Whereas Tizzy's grenade had gracefully disappeared over the top of the roof (greeted by the terrified screams of those hiding up there), mine did not get the desired height. So, instead of landing on the roof, it hit the top of the building and bounced back.

In slow motion, it tumbled back to earth and landed behind the wall where Jackson, Loomis, and Word were hiding.

Jackson stood bolt upright and glared directly at me. Then, with his final breath, and sounding neither scared nor angry but merely disappointed: "You are such a douchbag."

Boom!

99 Problems But a Pulse Ain't One

The AAR (After Action Report) was harsh. The accidental deaths of Sgt. Jackson Cole, Corporal Adelle Loomis and Specialist Paxon Word did not go down well. Drill Sergeant Hauser chewed me out for over an hour (and yes, the irony of that statement is not lost on me). He got so up in my face that I thought I might, if it were possible, drown in his spit.

"But wasn't the mission successful, Sarge?" I ventured meekly.

"No thanks to you," Hauser yelled in my face. "But for the recovered intel on the bank and hospital attacks, the entire mission would have been a disaster."

"And Chinese Embassy," I said without thinking.

"What?" Hauser screamed.

"They also got the plans for an attack on the Chinese Embassy."

"You are mistaken, Net-Head," Hauser said, with more

menace. "There were no such plans."

I nodded. Even I had enough common sense to know to drop it.

Something about the way he then looked at me, made me think he wanted to silence me forever.

As the grilling continued, and after at least half a dozen threats, I truly believed he was going to push the little red button that would detonate the explosive in my brain. I'll be honest, part of me welcomed it.

Only the testimonies of Alverez (who said I took enemy fire to save his life and then charged into an enemy-filled building), of Weis (who credited me with 'deliberately' taking out another with a bazooka), and a couple of other Marines (who claimed I jumped on a helicopter to take it out), kept Hauser's finger off that button.

However, it was Staff Sergeant Ballantine who eventually talked him down. It turned out that I had inadvertently neutralized close to half of the enemies in that compound.

"Hell, if this kid were alive, we'd be giving him the Goddamn Medal of Honour," Ballantine said. I think if they knew the truth, they'd pin a warning label to me instead: 'Do not allow to operate heavy machinery, vehicles, explosives or weapons of any kind.'"

Though no medal was forthcoming, I was allowed to leave the debriefing room with my head intact.

I was halfway back to my barracks when a Marine trotted up to me. She was in her early twenties. Her dark, wavy hair was tied up and mostly tucked under her cap. She had almond skin and big brown eyes. She reminded me of Beth. Not quite as pretty, but lovely nonetheless. As she approached, I was grateful that Andrew was not with me.

"You're Project 2219, Marco, right?" she said, with a friendly smile.

"Er, yes." *How did she know my name?*

She reached into her camo jacket, pulled out a ziplock bag and handed it to me. Inside was what looked like a liver, marinating in blood. I looked at it and then at her in confusion.

She said, "Alverez says thanks for saving his life and not eating him when you had the chance."

"Oh," was all I could say.

She turned to walk away but over her shoulder said, "Took out most of the enemy, huh? You're making quite a name for yourself. Keep this up, and you'll get recruited into the Morgue Horde for sure."

I shuddered. *No thanks.* Those guys actually *mean* to kill people.

I snuck the bag back to the barracks, but instead of going inside, I ducked around the side where it was quiet. I opened it and greedily devoured its contents. The liver was not human, but the blood unquestionably was. *Man, it tasted so good.*

By the time I was finished, my mouth and hands were caked in blood and gore. I wiped them on the grass and did my best to get rid of the blood around my mouth.

Before going to the mess hall for the regularly scheduled

evening meal, I knew I would have to empty my gut-bag. I unbuttoned my shirt and reached for the zip running the length of the abdomen. Only then did I notice that it was partly undone. The clip had come away from the teeth securing it. I had been so concerned with patching up the other injuries from the previous night, I had not noticed a problem with my zip.

I tugged on it with no success. I knew I could open it further, but there was no way it would close again. *Damn!* This meant I would have to see my Project Leader, Emily Aiken, which scared me almost as much as the mission last night.

However, it was inevitable. Any issues with standard fitted equipment must be reported to a Project Leader immediately. That was the protocol. Before seeing her, I knew I had to empty my stomach bag and replace it with a new one, lest it raised questions. I did not want to get Alverez - or the Marine who had given me the tasty treat - into trouble.

I unzipped my stomach further and reached inside. I fumbled around a little but eventually found the clip securing the stomach bag. I twisted it and it came loose. As I extracted it, I saw it was not the only thing to come out of my stomach. Sitting on top of the hand holding the bag was a huge black scorpion. I screamed, shook my hand and dropped the bag to the ground. After several shakes, the scorpion fell off my hand and landed softly onto the grass. It then scurried towards me and stopped dead in its tracks when it reached my boot.

I stared down at the creature and then remembered where

I had seen it before. “You’re the little fella from last night.” Somehow, when I was not paying attention, it must have climbed back up and into my shirt. It probably crawled into my stomach when I unzipped it to get the night vision goggles.

I bent down and placed my hand near my boot. The scorpion ran up a finger and onto my palm, making no attempt to sting me. In fact, it seemed rather calm as I lifted my hand to get a better look and it seemed to look back at me. “Well, you’re actually kinda cute. Hmmm, I think I’ll call you Eric. Sorry again about last night, Eric.”

Eric took a couple more paces forward on my hand. “Well,” I said, “if you’re going to hang around with me, I’m going to need to get this zip fixed pretty quick, because you won’t be able to hang out in my stomach until I do.” I unbuttoned one of the pouches hanging from my belt and moved my hand towards it. Eric scuttled from my hand into the darkness of the pocket.

I ran to a water fountain outside and washed off the rest of the blood, then headed out to find my Project Leader.

Every base where Zombies are stationed has a lab where the Project Leaders and staff of Batoltech Global work. We may be under the military’s control, but Batoltech has the contract to maintain us, as and when needed. However, it just didn’t make sense to ship us off for repairs and upgrades. So, in the same way that military bases have their own doctors, mechanics and storage facilities that house spare gear, they also have onsite zombie specialists. Employees of Batoltech, stationed at the bases, working from Company-designed labs.

This particular lab - three long, white Portacabins sandwiched together - was situated at the far end of the base. Generators and airconditioning units had been affixed to the outside, giving the whole thing the appearance of a more permanent structure rather than something that could be moved at a moment's notice.

No guards were stationed outside the only entrance into the long building, which led to a reception area where a single armed Batoltech employee sat behind a desk. We called her The Vice because, we all suspect, she could squeeze your nuts like they were, well, you get the picture. To get to the Project Leaders, you needed to get past her, so you had better have a damn good reason.

Beyond that room, the rest of the building really did look like a lab. Glass partitioned the offices, operating rooms (also known as repair rooms), and storage rooms. These were mostly filled with clear plastic tubing, bags, and fastenings that were used on the inside of Net-Heads and regularly needed replacing. Only one room, at the far end of the Portacabins, was not walled in glass. This one was sealed with a metal sliding door with a retina scanner and keypad. None of us knew what was in there, but we all suspected it was pretty important. All, apart from Andrew that is, who thought it was where the crapper was situated.

I walked along the length of the Portacabin towards the entrance, peering into the windows as I did so. This was my routine every time I had to come here. It's not that I was particularly nosey; it was just that I liked to see people outside of military life getting on with their own thing. Most of the time, I would see them tucking into their homemade sandwiches or sharing a quick joke between tasks and occasionally sitting about gossiping. Not today. As I walked past the windows, I noticed something strange. Every single Batoltech employee was studiously busying themselves. Not one looked up from their work. There was no joking, gossip, or talking of any kind. Even standing outside, I could tell the atmosphere inside was icy. I glanced further down the building and saw a black limousine with tinted windows parked at the far end.

As I got to Emily Aiken's office window, I stopped dead in my tracks. Standing on the opposite side of her desk was a stern-looking man in a black suit. He was in his early forties, with dark, slick back hair and skin that looked more leathery than mine. Emily was sitting on the other side of her desk looking worried. If she was, it could mean only one thing; this guy was a Batoltech head-honcho. I had never seen Anton Batolgore in the flesh, and had only seen a few of his direct reports a handful of times. However, I had seen enough to know that those that spoke on Anton's behalf were to be feared.

I took a step back to where they could not see me through the open window, and listened.

"The rogue NPC pod has to be here," the man was saying

"How do you know?" Emily asked.

"Because this is the only base that has been receiving unsanctioned communications."

"Have you been able to find the source of the signals?" she asked.

"No. And they are encrypted, so the only way to find out what information has been transmitted will be to discover which of those Net-Heads has the rogue pod inside their skull."

"And how do you propose we find out?" Emily asked, sounding a little concerned.

"Dismantle them all and send their NPC pods back for analysis," the man said flatly.

Woah! My mouth fell open. I chanced another peek through the window. Emily's jaw was likewise *agape*. "Dismantle sixty-five zombies and destroy millions of dollars worth of assets?" she said. "Not to mention the training that would be wasted. The Military would never sanction this. What do we say to them?"

"We tell them their current zombies have a fault in their pods. They will be suitably compensated, and we have a new batch of more competent zombies in production. The cost is of no concern to Mr. Batolgore. His primary concern is protecting Batoltech Global no matter what. Do we understand each other?"

Emily hesitated for a moment. "It may not be necessary to dismantle all of them. Allow me to interview them first. If any display irregularities in their answers, I'll dismantle them myself. It'll take me just three days."

The man gave this some thought. "How will you prioritize your interviews?"

"I'll do it in order of this pile," she said and held up a stack of folders. To my horror, I saw a picture of my face paperclipped to the top one.

The man shook his head. "Assume the recipient of the rogue pod was not chosen at random. I believe our saboteur would have read your subject's profiles and inserted it into the most resourceful, competent and intelligent candidate. Start with the zombies that fit that profile and work back from there."

Emily looked at my picture and promptly moved my file to the very bottom of the pile. "Agreed."

It may have bought me time but, I have to say, seeing her do that *hurt*. I had a good mind to storm in there and say, "Hey, lady. Didn't you hear I just got the highest kill count in our last mission?" However, that may well prompt both her and mystery man to bypass the interview stage and just pop my head open. Thus discovering what I feared to be true; what they were looking for *was* inside my skull.

It would explain how I knew things about Batoltech Global, Zombies, and TF Bundy that were not public knowledge. What I could not explain is why it had been put in my skull and for what reason. Maybe my brain's secret stowaway, Mr. Marshmallow, knew.

I slunk away from the lab, hoping no one had seen me. I didn't go to the mess hall that evening for dinner, nor did I watch Ned Cunningham and The Pastures show. I wanted to be alone. In part, because I was anxious about what I had learned and in part because I didn't want to open my big mouth and spread panic amongst my fellow zombies.

Instead, I scoured the grounds of the base, searching under rocks, in tall grass and around garbage bins for tasty morsels for Eric to eat. All the time my mind was reeling from the revelation. I tried to kid myself that it may not be inside my head. After all, surely Tizzy would have been the best candidate for this unwanted gift. But if my suspicion was right, should I say nothing and let her head get cracked open like a watermelon? She may not be my favorite zombie, but didn't she deserve to know?

However, deep down I knew it was *not* inside her head. It was inside mine. I needed to talk to Mr. Marshmallow.

I retired to the Blue Room as soon as I was permitted and lay on my plastic-covered bunk. Shortly afterward, the other zombies arrived, all heading directly to their respective bunks. Andrew was spouting to a couple of other zombies, who were only partially humoring him, something about the canteen lady panting for him.

As Tizzy walked by, she gave me the evil eye. She did not break her gaze from the moment she entered to the moment she got on her bunk. Her stare chilled me to my dead, resin-filled bones.

I mouthed, "What?" She shook her head slowly, saying nothing. *What had I done? Did she know?* Maybe I would not have to worry about Emily cracking my skull open. Maybe Tizzy would save her the effort.

Ash tapped me on the shoulder. He looked concerned. I

stared at the big white patch of bone on his forehead where skin had once been. It dawned on me that you gotta have pretty expressive eyes to look worried without the ability to frown. He smiled sympathetically, pointed at me, and then made the 'okay' gesture with his thumb.

I nodded. "Yeah, I'm okay, buddy."

Ash turned around, bent his head, and then did something I could not make out. When he turned around again, written in dry marker across his pearly white skull was the word, 'Sure?' He gave me a big cheesy grin, and I burst out laughing.

I reached out and patted him on the shoulder. Still smiling, I said, "Yeah, I am now. Thank you."

Ash nodded and rubbed off the dry ink with the back of his hand. It made a squeaking sound as he did so. He then climbed onto his bunk, the one below mine.

The lights dimmed and a dark blue haze filled the room. The soft sound of waves flowed from the speakers, and soon everyone was still and silent.

I undid my pouch button. Eric climbed out and crawled up the middle of my chest. I reached into my pocket and handed him the cricket I had found earlier. He grabbed it from my hand with one of his pincers and heartily munched down on it.

"Goodnight, buddy," I whispered and closed my eyes. I tried to quiet my brain. I tried to forget everything that had happened in the last twenty-four hours and focus solely on the sound of the waves and the dim blue light that penetrated my eyelids.

It took a while, but eventually my mind fell silent and I was no longer lying on an uncomfortable bunk in the Blue Room. I was standing in the middle of a dark forest, in front of a warm, glowing campfire. Sitting on a large log on the other side of the campfire was Mr. Marshmallow. He held a long stick, with three plump marshmallows skewered on the end, which he kept close to the flames. Another marshmallow-laden stick was stuck into the ground next to him. He looked up at me and smiled. "Right on time," he said. He pulled the other stick out of the ground and offered it to me. "Marshmallows?"

I nodded, took the stick, and lowered myself next to him on the log. We sat in silence as the outer layer of our marshmallows crisped up and went through all the shades of brown until they were eventually turned black by the flames. We withdrew our sticks simultaneously. He crammed the first marshmallow into his mouth greedily. I played with mine, testing the consistency between my thumb and forefinger. Here, on this log, I was not dead. I could feel as I had once been able to. I could eat marshmallows and remember their taste.

I would normally have enjoyed being here, but not tonight.

"What's wrong," asked Mr. Marshmallow. Tall and wiry with a kind face, he reminded me a little of my grandfather. His grey hair was short but a bit messy, as was his trimmed beard. If left to grow of its own accord, I suspected the hair on his face would stick out in all directions like an electrified scarecrow.

"Who are you?" I asked, realizing I had never taken the time to ask him that before.

He mused over this for a while. "I understand you have taken to calling me Mr. Marshmallow. I like that name. Why don't we stick with that?"

I looked at him squarely. "I heard a Batoltech employee talking about a rogue NPC pod."

Mr. Marshmallow sucked in air between his teeth. "Oh, so they found out."

I nodded. "It's inside my head, isn't it? You put it there and you're the reason they're looking for it."

He sighed and patted my knee. "I'm sorry, my boy, but that is correct."

"Why?" I asked.

"Because it's important," Mr. Marshmallow said. "There are things going on in this world that are not right and without your help, I don't know how to stop them."

I stood up and threw my hallucinatory stick and marshmallows into the fire. "But why me?" I shouted. "If this is so important, why give it to me? Why not Tizzy or Ash or *any* of the other zombies. You know I have been ranked as the most incompetent zombie ever to complete basic training? I once got tangled up in somebody else's climbing gear and he hadn't even taken it out of his bag. There's a zombie in our platoon called All Thumbs Joe. They call him that because I slammed his fingers in a door. TWICE! I killed three of my *own team* last night..."

"And a whole bunch of bad guys," he reminded me.

"Accidentally!" I yelled. "And besides," I added more calmly,

"I've been told I'm not supposed to call them bad guys. It's childish."

Mr. Marshmallow scoffed. "We're inside your head. Here you can call them what you want."

"But *we're* not going to be in my head much longer, *are* we?" I said, my voice rising again. "Soon they're gonna break open my skull and take *you* out and kill me in the process."

"That is regrettable," he nodded. "I'll see what I can do to buy us time."

"And in the meantime, what happens to my friends? How many of them will they 'dismantle' while you're buying us time?"

Mr. Marshmallow shrugged.

I shook my head and took a step back. "No, I *have* to tell them it's inside me."

Mr. Marshmallow stood up, dropping his stick. He pointed a finger at me. "No. You can't do that. What's in there," he pointed to my head, "what you know, what you *will* know, is too important. I'm afraid it's more important than the safety of your friends. You cannot let it fall into their hands."

"And I can't sit back and watch my friends die for me," I said.

Mr. Marshmallow's eyes softened and he gently took hold of my shoulders. "It was no accident that my NPC pod ended up in your head, Marco. I know you are not the smartest…" *Ouch* "nor the most talented…" *Oww* "or even the most competent zombie." *Ok, that one I'll give you.* "I chose you because of this." He placed a hand on my chest. "You have a good heart, and when it comes to the crunch, I know you'll do what's right, regardless of the price to yourself. That's why I chose you."

"They removed my heart," I said with a weak smile.

Mr. Marsmallow gave me a sincere, warm smile. "They removed the muscle, but they can never take away the part that counts."

I don't know why those words warmed me, more so than the crackling fire. Maybe it was just nice to hear someone else say there was more to being human than a beating heart.

"I still don't know how we're going to get out of this situation," I said.

"Neither do I, my boy, neither do I." With these words, Mr. Marshmallow faded into the darkness.

Dead Meat

Tizzy was the first one to be dragged to Emily Aiken's office. She came out looking more pissed off than she had the night before.

I overheard her talking to some other zombies. "I don't know," she was saying. "She said it was just some routine psych evaluation, but something's not right. It seemed…off."

I spent the rest of the day avoiding her, Andrew and Ash. Avoiding Tizzy was not too difficult since she always avoided me anyway. Andrew and Ash proved to be more difficult. Ash was concerned at first but eventually figured I needed some space, so he let me be.

Andrew was another matter. He just would not leave me alone. He was on me like flies on a corpse. Everywhere I turned, there he was.

Fortunately, he mostly wanted to talk about what was going on in his life. He did not seem to notice that something was playing heavily on my mind. He had managed to re-attach his ears using staples, and when he ran out of those, thread, but neither sat right on his head now. One flopped forward a bit, and the other tilted back ever so slightly. Still, he seemed pleased with the result. When he was not asking if his ears looked okay, he talked about the new female recruits. I reminded him why he needed to re-attach his ears in the first place, and this shut him up for a while.

With each zombie that was dragged off for interrogation, the mood in the yard grew more tense. Each spoke with hushed voices on their return and it was not long before rumors went round of recalls and mass 'dismantling' and conspiracy theories abounded.

Only Andrew seemed not to get the memo. Before long he was bleating on again, driving me insane. I was sitting on a bench near the blue room, trying in vain to ignore him.

Eventually, Ash came to my rescue. He drew a pair of boobs on his head, showed them to Andrew and pointed excitedly in the direction of the canteen.

Andrew sprung to his feet. "Sorry, Marco. Duty calls." He then legged off in the direction of the canteen.

Ash gave me a knowing wink but had no sooner done so, when a Marine prodded him in the back and said, "Come with me."

Ash pursed his mouth as if to say, "Oh, well," and turned to follow theMarine.

I called after him. He turned and I pointed to the pair of boobs drawn on his forehead. Ash grimaced comically and erased them with his palm.

Late morning of the following day, it was my turn. A Marine

barked at me to head directly to Emily's office

So this is it. I am the last one to be interviewed, and after this they'll start popping open skulls. I felt sick to the core, even though this was a physical impossibility. Nonetheless.

I was led into Emily's office by a Marine armed with a taser. I suspected it carried enough electrical charge to light up half of Manhattan, and more than enough to fry every single nanobot in my body.

I sat down on a metal chair opposite Emily. She eyed me for a moment and sighed. "Oh well, may as well get this over with," she muttered under her breath.

She reached for a pen and lifted the clipboard on her desk. Seeing both it and the pen gave me a horrid flashback to my last interview with her.

She sighed again. "Hello, Project 2219."

"Oh, we're old friends. You can still call me Marco if you want," I said.

"We're not, I won't, and I don't," she said bluntly, not looking up from her chart. "I'm going to ask you a series of simple questions. Now, I appreciate what may be simple to others may be a reach for you, but try to answer them as honestly as possible. You have nothing to worry about..." *yeah, right!* "this is just routine, to see how your hardware is functioning and how you are doing. Understand?"

I nodded.

"Good, then let's begin. Have you had any periods where you have blanked out or experienced missing time?"

I shook my head.

"Have you seen any bright lights, with eyes open or closed, that cannot be explained?" she asked.

I shook my head again.

"Have you had any unusual dreams that seemed very realistic? And in these dreams, are you given knowledge of things that you have no reasonable way of knowing yourself?"

I smiled. "Are you trying to make sure I'm working okay or if I've been abducted by aliens?"

Emily did not look amused. She reached across her desk, grabbed a jam jar full of sharpened pencils, and shook it once in my direction.

My eyes widened. "No, no, I haven't," I lied.

"Any uncontrollable seizures, fits or loss of muscle control, beyond the usual that is?" She asked.

"No," I said.

She bit her cheek and looked deep in thought. "I understand that on your last mission, you neutralized nineteen hostiles."

"Nineteen?" I gasped. "Wow, there was only fifty, so I took out like two-thirds of them?"

Emily's face scrunched up, as if my words had caused her actual, physical pain. Eventually she shook her head and continued, "During this time, did it feel like someone else was controlling your body and actions?"

"Honestly," I said, "if you'd been there, you'd have seen that every single person I took out was by complete accident."

"That I do believe," she said. She then flicked through at

least three more pages of questions on her chart. She huffed loudly and said, "I really can't be bothered with this. Putting it inside you would be like putting a handbrake on a slug."

"What?" I asked, though I knew full well what she was talking about.

"Never mind," she said, waving a dismissive hand. "You can leave, Project 2219."

I stood up, but before I left I said, "Oh, my, um, zip broke."

"See Dr. Hickman on your way out and get it fixed," Emily said without looking up from her clipboard.

Outside of her office I glanced back at her through the glass partition. She was rapidly ticking the 'No' box for every question on her sheets.

After getting a new zipper installed, I left as quickly as I could. As I walked away from the Portacabin lab, I was filled with a sense of dread. I may have been the last on her list to interview, due to her view of me being the most worthless zombie, but I suspected she would dismantle me first out of spite. The upside being, at least my friends would be saved.

Before I could make it to the barracks, the siren blared out to indicate it was lunchtime. I figured if this was to be my last meal, I might as well enjoy it.

I was the last to arrive at the mess hall due to its distance from the lab. Apart from the people serving the food, everyone in here was dead. Ten long aluminum tables, with affixed benches on either side, were packed with zombies. About sixty all told.

I picked up a metal tray with a blood-drenched hunk of meat on it and headed straight to where Andrew and Ash were sitting. I was almost there before I noticed Tizzy, sitting next to Ash. I faltered in my tracks but then decided I needed to bite the bullet. If this was the last time I got to sit with my friends, I could not let her chase me away.

I sat next to Andrew.

"Hey, pal," he said. "You back with us now?"

"Yeah," I nodded.

Ash quickly scribbled, 'All good?' on his shiny forehead; he had really gotten quite good at writing backward.

Andrew and I smiled. Tizzy just shook her head and forked another slice of raw flesh into her mouth.

"Hey Tiz…Angelique, ma'am," I said.

She did not look up at me.

"Oh c'mon," I wheedled, "what have I done wrong?"

She slammed her knife and fork onto the table. "You screwed me!" she barked.

"I don't remember," I said innocently.

"You'd think you would," Andrew quipped. "I know *I'd* remember. It's not something *you'd* forget either!" he said, winking at Tizzy.

She picked up her fork and stabbed it into his hand, pinning it to the table.

"Waah!" Andrew yelled. He grabbed the fork and tried to yank it out. Tizzy batted his hand away. "No," she said. "That stays there now for the rest of the meal so you can learn your lesson. Try to remove it and I'll cut your hand off."

Andrew's bottom lip quivered a bit and he slumped back in his chair, pitifully eyeing the fork impaling his hand.

"What did *I* do, Tizzy?" I asked, still waiting for an answer to my question. I no longer cared if she was going to punish me for calling her that.

She pointed her steak knife at my face and spat, "I've busted my gut to get recognized here. I put my neck on the line during that last mission and took out six, *six,* HoMS by *myself.* More than any living marine there. I was on my way to getting promoted out of this dead-end outfit and into The Horde.

"But then you came along, and Forest Gumped your way through the entire mission, and now you're all everyone can talk about."

"Oh, come on," Andrew said to Tizzy. "What Marco did will be forgotten in a couple of days. You just carry on doing what you do, and The Morgue Horde will see you're just the kind of psycho bitch they need on their team. Oh! Sweet Jesus, I did not just say that."

Andrew quickly tucked his other hand under the table before Tizzy could skewer that too.

"You have to believe me," I pleaded. "I didn't mean to steal your thunder. I didn't mean any of it."

"I know," she growled, "and that is what's pissing me off the most. You are the luckiest son-of-a-bitch I've ever met. But I swear to you, if you do anything to stop me getting into The Horde again, I... will... end... you!"

"I won't," I said defensively. "Besides, *we*," I pointed to Andrew, Ash and myself, "want nothing to do with The Horde. We just want to make it to The Pastures."

Ash and Andrew nodded.

Tizzy scoffed, leaned in close and whispered. "You and I know The Pastures is a bag of crap."

No, I don't, I thought. In my mind it was real, very real.

"There are only two ways out of this unit," she continued. "In a body bag or being promoted to The Morgue Horde."

Tizzy yanked the fork out of Andrew's hand and he groaned in relief. She then told him, "I need this. Stick your own in."

"Whaaat?" Andrew mouthed in dismay.

Tizzy gave him a stony stare. His bottom lip wobbling, Andrew reluctantly picked up his fork and stabbed it into the back of his hand.

Without looking up from her bloody meat, Tizzy said: "And Marco, call me Tizzy again and see what happens."

I winced at the fork sticking out of Andrew's hand. "Understood."

The door to the mess hall swung open. Drill Sergeant Hauser stood in the doorway, his chest puffed out and his shoulders thrown back. He looked like the cat that had got the mouse that had been dipped in cream and then rolled in catnip. Seeing him this maniacally happy made my nutsack retreat into the empty cavity inside my gut.

"Meatsacks," he yelled. "You have some new recruits. And I'll bet my bottom dollar, each of them is worth more than all your sorry asses put together."

With that, he stood aside, and my absent heart almost fell out of my butt.

Marching his massive frame through the doorway as if he already owned the place, was the zombified Jackson Cole. Behind him, Adelle Loomis strode in, casting a judgemental eye over all of us. Lastly, Specialist Paxon Word strolled in, looking way too casual under the circumstances.

Hauser gave me an evil smile. He turned and left without saying another word.

Jackson slowly scanned the mess hall. No prizes for guessing who he was looking for. I flipped up my metal tray, spilling its contents onto the table, and held it up to hide my head.

Ash quickly scribbled 'OMFG!!!' onto his forehead.

Andrew nudged me? "Marco, my chum, you are *so* dead-dead."

Tizzy looked at me, "I didn't think it possible, but I genuinely feel sorry for you right now."

"Maybe it's not that bad," I said, still hiding my face behind the tray. "I mean Dead Air, right? They won't remember how they died. Maybe no one told them it was my fault."

Tizzy scoffed. "Yeah, right. Keep telling yourself that."

"Oh, nuts. Do you think they saw me?" I asked.

Tizzy raised her eyebrows and nodded. "Oh yeah."

With that, the tray was savagely ripped from my hands and tossed across the mess hall, where it hit an unsuspecting zombie on the head. Jackson Cole towered over me, his immense shadow blocking out most of the light.

"Oh, hey, Jackson. I didn't see you there," I said innocently. "How are you doing?"

The zombies on our table scattered. Andrew made to follow suit, but as he stood up, he realized his hand was still pinned to the table, so he meekly sat back down again. Tizzy did not budge because, I suspect, she didn't give a damn, while Ash sat stoically and gave me a reassuring wink as if to say, "I've got your back, buddy."

Jackson sat astride the metal bench so he was facing me. The bench was secured to the table, and the whole thing shook violently as his butt hit the metal.

I have to say that, despite being taken out by a grenade, he didn't look too bad. Oh, who am I kidding? He looked a freaking mess.

Most of the skin on the lower half of his jaw was missing, exposing the bone beneath. Half of his nose had been blasted away, leaving a gaping hole where his left nostril used to be. His left eye was red and discolored, and a tiny piece of shrapnel was still visible under the sclera. Cuts covered his face and his trunk-like arms where shrapnel had torn through his flesh. The larger wounds were stapled shut, but others remained open and angry.

Adelle Loomis had not fared much better. The grenade blast had obliterated the right side of her face destroying the cheek. Instead of reconstructing it, her Project Leader had simply riveted a piece of metal over the hole. Part of her lower lip was missing, exposing the teeth beneath. Like Jackson and

Word, her face was peppered with cuts and holes. No longer would anyone think to refer to her as 'Marine Barbie.' More like 'Mortician's Nightmare Barbie.' Although, ironically, Andrew may stand more of a chance with her now, like one in a million maybe, but still more than when she was alive.

Judging by Word's face, I guessed that Jackson's forearm might have between it and the blast when the grenade went off. The flesh running down the middle of his face was unmarked. However, the skin on either side was torn to shreds. Both of his sticky-out ears were in tatters, and his cheekbones were visible under the torn flesh. Lost skin from either side of his head exposed the skull beneath. His left arm was missing below the elbow. In its place a deadly looking sword was grafted, all shiny and brand new. When not looking *daggers* at me, Word was mesmerized by his new toy.

"Well, you guys look good," I chirped. Tizzy almost dropped her fork in disbelief. Even Ash shook his head. "All things considered," I finished, less eagerly.

Jackson glowered. "No thanks to you."

"Ooh, so you know about that," I winced.

"Everyone knows," Loomis said coldly.

"I'm really, really sorry. It was totes an accident," I said. "But on the bright side, the mission was a success. Yay us?"

"A success would have been us coming back alive and leaving you Net-Heads out there to rot," Jackson scowled.

"But you're a Net-Head now," I said. I'm not sure why I said that. Maybe a part of me hoped that, now we shared a camaraderie, this Goliath of a man would cut me some slack. That seemed unlikely, as Jackson reached out both curled hands as if he was about to rip my head off.

Thankfully, Andrew distracted him. "Can I ask why you guys did it?"

It worked. Jackson and the others turned their attention to him.

"I mean," he continued, "you've seen firsthand how we get treated. How *you* are going to get treated now. So why do it? Why sell your body to these guys?"

Ash nodded in agreement. Even Tizzy seemed curious to know the answer.

Jackson leaned a little closer to Andrew. "We didn't do it for the money. We did it for our country. Unlike Nathan Hale, we *do* have more than one life to give our country."

Who's Nathan Hale? Was he one of the other Marines who died on the mission? And why did Nathan not elect to be made into a zombie? I looked at Andrew quizzically. He shrugged his shoulders.

I was about to put my question into words but then saw Tizzy shaking her head and mouthing a warning; "Don't."

"Besides," Loomis said, with a smile that exposed more teeth and gums, "we aren't going to be here long anyway."

Phew, that's a relief! I thought, but then saw Ash, Andrew and Tizzy all looking at me, mouths agape. "Ooh, those words actually came out of my mouth, didn't they?" They all nodded, cringing.

Jackson grabbed my face with one baseball-mitt-sized hand,

and twisted it in his direction. “Because we’re being fast-tracked to The Morgue Horde.”

This statement made Tizzy sit bolt upright, keen to hear what Jackson had to say.

“But rest assured,” he said, motioning to Andrew and Ash too, “before we leave, we’re going to make sure the three of you are dead-dead.”

Ash looked affronted and scribbled on his forehead. “Why me?”

“Because you’re friends with these losers,” Loomis said. She then leaned down, wrapped an arm around Tizzy and spoke softly in her ear. “And if you want to be in with a chance of coming with us, I suggest you put some distance between you and this lot.”

Tizzy nodded. “No problem there.” She stood, picked up her tray and walked away, finding an empty section of table at the far end of the mess hall. Loomis smiled approvingly.

Jackson let go of my face and he, Word, and Loomis left. At the counter they grabbed trays of meat and joined Tizzy.

Ash rubbed off the writing on his head with the back of his hand and scribbled more on it. He only had enough room to write, “We are so fu.” But I knew what he meant to say.

I wondered if Jackson would have a chance to make good his threat before Dr. Aiken cracked my head open. Either way I was screwed, but now it seemed that, even without Emily Aiken having a reason to destroy them, my friends were still doomed because of me. Well, that just wouldn’t do.

PART THREE

Book of the F'd

There's Something Rotten

That night was the longest night of my un-life.

Space had been made in the Blue Room for Jackson and his cohorts. And by that, I mean they forcibly moved three zombies out of their bunks and commandeered them for themselves. With more subtlety but with an equal amount of menace, Tizzy managed to convince a zombie to give up his bunk so she could be next to the new arrivals. To be fair, he seemed reasonably keen to relocate.

The soothing sounds of whale calls, ocean waves and the gentle breezes did little to calm my frayed nerves. I knew Emily Aiken and her crew were going to start the brain-ectomy of the zombies tomorrow. Somewhere in the back of my mind, I was sure I could hear Mr. Marshmallow whisper, "*Encephalectomy*," but I had no idea what that meant.

As awful as the encroaching doom of tomorrow seemed, I still had to deal with the very real doom of this night. I was sharing a room with three zombies that wanted me dead-dead, and possibly a fourth if Tizzy thought it would secure her a spot in The Morgue Horde.

There was no way I was closing my eyes tonight. I leaned over the edge of my bunk and looked down at Ash. His eyes were open and staring up at the underside of my bunk. I caught his eye and he gave me a 'thumbs-up.' Andrew was lying in the bunk next to ours, and he was also wide awake. He smiled weakly. I nodded back.

I lay back, took Eric out of my chest cavity, and placed him on my sternum. I fed him a squished cockroach and whispered, "Watch my back, buddy, and sting the crap out of anyone who comes near."

As it turned out, no one did. I saw the first rays of the new dawn break through the window-blinds and tucked Eric away before any of the other zombies stirred.

I was the first one out of my bunk as soon as the morning siren went off. Within a couple of seconds of my feet hitting the floor, Ash and Andrew were also up. We all looked over apprehensively at Jackson and his cronies as they rose from their slumber with the kind of military discipline that was now part of their DNA. Although not as quickly as us, they were up and ready before any of the other zombies. That was, apart from Tizzy, who sprang from her bunk, eager to impress her new friends.

None of them seemed overly interested in us.

I turned to Ash, "If I happen to get called into the lab today, don't worry about me. Just know…well, you're a good friend."

Ash's face scrunched up, cracking some of his burnt skin.

"Ooh, don't do that," I said. "Just watch his back, okay?" I pointed to Andrew.

"Why?" Andrew asked. "Where are you going?"

"I don't know," I replied. "Maybe nowhere."

As it turned out, Emily did not dismantle any of us that day. Something happened that put her plans on the backburner.

Just as we were leaving the mess hall after a breakfast of minced meat in a blood gravy, an anxious flurry of activity gripped the base. Marines huddled around smartphones. Others dashed to the breakout areas to watch the news unfolding on the TV.

"What's going on?" we asked, but at best we were ignored, at worst met with a barrage of insults and told to mind our own business.

As we walked past the building where we zombies would watch movies and The Pastures show, a zombie called Dwayne excitedly called us over. He had managed to get the news on the large screen in there. All the zombies quickly huddled in, standing in silence as we watched a live news report from Washington, D.C.

On the screen was a shot of a modern looking building surrounded by a high steel fence. Several cars were burning on the road out front, sending up clouds of smoke. About a dozen dead bodies, all in uniform, lay on the ground outside of the building. Broken windows, bullet holes in the guardhouse and the building itself, suggested one hell-of-a firefight had taken place.

I didn't need to read the white writing on the red panel at the bottom of the screen to confirm that I was looking at the Chinese Embassy. I recognized the building from the plans I had seen a few nights previously. The same ones Hauser had accused me of imagining. A sinking feeling filled the pit of my artificial stomach.

The reporter announced that twenty terrorists had stormed the building a little over an hour ago, killing at least a dozen guards and ten civilians. She said they had taken approximately thirty hostages, including five dignitaries visiting from China and American Congressman Herman Oetiker and Senator Sadie Mitchell. The reporter went on to say that no demands had been given for the safe release of the hostages. Also, China had yet to comment on the attack but was believed to be in talks with The President. "We cross shortly to The White House for a live press conference…"

I did not listen to the rest of what she had to say. "They aren't terrorists," I whispered to Ash and Andrew.

"What makes you say that?" Andrew asked.

"Do you remember the intel we found in that room?" I said.

Andrew nodded.

"I saw blueprints and floorplans for *that* building," I said, pointing at the TV. "Those were hired guns in that compound."

"Well, why wasn't China told there could be an attack on their embassy?" Andrew asked, barely loud enough for me to hear.

I leaned in close, as did Ash. I didn't want anyone to hear

what I was about to say. "I don't know. I think it was covered up for some reason. When I mentioned it to Hauser, he said I imagined it, and I got the distinct impression he would make me dead-dead if I didn't drop it."

"But why?" Andrew pressed.

I shook my head. "I don't know. Also, I'm sure I've heard of that Senator before, Senator Sadie Mitchell."

Nodding energetically, Ash pointed a finger at himself. He then looked desperately at Andrew, who nodded too.

"We've all heard of her, buddy. She was the one most opposed to The Stockon Bill. If she had got her way, none of us would be here. She's as anti-zombie as they get."

The moment Andrew said it, I remembered her. Every time an advocate of The Stockton Bill came on TV, she was there, destroying their argument. I had not paid much attention to her at the time, but in hindsight I wish I had.

I didn't want to hear anymore, as if doing so would fuel the growing sense of dread I was feeling. Between Emily's impending surgical procedure and Jackson's promise to make me dead-dead, I knew I had bigger problems than whatever was happening in D.C. However, I could not shake the thought that I had stumbled onto something I wasn't meant to see in that compound.

"I'm leaving," I said.

I walked out just as a black helicopter zoomed over my head. It was flying low, kicking up dust and debris from the ground. I shielded my eyes, cussing it. This was like no military helicopter I had ever seen before. With its sleek shape and dark-tinted windows, it was more like a flying sports car.

It was flying in the direction of the lab.

Uh-oh. This can't be good. Trying not to draw too much attention to myself, I jogged after it.

By the time I got to the lab, the helicopter had already landed by the building's north side. Its rotor blades slowed down, and the man in the black suit I had seen in Aiken's office a few days previous, stepped out.

He straightened his tie and casually glanced around. Instead of walking to the lab, he simply stayed by the helicopter as if waiting for someone.

Aiken did not come out of the lab, nor did anyone else. Maybe the man was not here to see any of them. As I was wondering who he was waiting for, I saw Jackson and an officer double-timing it towards him.

Jackson shot a look in my direction. With a nonchalance I didn't feel, I feigned interest in my shoes and then the sky and anything but him or the mysterious man by the helicopter.

They approached the man, who took a few steps further away from the helicopter. The man shook the officer's hand and they exchanged a few words. He then motioned to the officer that he wanted a moment alone with Jackson. The officer complied; he moved away from where they were standing, and waited.

The man looked Jackson up and down and smiled. He took a step closer, looking up at the zombie that dwarfed him. He started to talk to him, occasionally glancing around to make sure no one was eavesdropping.

Jackson listened intently, nodding on occasion. At one point, he gritted his teeth, clamped his fist with his other hand and nodded aggressively. He was like a dog ordered to attack someone who had just stolen his pork chop. The man seemed pleased with this reaction, and patted Jackson on the arm.

He then asked Jackson a question. Jackson's face lit up like a kid who had just got an early Christmas present. He turned and looked directly at me. Even at this distance I saw the wink and the malicious smile that spread across his mouth. He then turned back to the man and nodded enthusiastically.

Double uh-ho. Had the man discovered that the 'rogue' NPC pod was inside my head? Was he asking Jackson to remove it personally in the most painful way possible? That seemed unlikely, but whatever the mysterious man had asked him to do, Jackson seemed intent on factoring me into the equation, and that could not be good.

I'd seen enough. Or at least enough to know that my day was not about to get any better.

I turned on my heels and hurried back to look for Andrew and Ash. I figured now was as good a time as any to say my goodbyes.

It took me forever to find them. They were not by the mess hall or where we had watched the news report. I even tried the Blue Room. Still no luck. As it happens, I couldn't find them because they were also running around the base looking for me. Fortunately, this gave me some time to reconsider telling them about my apparently impending doom. When we finally found each other, I decided to say nothing; they already looked worried enough.

"Where did you go?" Andrew asked.

"Just for a walk. Why? What's going on?"

"When you were gone, we saw Jackson get marched off by an officer," Andrew replied. "A few minutes later, someone came and got Loomis and Word. Something is going down, I tell you."

Ash quickly jotted the word; 'China' on his forehead and looked at Andrew questioningly.

Andrew nodded. "Yup. That's what my money's on. Hey, who knows, with any luck they'll get made dead-dead if they go into that embassy, and we won't need to worry anymore. I mean, did you see all those dead guards? Yeah, anyone dumb enough to storm that place is dead meat."

The siren blasted across the yard and we exchanged worried looks. We knew what this meant - the signal for all zombies to report to the briefing room immediately.

By the time we arrived, most of the zombies had already taken their places on the plastic chairs, arranged in rows facing the front of the room.

The three of us sat down and waited nervously. The door opened. Drill Sergeant Hauser and a corporal I had never seen before, entered the room. We all stood to attention and saluted.

The corporal, a young man with a California tan and blonde

hair, nodded at us. Hauser took up position in the corner of the room and barked, "Sit."

We did so, making a symphony of noise as plastic chairs scraped across the floor, and creaked and clanked under our weight.

The corporal held up a clipboard and said, "When I call out your number, stand. Right, Project 3222..."

Tizzy, who was sitting in the front row, shot up from her chair and stood rigid to attention.

The Corporal continued, "Project 2626."

"Aah, you have gotta be kidding me," Andrew muttered and stood up.

Satisfied that this roll-call had been answered, the Corporal returned to his list. "Project 2314."

Ash bowed his head for a moment and then stood up. He looked down at me sympathetically. I suspected he knew what number would be called next in this game of Dead Meat Bingo.

I was on my feet before the Corporal could even finish saying, "Project 2219."

He then lowered his clipboard and looked at the four of us. Tizzy turned around to see who had been called out in addition to her. When she saw our trio standing side-by-side, her expression turned to one of irritation. She shook her head and mouthed something. I couldn't say for sure, but I'm reasonably certain it was an F-bomb.

"Follow me," the corporal ordered.

"We're not just dead meat, we're dead-dead meat," Andrew

whispered to us as we shuffled along the row of sitting zombies. I had to agree with him.

We were led to an official-looking building in the center of the base. It was three stories of brick and mortar, a far cry from the single-story modular barracks for the Marines and Zombies. I had never been into this building before, I don't think any zombie had. The only people I ever saw coming out of this building had more stars and stripes on their uniforms than the American flag.

We were marched inside and down a long hall until we reached a small briefing room, probably only large enough to comfortably seat a dozen people. The corporal opened the door and motioned us inside.

I took a step inside and momentarily froze. Waiting for us and already seated were Jackson, Loomis, and Word. They looked suspiciously a lot happier to see me than I was to see them. Though my feet begged me to go in the opposite direction, I stoically walked forward.

Tizzy seemed a lot more relaxed the moment she saw them. Andrew, on the other hand, took one step inside, spied Loomis, and immediately spun round to walk back out. Ash had to push the quietly whimpering Andrew back inside.

I was so fixated on the dead Marines that I hadn't noticed the two people standing at the front of the room. Only when the corporal saluted to one of them before leaving did I realize we were not alone.

Standing against the wall was the man in the black suit, and a Section Chief. I figured the latter was in his late fifties. His hair was as bone white as his neatly-trimmed mustache.

Tizzy saluted the moment she clocked him, and we followed suit with a lack of enthusiasm matched only by the Section Chief's salute back to us. He motioned for us to sit. Tizzy sat next to Loomis, but Ash, Andrew, and I sat as far away from everyone else as possible. If I'd had any choice in the matter, I would have grabbed my chair, sat in the adjacent room and just asked the Section Chief to speak up.

The man surveyed us. "I am Section Chief Priestly. This is Mr. Thomas from Batoltech Global."

"Hi. I'm Marco," I said with a friendly wave.

Mr. Thomas looked at me like I'd just announced I wanted to poop on his shoes.

"Shut up. No one cares," Chief Priestly scowled at me.

He took a couple of moments to cool his temper, and continued. "As you know, terrorists attacked the Chinese Embassy in Washington, D.C. this morning. Because the Embassy is classed as Chinese territory, we cannot send American troops in without their permission. Due to the somewhat strained relationship between our two countries, and the Chinese government's view that this would be seen as a weakness on their behalf, permission has not been granted."

"Oh well, can't say we didn't try," Andrew said. "Thanks for letting us know."

He went to stand, but Priestly yelled, "Sit down!"

Andrew swiftly re-planted his butt on the chair and blinked at Chief Priestly in fear.

The Section Chief then said to Jackson, "The zombie formally known as Sergeant Jackson Cole, you have my permission to rip the head off of the next zombie that speaks. Understood?"

"Sir, yes, sir. Gladly, sir," Jackson trumpeted back.

Yeah, I bet. He'd probably play a couple of games of two-on-two basketball with it as well.

Mr. Thomas stepped forward. "As your section chief just mentioned, US Marines have not been granted permission to enter the Chinese Embassy. However, China will allow its Embassy to receive delivery of products they have purchased."

"And let me guess," Tizzy said with a wry smile, "they've just bought themselves seven brand new zombies."

With a slight smile, Mr. Thomas shook his head, "No, *we* are not allowed to sell zombies to China."

Section Chief Priestly took over. "However, the US Military *is*. For the next twelve hours, you are possessions of the People's Republic of China. You will be delivered to their embassy in three hours. From there, you will have two hours to successfully complete your mission, thus allowing China to save face."

I raised my hand.

"What?" Priestly said, his lips lifting in a snarl.

"And if we fail?" I asked.

Priestly took several steps closer to where I was sitting and glared down at me. "Failure is *not* an option."

*

He spent the next half an hour going over the plan and the objectives. I really should have been paying more attention but I was more concerned about why Andrew, Ash, and I had been roped into this mission. This was too high profile and too important to screw up, so I could understand if they wanted to send the likes of Jackson, Loomis, Word, and even Tizzy. But us? We were the zombie equivalent of Ed, Edd, and Eddy. Nope. Jackson had handpicked us and for one reason only; so he could make good on his promise; if the mercs didn't get us, *he* sure as hell would.

For that reason, when Priestly was saying, "You enter via the roof, yadda, yadda, yadda… secure hostages, yadda, yadda… eliminate the threat, yadda, yadda, and extract here, yadda," I was wondering; how the hell *we* were going to get out of this. Screw the hostages!

I was so engrossed with how I would get out of this one, that I had not even stopped to consider why Priestly was wasting valuable time briefing us here instead of en route. It was only when he said, "You leave immediately and will be flown to Washington D.C. and capsuled in transit," that I realized why.

When he said 'capsuled,' what he was really referring to were 'Splat Capsules.' Another nifty invention of Batoltech Global, explicitly designed for zombies because anyone living and dumb enough to try it, would die.

A Splat Capsule is like a big ol' jello mold, big enough for a zombie to lie down in. It is then filled with a gel-like liquid that forms a rubbery outer skin around the gooey center. Then, like a giant cod-liver oil capsule, the zombies are thrown out of planes at high altitudes. Wingtips and thrusters are attached to the rubbery gel, not to slow descent but rather correct its course. At the last moment, the capsules are maneuvered to land horizontally and then…splat! Hence the name.

Splat Capsules serve several purposes - first, rapid descent to a target without the need for parachutes. Second, the gel cushions the majority of the impact. Not enough to ensure a living occupant's safety, but enough to stop a zombie from being obliterated when it hits the ground at terminal velocity. Lastly, the gel acts like an adhesive, preventing its passengers from bouncing off in different directions. After landing, the zombies peel themselves out of the gel, and violà.

However, this was catastrophic news for me. Not only did it mean that *yet again* I was going to get tossed out of a perfectly good aircraft, but the gel-filled Splat Capsule would make it impossible for me to talk. Now I would have no chance to warn Ash and Andrew.

It's Raining Dead! Hallelujah!

We were quickly outfitted with our tactical gear, bundled into the back of a troop truck and driven to the airfield. Jackson, Loomis, Tizzy and Word sat on the bench on one side, facing Andrew, Ash, and me on the other. We traveled in complete silence. Jackson and Loomis stared at me the whole damn way as if daring me to speak. Word had also started the journey staring at me but quickly bored of it. He turned his attention to the blade grafted to his arm, using it to peel off tiny slithers of skin from his other arm.

I chanced a glance at Tizzy. As soon as our eyes met, she looked away. For the rest of the journey she stared at the floor of the truck as if looking at Andrew, Ash or me might cause the skin on her face to fall off. Had Jackson filled her in on his plan, or had she come to the conclusion herself that the three of us were in deep trouble?

We were herded into a C-17 military plane, with Jackson shoving me in the back all the way as if I intended to make a break for it if he didn't keep me moving. The troop pen was huge. Seven glass pods had been wheeled in along with steel tanks full of gel. Tubes and pipes led from the tanks to the pods. It looked like something from a science fiction movie; all that was missing was mist from dry ice and funky futuristic sound effects.

Batoltech Global lab technicians in white coats were working on the pods, checking gauges and instruments. When we reached the top of the ramp at the rear of the plane, one of the technicians motioned for me to climb into an open pod. I hesitated. This was my last chance to warn Ash and Andrew, but what the hell could I say? Jackson's fist dug hard into the small of my back to keep me moving in the direction of the technician, causing me to stumble and almost fall.

"Enjoy the flight, meathead," he scoffed.

I shuffled apprehensively towards the empty glass pod. It looked like an open casket shaped like a giant suppository. The technician took my rifle and again asked me politely to climb inside. I obeyed and slid in, but before lying down completely, I looked over at Jackson who was on the other side of the plane.

He was staring at the pod and the technician in despair. The technician shrugged sympathetically. It dawned on me what the problem was. These pods were designed to fit average size people, not Godzilla-sized freaks like Jackson.

Enjoy your flight, meathead.

"Haha," I shouted over to him, "You too, you sasquatch," and flipped him the bird.

He looked like he was about to storm over to me, but the technician placed a hand on his chest and motioned once more to the impossibly small capsule. Jackson huffed, threw his assault rifle to the technician and tore off his tactical vest. He then squeezed himself into the pill-shaped tube, pressing his arms awkwardly to his chest and clampings his legs together. He looked as uncomfortable as anyone I had ever seen. And that was before the technician jammed the assault rifle into the tube with him. I watched his discomfort with a tremendous amount of satisfaction.

When the technician pulled down the glass lid on Jackson's capsule, it stopped about an inch from the latch. At this point the technician, like a tourist with a suitcase crammed with souvenirs, sat atop of the lid and bounced up and down a couple of times until the latch clicked into place.

So much of Jackson's skin was pressed up against the glass, I wondered what space would be left to fill with gel

It was only now that I realized this little spectacle had drawn an audience. Everyone on the plane had stopped to watch Jackson get squeezed into the Splat Capsule, like someone trying to shove a pillow into a Pringles tube.

Only the living dared openly laugh at this farce. Loomis, her shoulders shaking uncontrollably, covered her mouth and seemed unable to look away. Word was peeking from behind a technician, retreating every time he failed to control his laughter. Ash and Andrew were doing little to hide their amusement yet aware that Jackson would soon be free of his confinement. Only Tizzy seemed unamused at the whole thing. She shook her head and climbed into her capsule.

I lay back in my pod. My technician placed my assault rifle on my chest and closed the lid. There was a sucking sound as all the seals were squeezed together. I look up through the glass and saw the technician turn a nozzle on the steel tank. Clear, gloopy liquid started to fill the capsule.

I have been put through many indignities since becoming a zombie, but this was definitely the funkiest. As the liquid covered my face, the primal part of my brain was screaming at me not to breathe. Of course, zombies cannot breathe. But that doesn't stop your mind from going into full panic mode. Also, the worst thing you can do is open your mouth before the gel has time to set. About twenty minutes after being released from the tank, the gel forms a rubbery skin that peels off the glass and your body pretty easily. But if that stuff gets down your throat, you are going to have a bitch of a time getting it out. Speaking will be impossible, and in all likelihood, a Project Leader will have to rip out and replace all of your plastic innards.

After a while, my sense of claustrophobia and fear subsided. When the plane took off, and all I could hear through the setting gel were its muted engines, it felt relatively peaceful. More importantly, it gave me time to think.

Ok, what's the sitch, Marco? You are about to be thrown, quite literally, into another hostile situation against a whole bunch of well-armed mercenaries. There is no doubt they will know we are coming, so they'll be better prepared than the last bunch. In the unlikely event you survive that lot, Jackson will take the first chance he gets to make you and your buddies dead-dead. If, by some miracle, you survive that, Emily Aiken is going to pop your head open like a Pez dispenser. Sigh.

Dear Diary, today sucked balls!

If that wasn't bad enough, another nagging thought wormed its way into my mind. Why had Mr. Thomas wanted to speak to Jackson alone? What had he told him that he didn't want that officer, and no doubt Priestly, to hear? I couldn't help but feel that something else was at play here.

I needed Mr. Marshmallow, but I was miles from the Blue Room. Hmm, but maybe I didn't need to be in the Blue Room.

The gel hardened against my ears, tuning out all sound but the low hum of the engines. A hypnotic vibration rippled through the liquid, and I felt I was floating. I closed my eyes and tried to relax and drown out everything else around me. Although it was still daytime, the light outside of my glass capsule grew steadily darker until it was pitch black. Out of the darkness, trees gradually materialized and a small orange glow, no bigger than a golf ball, expanded and expanded until it became a fully formed campfire.

Mr. Marshmallow walked out of the shadows and sat on a log next to the fire. He held in the palm of his hand a large, black scorpion.

"He's kind of a cute fella. What have you called him?" he asked.

"Eric."

"Eric. I like that," he said.

"What's going on?" I asked.

Mr. Marshmallow blew on the palm of his hand, and Eric broke apart like dandelion seeds and disappeared in the air.

"You mean beyond what you already know?" Mr. Marshmallow asked.

"Yeah. I mean, I know I am in deep trouble," I replied. "I just don't know how deep."

"Pretty deep, I'm afraid."

"Terrific," I slumped on the log next to him. "I know why Jackson wants me, Ash and Andrew there. It gives him an opportunity to waste us. But what I don't get is why Mr. Thomas, that guy from Batoltech, wanted to speak to him in private."

"Well, let's look at this logically, shall we." He patted my knee. "Why do you think?"

"Not a clue," I replied flatly.

"Think hard now."

"The embassy was attacked by mercenaries. They're not terrorists, and not politically motivated, so I don't know why they want to do this," I said. I looked to him for a clue.

"Well, why don't we forget their motives for a moment and focus on Jackson and Mr. Thomas," he said.

Nope. I was still coming up blank. I gritted my teeth. I looked up at the night sky, praying for a sudden thunderstorm. If inspiration couldn't hit me like a metaphorical thunderbolt, maybe it could do so with a literal one. With any luck it would also fry my nanobots and NPC pod. That would please Jackson, Emily and, to no small degree, me. Oh, and maybe that zombie-hating Senator.

"Wait!" I yelled, jumping off the log. "A Senator, Sadie something. Yes, Sadie Mitchell! She's one of the hostages."

"And how do you know that name?" he asked, and once again, the purpose seemed to be to nudge me in the right direction.

"She was the one most opposed to the Stockton Bill. She never wanted zombies to be created, forget being sold for military use." I was getting excited. For the first time, I felt I was the detective in one of those great TV shows and not one of the dumbass extras they interview who always seem to say, "I dunno know nuthin.'"

Mr. Marshmallow nodded eagerly and motioned for me to continue.

"*She's* what they were talking about. That's it, isn't it?"

He shrugged. "Maybe. But let's assume you're right. What does Jackson want?"

"I'm guessing, when he was alive, to make hairy offspring with King Kong. Now he's dead, to get promoted into The Morgue Horde."

"And what does Batoltech Global want?" he asked.

"To sell more zombies," I said.

Mr. Marshmallow raised an eyebrow, "And if Senator Sadie Mitchell lives long enough to get the Stockton Bill overturned?"

"No more Morgue Horde, no more Batoltech, and no

more zombies," I said. A lightbulb appeared above my head, illuminating the darkness. "Oh, my God. Mr. Thomas gave Jackson the order to kill her."

Mr. Marshallow touched his nose and clicked his tongue.

"Probably promised him a guaranteed spot on The Horde," I muttered. "How do I stop him? How do I save her?"

Mr. Marshmallow shrugged. "I don't know. The question you have to ask is, do you want to?"

I looked at him quizzically, squinting as the bulb above my head grew brighter.

He said, "If Senator Mitchell gets the Stockon Bill thrown out, it won't just mean no more zombies in the future. Those already in existence will also be dismantled. Including you and your friends."

"Oh," I said. It had never occurred to me before that between a rock and a hard place, there could be a field full of mines, beartraps and rabid squirrels.

The light from the bulb was now unbearable. It was everywhere. My eyes stung and I shielded them with my arm.

"I'm sorry, Marco," said Mr. Marshmallow as he disappeared in a brilliance of white. "I'd offer you a marshmallow, but you're about to be thrown out of a plane."

I opened my eyes just as I was being wheeled towards a ramp at the rear of the plane. The entire tail section was open, letting in blinding sunlight and wind so fierce it blocked out the sound of the engines.

The top half of our glass capsules had been removed by the

technicians. We were now lying, encased in clear gel, on the bottom half that acted as a glass gurney. I saw that metal fins had been stuck on the rubbery capsule. Two small boosters were also attached, near my shoulders, to push the Splat Capsule into a horizontal position when needed.

They wheeled us closer to the ramp until all I could see through blurred vision was bright blue sky.

My technician leaned down and shouted over the roar of the wind, "Try not to move. You don't want the capsule to break before you hit the ground."

I wanted to say, "Great, can we also do something about me hitting the ground because I'm not too keen on the idea of that either," but the rubbery film over my face prevented me from doing so.

I moved my eyes left and right. I could just about make out the other Splat Capsules lined up either side of me. Jackson's was right next to mine and I was pretty sure I saw an elbow and shoulder sticking out of the gel. His technician looked down at the protruding body parts and grimaced to a colleague.

A red light blinked on in the hold. A technician standing next to a lever attached to the plane's hull, reached up and pulled it down.

We were all propelled forward at high speed. At the last moment, our gurneys were flipped upright and we were catapulted out of the plane.

Once again, I found myself plummeting towards the earth. However, this time it was from a dizzying height. As I fell, small wispy clouds hurtled towards me. I smashed through them. The Splat Capsule wobbled like a bowl of jelly in the hands of a drunk with hiccups, rollerskating over cobbles. The closer to terminal velocity I approached, the more sure I was that my flimsy rubber casing would tear apart.

Despite the removal of all of my innards, it still felt like my stomach was in my throat. My nonexistent bladder wanted to relax and let liquids, not present in my body, trickle down my legs.

Dear Diary, today I discovered it was possible to crap yourself without a bowel.

A motor whirred into life. The fins on the outside of the capsule pivoted slightly but changed my course dramatically to the left. Below me, the city slowly came into view. What initially had looked like little Lego pieces on the ground, now grew larger and larger, until I could see cars and rooftops. I zipped past a flock of geese flying in formation. They responded with a cacophony of panicked honks.

"Sorry," I said, but my voice got no further than the rubbery film covering my mouth.

My capsule tilted forward slightly. While it gave me a better view of the onrushing buildings, it also meant I could hit the ground face on, which was not appealing. I almost laughed. *As if I had a better option.*

Beneath me, the Chinese Embassy loomed into view. I had to say from this vantage point it was really quite impressive. Even nature had not been left to chance, as all the trees around the building seemed to have been meticulously placed. But the Embassy itself seemed like an architectural oasis surrounded by a sea of drab and grey buildings.

The central part of the building was light grey, and overlooked a large courtyard made of stone, so white it almost looked like marble. The roof of the central section had three skylights. The middle one was square and the largest of the three. The other two were small and diamond-shaped. A tapered roof connected the three skylights. In fact, the top had such a sharp angle I feared, if we landed there, we'd slide straight off it and fall to the ground. Either that or crash straight through one of the glass skylights.

However, my pod corrected its course again. To the right of the roof was a small east wing with a flat roof. To the left was a large west wing, also with a flat roof, with a raised central section in the shape of a crooked L, on which four large fans whizzed around on the top of the far end.

My descent veered towards the west wing, and for an awful moment I was sure I was going to crash directly into one of the fans and get minced on impact. At least it would be a quick death-death.

Then the tiny wings popped off with a small explosion. The boosters engaged on my chest and I flipped 90 degrees so that instead of coming down face or feet first, I was tilted onto my back. I looked up at the bright and somewhat wobbly blue sky, smattering of feathery clouds and squadron of pissed off geese. As I did, I thought to myself, *yes, the Embassy of the People's*

Republic of China truly is a beautiful building.

However, it lost some of its allure a second later, when I slammed into it at a hundred and fifty miles per hour.

SPLAT!

Let the Bodies Hit the Floor

The Splat Capsule lived up to its name. It splatted over a two-yard radius with me in the center.

Even cushioned by the rubbery, viscous liquid surrounding my body, I hit the roof so hard my jaw slammed shut on impact and broke at least two of my teeth.

I heard, to the left and right of me, six more Splat Capsules pound the roof. Each sounded like a wet thump followed by a squishy explosion.

I struggled to my feet encased in the gooey, rubbery substance. The outer shell was now scattered all over the gravel-covered rooftop - the inner cover encased my body. I clawed at it, surprised how cleanly it came away from me and my clothes. It didn't, as I'd expected, look as if a giant had hocked a runny loogy on me.

Instead it came away in one big snakeskin-like sheath, except for my right foot where the stretchy substance still clung stubbornly.

I looked around. I had heard my fellow zombies land but I couldn't see them. Then I realized I had landed on the raised section of the roof, narrowly missing, by about a couple of yards, the monstrously large fans that whooshed and roared.

Phew, that was close! I inched a little closer to the fans. I figured they were attached to the airconditioning units that ran throughout the entire building. That was a lot of floors and a lot of rooms to circulate air through, no wonder they were so huge.

I peered over the edge of the roof. On the lower level, about two-and-a-half yards below me, I spotted my teammates.

Ash had peeled himself free of his splat capsule and was feeling his forehead, no doubt checking that no more skin had fallen off.

Andrew looked shell-shocked. His gaze flitted frantically from the sky to the roof and back up to the sky again. He then hurriedly ran his hands all over his body to make sure he was still in one piece and, for reasons beyond me, checked his crotch.

That ship has already well and truly sailed, Action Man.

Word was climbing out of his slimy casing, like a man taking off his PJ's. He even paused to remove the foam sheath they had used to protect his arm-blade. He checked it for damage. Then, with methodical precision, he used the blade to cut away more of the substance.

Loomis was frantically tearing the rubber-like skin away in chunks and angrily throwing it on the ground.

Jackson was halfway out of his casing but paused to inspect

his elbow, where a massive chunk of skin had torn away, exposing the bone underneath. He then started to pluck at the pieces of gravel deeply embedded in his right shoulder, which had clearly not been covered by the Splat Capsule.

By the time I noticed Tizzy, she was already clear of the goop that had surrounded her. She was kneeling and was pointing her assault rifle in my direction. I knew she didn't like me, but figured she knew she was fourth in line, even behind Word. *Oh well.* I raised my hands in surrender.

She looked up at me and her lip curled in confusion. She then clenched her jaw and shook her head. She jabbed the air with her weapon and it then dawned on me; she may not be aiming it at me. I took a step closer to the edge of the roof and looked down. Right below me was a door that I then understood she was covering.

I shot her an apologetic smile.

Jackson and his two cohorts were now free of jelly and, like Tizzy, had their guns trained on the door. Ash followed suit. Andrew took a couple of steps forward and mimicked them. He stopped when it became apparent that he was only pointing his fingers at the door. He spun around and frantically scoured the roof. Lying inside the blubbery remains of the capsule was his assault rifle. He snatched it up and pressed his eyes shut, shaking his head slowly. I bet, if the roof had opened up just then, he would have gladly leaped in, head first.

Jackson spotted me. "Get down from there, you idiot."

Right-ho. I picked up my rifle and flicked my right foot to dislodge the only part of the rubber skin still attached to me. It didn't come free. Instead, the stretchy Marco-sized membrane shot forward, extending to about twice the length. The far end was sucked straight into the gigantic fan.

Oh, nuts!

The moment it caught in the fan, I was flung off my feet and onto my back. The rubber twisted around my foot, and now, unlike a single easy-to-tear sheet of cellophane wrap, it took on a rope-like quality. I was instantly dragged along the gravel towards the fan's blades as it gobbled up more and more of the elastic material attached to my foot.

"Help!" I yelled. I rolled over onto my stomach, trying to get a purchase on something. I clawed at the loose gravel that came away in my hands. My boot was now less than a foot away from the fan. Finally, I manage to reach out and grab hold of the edge of the roof.

Pulling myself close to the edge, I gawped down at the others with eyes so wide I thought they might pop out of my head.

"Please! Help!" I spluttered.

Jackson lowered his rifle to his side and took a couple of strides forward. When Loomis tried to do the same, he stretched out his gravel-encrusted arm to stop her. She looked at him, momentarily confused. He gave her a glance, then stared up at me and smiled.

Loomis looked at me and then at Jackson. Then, as the penny dropped almost audibly, she smiled an evil little smile and gave me a mocking wave with just her fingertips.

Bitch is what I would have screamed at her if I didn't think the effort would somehow cause me to lose my precious grip on the edge of the roof.

Ash pushed past Jackson and ran towards me. Andrew stood stock still, looking on in shock.

Tizzy growled, "Jackson!"

The membrane around my foot was now being stretched to its limit. I doubted it would give before my grip did. Or worse, my leg detached from my body.

Ash jumped up to grab my hands that were clamped to the edge of the wall, but his fingertips barely grazed mine.

He tried again with no success. I dared not let go to reach out for him. Then I heard a tearing sound and prayed to God it wasn't my leg.

"Jesus," Tizzy yelled. She dropped her rifle and sprinted towards Ash, yelling his name at the last second. He turned, just as she used his body as a springboard and scaled the wall in one fluid parkour-style move. She landed on the roof beside me, just as my fingers lost their grip and I was snapped towards the fan's metal blades.

She drew her knife with the speed of an Old West gunslinger and brought it down on the elastic rope. It snapped, just as the toe of my boot was clipped by the fan, sending a chunk of it flying off.

She grabbed me and pulled me to my feet. Before I could say thanks, she had leaped down to the lower level.

"What the hell was that about?" she roared at Jackson as she stormed off to retrieve her rifle.

"Keep your voice down," Jackson hissed back. "They'll hear you."

She snatched up her weapon. "Oh, please. A deaf man could have heard us land. Why didn't you help him? You could have grabbed him, no problem."

He marched toward her, his massive frame towering over her. I instinctively jumped down now, unsure what I would do if Jackson got physical. Probably get snapped in half. I matched Jackson's speed and reached Tizzy just after he did.

"Because *he*," pointing at me, "is a liability. As is that dickless wonder and the walking barbeque over there."

"Then why bring them?" Tizzy challenged.

"Because every mission has heroes and casualties," he barked back. "The greater the casualties, the bigger the heroes. And only heroes get into The Morgue Horde. Do you still want to come with us to The Horde?"

Tizzy blinked as if slapped. "Yes."

"I ask again," said Jackson, "do you want to earn a place on The Horde?"

"Yes," she said with more determination, but it sounded hollow.

"Then you need to learn how to cut away the dead weight," he said with a low menace, "before it drags you down. Clear?"

Tizzy nodded.

"Clear?" Jackson repeated.

"Clear," she replied.

He strode away from her with his rifle firmly trained on the door. Loomis followed, her rifle likewise fixed ahead of her. Word lifted his, rested it on the nook of his bladed arm, and moved forward with the other two.

Ash, Andrew and I did not move; instead, we shared furtive glances.

I leaned towards Tizzy and said quietly, "Thank you."

She did not look at me. She raised her rifle and said, "Get moving."

Once at the door, Jackson and Word took up position to the right of it and Loomis to the left, with Tizzy right behind her. Andrew and I were left standing in front of it with Andrew pointing his rifle shakily at the door. Ash grabbed him by the collar and gently pulled him to the side, next to Loomis and Tizzy.

Suddenly, I was the only one standing directly in front of the door, in line of fire of anyone standing on the other side. I quickly jumped towards Jackson, who glanced at me with disdain.

He nodded to Loomis, then reached for the door handle. He twisted it and the door quietly clicked ajar. He placed his meaty hand on it, ready to push it open.

"Wait," I whispered.

All eyes were on me. "Shouldn't we check?" I said. "There could be a booby-trap on the other side."

Jackson shook his head and shoved the door open. I winced,

waiting for an explosion. There was none. Still, I couldn't help but think that was pretty damn reckless on his behalf.

The door opened onto a concrete stairwell. Jackson took the lead. Somehow Tizzy had managed to push her way past Loomis and was directly behind Jackson. Andrew, Ash and I took up position behind Word and Loomis and cautiously made our way down a flight of stairs.

We were halfway down when Ash tapped me on the shoulder. He pulled out a dry marker from his tactical vest and drew a circle and crosshairs on his forehead. He pointed at Jackson, then the crosshairs, then at each of us.

"I think so, buddy," I whispered, looking down the stairs at Jackson and his henchmen. "Watch yourselves."

We got to the bottom of the first flight and inched open a door on the landing. It opened out into a long corridor with office doors on either side.

"Looks like they didn't hear us," Tizzy said.

"Let's keep it that way," said Jackson. He reached into his shirt and we heard the distinct sound of a zip. After a couple of seconds, he retrieved a silencer from his body cavity, which he screwed onto the muzzle of his assault rifle. Although it was more difficult for us as we were still wearing tactical vests, we did the same.

I was groping around inside my chest, looking for the silencer, when I felt something crawl over my hand. I almost yelled out in fright. *Damn, it's Eric.* I hadn't had a chance to take him out before heading out on this mission. If I was going to be toast, he probably was too. I contemplated letting him loose here but didn't rate his chances of survival in Washington, D.C., home of the *really* venomous. I figured the safest place for him was hidden back inside me.

I pushed him back in, zipped myself up, then quickly screwed on the silencer.

Jackson ducked his head under the doorway and took a step forward into the hallway. Before he could take another, Tizzy grabbed his arm.

"What?" he hissed.

Tizzy pointed upwards. Nestled in the corner by the ceiling, just on the other side of the door, was a security camera.

Jackson looked at it briefly. "It's not on."

Tizzy's brows furrowed. "How do you know?"

"The cameras can be accessed remotely in the event of an attack," he said. "Anyone worth their salt would know this and would have shut them down."

"Really?" Tizzy asked, unconvinced.

"Sure," Jackson replied. "Take point." He motioned for Tizzy to cover the corridor. He then turned to Loomis. "You take Word, Action Man and the human whiteboard and clear the level below us. We'll sweep this level and meet you by the opposite stairwell."

Gripping my arm, Ash pointed desperately to me and then to himself.

Jackson shook his head angrily and said, through gritted teeth, "You'll go where I damn-well tell you."

Loomis grabbed the back of Ash's tactical vest and tugged it. "Come on, burnt toast. You'll be with your boyfriend soon enough."

Ash looked at me, mournfully.

"I'll be ok," I said quietly. "Just go." I pointed to Andrew. "Take care of him."

"We'll look out for each other," Andrew said. "C'mon, big guy, let's go."

They stepped back and let the stairwell door close shut. Now it was just Tizzy, Jackson and myself standing in the hallway. I looked down at my rifle and wondered if I would live long enough to shoot any bad guys with it.

Jackson pulled from his collar an earpiece attached to a curly length of white wire and popped it into his ear. He motioned for us to do the same.

He tapped the earpiece twice. "Copy?" he whispered.

Loomis's voice sounded through the earpiece, "Roger that."

"Out," Jackson replied, and made his way forward.

We headed cautiously down the hall. As we passed each office door, Jackson carefully opened those to the right and Tizzy, those on the left each time whispering "Clear" before moving on to the next.

I followed in Jackson's wake, preferring to keep the colossus in front of me. His enormous shoulders were pitted with chunks of gravel that made him look even more like a stone golem.

Had I known he would come back this pissed-off at me, I probably would have made sure he stayed dead when I had the chance. I smiled inwardly as it occurred to me that, if I could iron out a wrinkle in the timeline, my only thought would be to make sure Jackson was dead-dead. As opposed to say, oh, I don't know - not throwing the grenade that killed him in the first place?

We were a little more than halfway down the corridor when I thought I heard something shuffle around the corner at the far end. I made to warn Tizzy and Jackson, but it was too late.

Red, Dead & Blue

Two figures, both dressed in black tactical gear and armed with automatic assault rifles, lunged into view and opened fire.

The first one's shots went wild, almost as wild as his scraggly ginger hair, and peppered the floor and wall.

His blonde companion was more capable. A bullet from his assault rifle slammed into Jackson's chest, and came out of his back, from where it smashed into my shoulder, knocking me off balance. More bullets streaked past us, a couple grazing Jackson's flesh.

Jackson roared and opened up with his gun. Bullets ripped through the blond man's chest and he fell to the ground dead. Tizzy took aim at the ginger man, but Jackson shunted her with his hip, buffeting her into an open office. The man fired another ill-aimed burst from his assault rifle and ducked back around the corner. It all happened so fast I hadn't even thought to shoot back.

Tizzy burst out of the office. "What the hell was that about?" she screamed at Jackson.

“I was trying to save your life,” he said.

“I don’t need your help,” she shouted and charged off down the corridor before either of us could react.

I made to run past Jackson and had only partially overtaken him before he took off. His foot caught the back of my heel and we both crashed to the floor.

“Aargh!” he screamed. He grabbed me roughly by my tactical vest, clambered to his feet and hauled me off the floor as if I were weightless.

“Idiot!” he bellowed and hurled me backward. I crashed through an office door and landed roughly on my back. My assault rifle fell from my hand and skidded across the floor.

Jackson’s gigantic frame filled the open doorway. He glared down at me, with eyes full of rage and fury. He leveled his assault rifle directly at my head.

More automatic gunfire rang out down the hall, followed by a man’s scream. Jackson turned, shot me one more murderous look, and thundered off in the direction of the gunfight.

I scrambled for my weapon and sprinted after him.

I heard the soft *prrrut, prrrut* sound of fire from Tizzy’s silenced automatic weapon. But whoever was shooting back at her must have run out of rifle ammunition, as single repeated cracks from a pistol replaced its rapid fire.

A terrified scream was cut short by a burst from Tizzy’s gun.

We reached the corner and saw Tizzy standing over the body of the ginger mercenary. Jackson paused to look down at the blond corpse by his feet. Only now did I notice that the man was wearing a red armband. Jackson bent down and ripped it off, then strode towards Tizzy.

She had taken a step back from the man and was inspecting bullet holes. She leaned closer to the wall and looked through one of them.

Then she stepped away, knelt beside the dead mercenary and picked up his pistol.

Unable to contain my curiosity, I too, looked through the hole in the wall into the office beyond. The bullet, I saw, had also made a perfectly round hole through a chair, and the wall beyond that. In fact, it seemed to have continued its unstoppable trajectory until the holes it made pinpointed into oblivion.

Jackson was staring down at the body of the ginger mercenary. His expression was rigid. Maybe he was upset he had not managed to kill this one himself, or perhaps the hunger was hitting him for the first time.

Curiously though, this merc sported a blue armband on his bicep and Jackson seemed more intent on this than the ready-meal wearing it. Maybe, like me, he was perplexed at the purpose of the armbands.

Tizzy had removed the clip from the man's sidearm and was inspecting its single remaining round. I peered closer to get a better look. The bullet was unlike anything I had ever seen before. It was made from a brighter metal than traditional bullets, and the tip was almost corkscrew-shaped with a pointy end. She held it up, twisting it this way and that.

She eyed Jackson with a grim expression. "Zombie-killers.

They knew we were coming."

Jackson licked his lips but said nothing. He pulled off the man's blue armband and stuffed it in his pants pocket, along with the red one.

"Come," was all he said as he made his way down the corridor.

Tizzy pushed the zombie-killer bullet back into the clip, snapped that into the pistol and tucked it into her belt.

Jackson moved with less caution now. He kicked open doors as he reached them, taking only cursory glances inside before declaring "Clear," and pushing on to the next one. Tizzy, on the other hand, was moving with even more caution than before. For every door she opened on one side, he had opened two on the other.

She huffed and said to me, "You take that room, I'll take the one after that, and so on. Understand?" I nodded. Taking alternate doors, we were able to keep up with Jackson. Eventually, we reached the last door, which had a green label attached with Chinese characters and an English translation beneath them: Fire Exit.

Jackson pushed it open with the muzzle of his rifle. All three of us hurried through it, guns at the ready. Beyond was another stone stairwell. Halfway up the stairs, with weapons aimed straight at us, were Loomis, Word, Ash and Andrew.

I let out an audible sigh of relief when I saw them. Ash smiled broadly and gave me a 'thumbs-up.'

"You're alive," Andrew exclaimed. "Or rather… still not."

We lowered our weapons.

"Report," Jackson said gruffly.

Loomis proudly held up two red armbands. "We KIA'd two below. That floor is clear. And you?"

"We nailed two as well," Tizzy said quickly.

Jackson pulled out the red and blue armbands from his pocket and held them up. Loomis looked at them and then at Jackson, who gave a slight shake of his head.

I wondered how convenient it was that the bad guys wore something that allowed us to keep score. Maybe you got five points for bagging a blue one.

Loomis glared at Tizzy. "You made one hell-of-a racket in the process."

"They jumped us," Jackson said. "It wasn't her fault. Either way, they'll know for sure now that we're here, so expect maximum resistance."

"They've got zombie-killers," Tizzy said, showing Loomis the pistol she had acquired.

Loomis barely acknowledged her, but Andrew asked fearfully, "Er, what are zombie-killers."

"Armor-piercing bullets," Loomis said, prodding Andrew hard in the forehead. "Designed to punch through your resin-filled cranium and scramble what little brains you have left."

Andrew gulped.

"What little brains *we* have left," I corrected her.

"What do you mean?" she sneered.

"Those bullets are made to dead-dead all zombies," I said.

"And you're a zombie too now, remember? You're just like us."

"I am *nothing* like you," Loomis hissed. "We," she said, gesturing to Jackson, Word, and Tizzy, "are nothing like you. We are patriots, professionals, killers. You're nothing but a bunch of civilian rejects that failed at living and are failing at being dead."

I took a couple of steps towards her and narrowed my eyes, channeling my inner Clint Eastwood. "Well, whaddya say we focus on not failing at saving the living in this building and making the bad guys dead? So us dead folk can carry on living… or not, and try to stop failing at being dead by succeeding in not being dead-dead, so the living can keep living, and the dead can keep… deading, and… by working as a team…to protect the living and dead… unless they're bad guys… in which case, we definitely need to make them dead..."

Loomis shook her head and softly face-palmed herself.

Jackson shoulder-barged past me. "Freaking moron."

"I thought you *started* really well," Andrew said sympathetically. Even Ash gave a nod of encouragement and patted me on the shoulder.

"You are such idiots," Tizzy sighed and stormed after the others.

"I think she's beginning to like me," Andrew whispered in my ear.

"Not if you were the last zombie on this planet," she called back up.

For the first time, I noticed the red smears around Word's

face and watched as he used his arm blade to cut strips off a piece of raw flesh he was holding. He popped a bit into his mouth, then followed Loomis and Jackson down the stairs.

The floor below was indeed clear, and the corpses of two mercenaries confirmed what Loomis had told us.

We headed along the halls until we reached an open set of stairs leading further downward and halted at the top, looking down.

Jackson leaned over and pointed his rifle down. Satisfied no one was on the stairwell, he said, "Below us is an entrance to the central section of the building. On the ground floor is another one. You three," he said, pointing at Ash, Andrew, and me, "secure that floor. Investigate potential extraction points. Clear?"

"Er, shouldn't we take someone like Tizzy or…um," I said.

"Or anyone with experience?" Andrew finished.

Jackson slapped Andrew up the side of the head, tearing his left ear free of its staples and stitches. Andrew caught it before it hit the floor. "Aah, man. Why d'you do that?"

"'Cause you're an idiot," Jackson replied. "There are no hostages in this wing. They're being held in the main building. At most, there will be a couple of sentries patrolling that floor. I'm sure you morons can handle them, right?"

How do you know that? Is what I wanted to ask, but did not like the idea of getting a slap from Jackson. Maybe it had been in the brief I paid so little attention to. Loomis and Word didn't seem to doubt it, so perhaps it was. Tizzy squinted her eyes a little. *Aah, you weren't paying attention either.* She was no doubt more interested in how many kills she could rack up this mission to secure her place out of our unit.

"Clear?" Jackson repeated.

"Clear," Andrew and I replied. Ash gave a two-finger salute.

The three of us proceeded down the stairwell to the ground floor. Jackson and his team had peeled off through a door on the floor above us.

The stairwell ended in a wooden door with a small glass window set into it. I peered through into the corridor beyond. It stretched off in both directions. I couldn't see or hear anyone on the other side. It was ominously quiet. I had always found offices eerie places after everyone had gone home.

After college, I worked for a cleaning company for a while before landing my cushy job serving burgers. They had a contract with a large insurance firm, and I was sent in at night to empty bins and vacuum. I hated being there alone at night. Offices are supposed to be occupied. Unlike homes, they have no soul of their own. In the absence of people, offices have all the warmth and humanity leached out of them. This is how the offices on the other side of this door felt - like a graveyard.

Human Waste

"I don't like this," Andrew whispered. "Why the hell send us by ourselves?"

"You heard Jackson up on the roof," I replied. "He wants us dead-dead, so he can come out of this looking like a hero and get into The Morgue Horde. Also, I think he's still sore about me blowing him up."

"Well, *you* did that," Andrew protested. "We didn't."

Ash made a circle motion with his finger, indicating to the three of us, and then crossed his fingers to show that we were tight.

"Oh, so we are going to die because we're friends with him?" Andrew exclaimed, his glare on me. "You're a lousy friend, Marco."

Ash punched Andrew on the shoulder.

"Hey! It's true."

Maybe Andrew was right. I suppose I was a lousy friend. I still hadn't told them everything I knew. I hadn't told them about Emily Aiken's plans to dead-dead us. I hadn't told them about Mr. Marshmallow, or Mr. Thomas's involvement in all of this. I hadn't even told them that one of the hostages had plans to destroy all zombies, if Jackson didn't kill her first, along with any witnesses - which could very well mean the three of us.

"Maybe we should just focus on the mission," I said.

Ash nodded, nudging Andrew away from the door. We raised our rifles. I gently opened the door and Ash poked his head through, aiming his gun left and right. The hall was clear. Ash stepped through the doorway, Andrew and I followed.

Grey tiled carpets lined the hall. The white walls were adorned with pictures of Chinese leaders and dignitaries. Occasionally there would be a stunning work of colorful art on the walls. Still, they did little to warm the abandoned building. The only sounds were those we were making as our boots hit the floor, our gear rubbing against tactical vests and clothing, and Andrew's teeth clacking together.

Both Ash and I halted, glaring at him.

"What?" he asked quietly.

"Stop doing that," I said, mimicking his teeth snapping together.

"Sorry," he said. "It helps me focus."

"It doesn't help us," I said, and Ash nodded.

Just then, we heard a dull, echoing clunk above us. I looked up. I wondered for a moment if it had come from the floor above, but it seemed too close, as if coming from within the walls.

I heard more noise. This time it sounded like shuffling and

the occasional 'donk' like a thin sheet of bent metal snapping back into position.

The sounds got closer. Ash tapped me on the shoulder and pointed up to an air-conditioning vent close to the ceiling. Someone was crawling inside the ventilation system.

The person up there was getting dangerously close to the vent that looked down on us. Ash pulled Andrew and me to the side. We stood silently with our rifles pointed upward.

Whoever it was in there was making one hell of a racket. They may have been trying to move soundlessly along the shaft but were failing miserably. Then, judging by how long it took them to move past the vent, I began to suspect there was more than one person in there.

Eventually, the person, or persons, moved beyond the vent and the sounds started to move away from us.

"Who do you think that was?" I whispered. "Bad guys?"

Ash shook his head. No, of course not. He was right. Why would the mercenaries take to the ventilation shafts when they could just stroll along the corridors? No, whoever was up there, was hiding.

"So, who could it be?" I repeated.

"Right now, I'd give my nuts for it to be John McClane," said Andrew.

We looked at him in shock.

"What?" he said and shrugged his shoulders. "Well, what's the use of keeping the bullets if you no longer have the pistol."

I guess he had a point. But I suspected he would be able to

keep his nuts, for now at least. I seriously doubted Bruce Willis in any incarnation was about to pop out from the ceiling and save the day.

"We should follow," I said. "Y'know, just in case."

We cautiously approached. We reached the door of a gent's W.C., where the sound seemed to move away from us and into the restroom. I grabbed the door handle.

Before opening the door, I turned to Andrew and whispered, "On the off-chance it is John McClane, are you going to present them to him yourself or give Tizzy the honors?"

Ash's shoulders shook, and Andrew gave me a wry smile. "C'mon," he said. "you know if Tizzy ever got a hold of them, she'd never want to let them go."

"I dare you to tell her that," I said, causing Andrew's eyes to grow wide. He shook his head.

From inside the restroom came a clang of something metallic hitting the floor. Ash raised his gun and motioned for us to cover the door.

On the other side someone landed heavily, the sound followed by a female grunt. This was followed by someone else hitting the ground feet first.

I looked at Ash and Andrew. They nodded. Weapons raised, we flung open the W.C. door.

There was a cry of alarm as we burst through. The W.C. was large enough to accommodate four people standing at the urinals and another three using the stalls. A large mirror built into the wall overlooked four sinks. Running across the ceiling towards the rear of the restroom was a square metallic tube. Midway along it, a grate had been pushed out, which was now lying on the floor in front of the urinals.

In the middle of the floor stood a yellow plastic sign that read, 'Caution! Wet Floor.' Just above the lettering was a little black drawing of a stick figure falling over.

Standing just below the open air vent was a shocked man and woman.

The man was a frail Chinese gentleman, probably about sixty years old, with neat grey hair and a weathered face. He was wearing grey suit pants and a grime-covered white shirt. When he saw us his hands shot straight up in the air.

The lady was African-American, probably in her late thirties. She wore a light grey skirt with a matching jacket and a pale blue shirt, likewise covered in dark, oily stains. What little jewelry she wore was gold and elegant. Despite clambering through an air vent for God knows how long, not one strand of her shoulder-length black hair was out of place.

Unlike her male companion, she did not put her hands in the air. She simply fixed us with a steely glare.

I recognized her immediately. Senator Sadie Mitchell.

It appeared that Andrew had recognized her too. "Oh look, it's the zombie-hater," he said, lowering his weapon.

"Zombies," the man said in horror, as if realizing what we were for the first time.

"Yes, yes, we're zombies," I said dismissively, "but we're the good guys. We're here to save your butts."

"Yeah, but it's not like you need to *thank* us or anything," Andrew told Sadie.

She reached for the man's arm and gently pulled it down. He lowered the other.

A female gasp come from within the open air vent. I instinctively raised my rifle towards it, as did Andrew and Ash.

The face of a Chinese lady peered from the hole.

"It's ok," Sadie called to her. "They're here to help."

The lady cautiously poked her head further out. However, the moment she saw us, she shrieked "Zombies!" and quickly retreated.

"I know, but they're not going to hurt you," Sadie said, and then to us, "Right?"

Ash and I nodded. Andrew shrugged. "Meh."

The lady appeared once more in the open air vent. Ash approached and raised his arms to help her down. She clambered out, and Ash grabbed her by her slim waist and gently lowered her to the ground.

She was a little over five feet tall, with long dark hair pulled back in a ponytail. She wore a black pencil skirt and a black jacket over a white blouse. Unlike her fellow vent-crawlers, she was not covered in muck and grime. Not a single oily blotch or smear sullied her still fearful face.

The moment her feet touched the ground, she backed away in dusgust, wiping the area where Ash had grabbed her as if trying to rid herself of rancid filth.

"Please don't touch me again," she said meekly.

"Geez, prejudice much!" Andrew exclaimed.

"What were you doing in there?" I asked.

"We managed to escape," Sadie replied. "They were leading us into the canteen, but as we got close, one of the terrorists pulled us to one side. He wanted to lead us to the diplomate chambers on the other side of the building. I managed to grab a statuette and bashed him on the head with it." She mimed the action, a vicious blow.

"Nice!" I exclaimed. This lady had balls. I raised my hand for a high-five.

Sadie stared at it for a moment and then at me.

"Nope. Okay. Just going to leave me hanging, huh?" I lowered my hand. "Then what happened?"

"We ran and climbed into a ventilation shaft to hide," she said. "I figured if we crawled long enough, we'd find a way out. The rest, you know."

"Right," I said. "Well, we definitely have to get you three out of here."

"How?" Sadie asked, folding her arms across her chest.

Good question. Better make her believe that I know what I'm doing.

"Alright," I said. "I'm going to leave first, along with An…"

Andrew spluttered the phoniest cough I had ever heard and shook his head in warning.

Oh right. I had forgotten we were forbidden to give our living names to civilians. Come to think about it, the military didn't particularly like hearing them either.

"Project…" I spluttered, "…um…" *Nope, not a clue.* I could barely remember my own project number, let alone anyone else's.

"Hi, I'm Project 2626," Andrew said with a cheesy grin. He extended his hand towards the Chinese lady. "And who might you be?"

She stared at Andrew's cracked, grey and rotting hand. Her face screwed up in disgust. "I am Qinyang," she said, stepping away from him.

Andrew winked at her. "Don't worry; I'll get you out of this. Then maybe afterward we can talk about improving Chinese, American diplomatic rel- …*yurgh!*"

The clout from Ash to the back of Andrew's head, ricocheted it forward in mid-sentence. The blow hit so hard that his remaining ear came free of its stitching and now hung by a single thread and dangled by his jawline.

Qinyang stared at it, repulsed. She clamped her mouth shut as her cheeks puffed outwards. She spun around and unleashed a torrent of puke into the sink.

"Dude!" Andrew protested loudly to Ash. "Why d'you do that. We were hitting it off."

"No…*blech*…," Qinyang said between gushes of vomit. "we…*retch*… honestly weren't…urgh!"

Okay, so Andrew may have damaged our credibility a bit, but I was still confident I could turn this around.

"Who are you?" Sadie asked me.

Oh, nuts! It turns out that in a crunch, I couldn't remember my own project number either. I wracked my brain. I *knew* this one. Dammit!

With each passing second, Sadie looked at me with growing expectancy.

Wait a second. She has no idea what my project number is, so it wouldn't matter if I made it up and looked damn awesome in the process.

"I'm Project 007," I said cooly.

Ash and Andrew swapped glances.

Sadie slowly nodded. "Right…okay. 007, gotcha."

Yeah, she bought it.

She motioned with her head towards Ash. 'And him?'

"This is Project…*er*."

Ash winked, quickly rubbed off the crosshairs on his forehead, and scribbled with his dry marker: 2314.

Sadie's mouth fell open. She looked at Ash and then at me.

"Can't he talk?" she asked.

I shook my head.

She leaned in closer to get a better look at Ash's forehead. She then turned on me, pointing an accusatory finger as if I was somehow responsible for his state. "Did they tear off the skin on his head so he could use it as a dry board?"

"No!" I said, shaking my head. "No one tore his skin off. That was an accident. It happened when they pushed him out of a helicopter." I winced the moment the words left my mouth.

"They pushed him out of a *helicopter*?" Sadie's mouth opened wide in disbelief.

"Yeah," Andrew said. "They did it to all of us. I thought you'd be happy to hear that, zombie-hater."

Sadie barked at Andrew, waving a finger, "Do you think that's what I'm about?"

Andrew took an involuntary step backward. "Umm…" I am pretty sure I saw his hand move briefly towards his nether region to safeguard the items that supposedly Detective McClane and Tizzy already had dibs on

"Can we keep it down please," I pleaded quietly. "Or am I the only one who remembers we are surrounded by bad guys."

Sadie pursed her lips and muttered. "Sorry, you're right. What do you propose we do? Where's the rest of your team?"

I said, "With any luck, they've already taken out the rest of the mercenaries."

"Mercenaries? Not *terrorists*?" Sadie asked, her eyes narrowing.

I didn't want to get into this now. "Mercenaries, terrorists, what difference does it make? Either way, they still want to kill you. You need to follow us. We're going to get you out of here safely."

"You three?" Sadie said with a raised eyebrow. "You're going to get us out of a building full of armed killers?"

I moved closer to her. "Look, lady, I don't know what you've heard, but zombies are not mindless idiots like you see in the movies. Well, some are, like the Dead-Heads. But we're Net-Heads. Smart, capable, and trained professionals. You're in good hands."

She still looked skeptical.

"I'm going to take the lead," I said. "Project…the one with no ears…"

"What?" Andrew gasped. He raised a hand to the side of his head. "Aah, man!"

I continued, "he is going to take point with me. You three stay close behind. The big fella," Ash casually saluted, "will cover the rear. Got it?"

They looked at me hesitantly. I knew they were scared. That's why I had to show them I had nerves of steel, that I had the skills to get them out of here alive. I had to make them believe I was just as dangerous as the bad guys who had taken over this building. I was a killer, but in a good guy kind of way. I was the hero they'd been waiting for.

I readied my weapon and threw open the W.C. door. Standing on the other side, armed with heavy assault rifles pointed directly at me, were two vicious-looking mercenaries.

I heard a girl scream. I couldn't tell if it was Sadie or Qinyang. Oh, wait, it was me.

The Quick and the Dead-Dead

I leaped backward and slipped on the 'Caution! Wet Floor' sign. Just like the man in the picture, I was flung into the air as my legs shot out from underneath me. Arms and legs akimbo, I slammed into the tiled floor on the flat of my back. The jolt from the harsh landing rippled down my joints and my finger squeezed the trigger of my assault rifle.

A hail of bullets burst from my weapon. Cries from the mercenaries were abruptly cut short as bullets riddled their bodies and they fell like sacks of potatoes.

A third mercenary burst into view, stepping over his fallen comrades. He roared and aimed his automatic weapon at Qinyang and Doctor Liang.

"No!" Andrew shouted, leaping in front of them just as the mercenary unleashed the entire clip. Bullet after bullet slammed into Andrew. Each one caused his body to jerk as if a hundred vaults were flowing through him.

Ash fired back, hitting the merc twice in the body and once in the neck.

I scrambled to my feet, shakily pointing my rifle at them, half expecting them to get back up again, like *real* zombies. I approached cautiously.

"Wait," Andrew said.

"What?" I snapped, anxious to get the hell away from here before more mercs arrived.

"Level with me," he pleaded. He took a step back and motioned the length of his body with both hands. "How bad does it look?"

"Seriously?" I huffed. I gave him a quick scan, knowing we would not hear the last of it until someone answered him. His torso was riddled with bullet holes. Two more had struck the right side of his forehead, and the flattened lead bullets poked out of the flesh like metallic badges of honor.

"I've seen worse," I said honestly. "You should be thankful they weren't zombie killers. If they had been, they'd have gone straight through you, through *them*," I pointed to Qinyang and Doctor Liang, "and straight out through that wall. Now, can we go?"

"Woah!" Andrew exclaimed. "How come *these* guys didn't have zombie-killers?"

I didn't know - *a problem for another time. Right now, we need to leave!*

I walked into the hallway and stopped when I was looking directly down on the mercenaries. None moved. Perfectly round bullet holes dotted their torsos and fresh blood oozed from the wounds. The crimson nectar seeped out from underneath their warm bodies. All thoughts of leaving were now replaced with a need to feed.

Suddenly I noticed I was not alone. Ash and Andrew were standing right next to me, gazing down at the fresh kills. Andrew sucked in his lower lip and Ash wiped his mouth with the back of his hand.

"We should take their armbands," Andrew said, licking his lips, "y'know, so we can prove that we bagged three."

All three wore red armbands, but that was not the red that had us transfixed us at that moment. We exchanged glances. We didn't need to speak. We all knew what we were thinking.

I turned and said to the occupants of the restroom, "You stay here. We're just going to, um, secure the area."

I gave them a toothy smile and let the door close shut. As soon as it had, I pointed to the ladies' W.C. entrance directly opposite. We snatched up the bodies like hungry junkyard dogs and dragged them into the other restroom.

We had been in there maybe thirty seconds when three slow knocks rattled the door.

We gasped. "Be cool, be cool, be cool," I whispered.

"Just a second," I called out and pointed to the toilet stalls. Ash and Andrew quickly dragged the bodies into them. When I was sure no evidence of our activities remained visible, I said as casually as I could, "Come in."

The door opened and on the other side stood Sadie, looking decidedly unimpressed, an open-mouthed Qinyang, who looked like she was going to spew again, and the elderly Chinese man grimacing in disgust.

Ash, Andrew and I stood next to each other, trying to look as nonchalant as possible.

"Did you just eat the bad guys?" Sadie asked.

This was followed by a chorus from Andrew and me of,

"No!"

"Of course not."

"What are you talking about?"

"We wouldn't do that."

Ash followed suit. He shook his head, waved his hands dismissively and pulled every facial expression he could to convey the absurdity of the accusation.

I finished with: "What made you ask that?"

Sadie said nothing. She looked at us with a stony expression, slowly pointing in the direction of the mirror.

We turned simultaneously to look at our reflection. *Ooh!* Each of our faces was smeared with bright red blood. A half-chewed finger still stuck out of the side of Ash's mouth, which he tried to covertly spit out onto the floor.

I made to speak, but Sadie held up a hand, "Don't. Just *don't.*" She shook her head in disgust. "Just clean yourselves up and if it's not too much bother, can you try to get us out of here alive?"

*

Feeling more than a little ashamed, we stalked the corridors in silence. Much to my relief, no more gun-toting mercs jumped out at us. A part of me wondered if maybe Tizzy, Jackson & Co. had wiped out the rest of them and were already proudly marching outside with the other hostages. However, that seemed unlikely. We'd heard no screams, gunfire, or commotion of any kind. Maybe they had cleared the floor above and were holding their position, waiting for us to regroup with them. It was more likely that they hoped we would somehow screw up and cause a diversion so they could swoop in and save the day.

I contemplated radioing Jackson to confirm but then thought better of it. If I distracted him in the middle of a firefight, there would be hell to pay. Besides, I didn't want him to know we had located Senator Mitchell. I knew for sure that if Jackson did learn this fact, it would not bode well for her. I was not totally convinced that hanging around with us was her best option either.

Ash and I crept down the corridor with the others right behind us.

"What's that?" Sadie whispered.

"What?" I asked, pausing to face her.

"That number tattooed on the back of your neck?" she asked.

"It's my project number," I replied without thinking.

"Oh," she said with a wry smile. "Double-o-seven indeed, Project 2219."

That was it! Why did I struggle to remember that number?

"What's your real name?" she asked.

"Does it matter?" I replied, turning my back to her.

"To me, it does," she said sincerely.

"Marco," I muttered. "But everyone calls me Project 2219."

Ahead of us, at the very end of the corridor, was a glass door. Bright sunlight shone through like a beacon of salvation. I quickened my pace, hoping that the way out was clear of more unwelcome surprises. I kept my rifle aimed straight ahead of me, just in case.

We reached the door and I was bathed in warm sunlight through the glass. I looked through and saw a paved path with lush green grass on either side. I could not believe how easy this had been. I grinned and reached for the door.

Ash shot out a hand and gripped my wrist tightly before I could touch the handle.

"What?" I said.

He motioned with his head towards the door. There, attached to it like a grey playdough brick, was about a pound of C4. Wires stretched out of it and disappeared into round sensors with red blinking lights.

"What's wrong?" Sadie asked.

"The door is booby-trapped," I said, pointing at the device. "It'll blow us all to smithereens if we try to open it."

"Do you know how to disarm it?" asked the elderly Chinese man.

"No," I replied and asked hopefully, "I don't suppose you know?"

He shook his head like I had just asked him if he knew how to reverse a fart.

"Well, we aren't getting out that way," I said. "Let's see if there is an open window or something."

We backed up and opened the first door we could find that seemed like it would have at least one wall that overlooked the outside of the building. The one we found opened into a large, plainly decorated office with at least half a dozen small desks, arranged in a neat row. Sizeable windows lined one wall.

Smack-bang in the middle of the window was another brick of C4. A small electronic device was attached to the front of it. From it stretched four silver wires, reaching almost to the corners of the window where they were attached by round suction cups.

It didn't take a genius (thank God) to realize that if anyone tried to break the glass it would trigger the explosive, vapourising anyone in the room.

We tried the adjacent office and discovered a similar device attached to its windows. And again in the office after that, and after that.

No one was getting in or out of this wing of the Embassy without bringing the whole building down on themselves.

We stood in the final office, staring at the window in defeat.

"What do we do now?" the Chinese gentleman asked.

"I don't know," I said. "Have you got any ideas?"

"Are you for real?" Sadie gasped. "You're meant to be

rescuing us. Not the other way around."

"In our defense," said Andrew, "we're kind of the rookies of the team. The real experts are clearing the floor above us."

Sadie's face screwed up in confusion for a moment as she struggled to find the words. Eventually she said, "Why the hell did they send you down here by yourselves then?"

Good question. I believe I knew the answer. I wanted to shift the focus as soon as I could. "Well, why did the mercenaries separate you from the rest of the hostages?"

Sadie shifted nervously and briefly looked in the direction of the man.

"Who are you?" I asked him.

The man swallowed and said in perfect English, "I am Doctor Jianjun Liang. I think they want my invention."

"Which is what?" I asked uneasily.

"I have created self-replicating nanobots," he said softly. "They are not as sophisticated as those created by Batoltech Global, but they are capable of reanimating the dead."

Ash mouthed an F-Bomb.

I tried to picture it in my mind. "So, your nanobots can have sex and make babies?"

"Huh?" said Doctor Liang. "No. That is not how it works. But they can construct more of themselves. Under the right circumstances, they could spread like a plague."

"And these zombies, would they be as smart as us?" I said, but the moment the words left my mouth, I realized we might not be the best product endorsement.

Doctor Liang shook his head. "I think the term you use is Dead-Heads."

"Well, that ain't good," said Andrew, in a high-pitched voice.

Doctor Liang nodded. "I know. China does not want this."

"So why create them?" I asked.

"For the same reason every country that can, has created a nuclear bomb," he replied. "To ensure that others do not use them."

"MAD," said Sadie.

"You bet I am!" I replied. "I'm pissed."

"What? No," she said, shaking her head. "MAD. Mutually assured destruction. If one country launches nukes, the others will too, destroying the entire world. Thus ensuring no one ever launches."

"You hope," Andrew scoffed.

"That's why Doctor Liang is here," Sadie continued. "He wants to show the President and the US Senate what they have, in the hopes that it will force their hand to shut down Batoltech Global and stop the creation of zombies." She then said, sounding a little apologetic, "I'm here to help him do just that."

Andrew stepped right into Sadie's personal space. "And let me guess," he snarled, "any zombies already created will be made dead-dead."

"If by that you mean destroyed," she said, and nodded slowly.

"Great," Andrew spat. "I say we hand her back to them."

"We're not doing that," I said.

"Why?" he barked back.

"Because if we do," I said, trying to remain calm, "we become everything she and people like her *think* we are."

"You don't know what I think about you," Sadie said softly.

"How about you?" Andrew nudged Qinyang who took a sideway step away in revulsion, as if he had just prodded her with the prickly end of a used toilet brush. He said, "Did you see how I selfishly saved your life back there? Do you see me as a monster or do you kinda like me now?" He shot her wink.

Qinyang grimaced. "I don't. I truly, truly don't."

Andrew's shoulders slumped. "Why are all the women in my life so mean?"

"I'm not in your life," Qinyang protested.

There was a *kshh* sound as my earpiece burst into life. Andrew and Ash jumped as well, as theirs did too.

"This is Red Six; where the hell are you? Over," Jackson growled in my ear.

"We're on the ground floor," I replied. "We have secured it, but there are no viable extraction points on this level. Repeat. No viable extraction points. Over."

"Bagged a few more HoMs," Andrew said proudly. Then, before I could stop him, he said, "We also saved three hostages. One of them is Senator Sadie Mitchell, another is a Doctor."

"Nooo," I mouthed at him and slapped my forehead.

A short silence followed. Then Jackson said, "We have secured the floor above you. Rendevous with us and bring the hostages. Over."

"Hmmm, that's a negative," I said, much to Ash and Andrew's horror. "I'm pretty sure they'd be safer hiding somewhere on this level."

"Don't question me," Jackson snarled. "Bring them to us *now*. Clear? Over."

I made a *crrrrrr* sound with my tongue. "Sorry, what was that? Bad reception… didn't, *crrrrr*, hear you. Must go. Got another call coming in."

I pulled out my earpiece and removed its jack from the port clipped to my tactical vest.

"What the hell are you doing?" Andrew said, putting his hands to his face like the kid from Home Alone.

I ignored him. I said to Doctor Liang, "Your technology would be worth millions on the black market, right?"

"Try billions," he replied.

Zombie Killers

"Why do you not want us to go to your friends?" Doctor Liang asked.

I couldn't help but glance at Sadie. "I think that would be a bad idea. You're safer with us."

"So what do we do now?" Sadie asked.

I contemplated our next move and licked my lips, which still had the salty taste of blood. I was starting to get hungry and it was clouding my mind - not that there had ever been a clear blue sky in there to begin with. Maybe if I could go back to W.C. and munch a little more on a dead merc…

"I've got an idea," I said, which seemed to take everyone by surprise, including me.

"What's your idea?" Sadie asked.

"We put you back in the air vents," I said. "You hide there, and we'll say that we were able to get you out."

"But why can't we go to the other soldiers?" Qinyang asked. "I don't understand."

"That makes two of us," Andrew muttered. Then to me, "Buddy, can we have a quiet word in the other room?"

No, is what I wanted to say. Instead, I reluctantly nodded my head.

There was a second door in this room that led to an adjacent office. Andrew headed towards the door and motioned for me to follow him, which I did, with Ash right behind me. As an afterthought, Andrew turned around as he reached the door and said to the living people in the room, "Er, just wait here for a bit. We are going to, um, discuss strategies. Need to know stuff."

"Don't we need to know?" Qinyang asked timidly.

"No," Andrew said, wagging a finger at her. "No, you don't. You had your chance and you blew it. You could've been part of the inner circle, but you had to be mean…"

Ash shoved Andrew through the doorway before he could finish and turned, mouthing, "sorry," to Qinyang.

In the adjacent office, with the door closed, Andrew moved right in front of my face and whispered, "Marco, what the hell are you playing at?"

"What?" I asked innocently.

"Don't!" Andrew said warningly. "You know what I'm talking about. Don't play stupid."

Why not. I've been told I'm a natural. I resisted saying that and bit my cheek instead.

"Why don't you want to take them to Jackson?"

Okay, the jig was up. It was time to come clean. "I saw Jackson talking to that Thomas guy from Batoltech Global. I think he was ordered to make sure Sadie Mitchell doesn't get out of this alive. In fact, I'm certain of it. If we take Sadie to Jackson, he's gonna kill her."

"So what?" Andrew exclaimed. "In case you haven't realized, she wants to dead-dead all of us. Are you trying to say the life of this stranger is more important to you than the lives of your friends?"

"We don't have lives!" I retaliated. "In any sense of the word. I don't like what she wants to do, but handing her to Jackson to be killed? It's not right. "

Andrew pointed a finger at my face, "Yeah, well, I say we take her to him. Because I choose to do what is right by my friends, like you, Ash and Tizzy."

I raised an eyebrow. "Tizzy is not your friend."

"Are you kidding?" Andrew scoffed. "That girl is hot for me."

"Nope. No she's not," I said bluntly. Ash vigorously shook his head.

"You've got more chance with Ash than you have with Tizzy," I said.

Ash shot a wink at Andrew and blew him a kiss. Andrew looked mortified and quickly glanced away. As he did so, Ash gave me a huge grin, as if he found the idea of making Andrew uncomfortable hilarious. I smiled back.

After a couple of seconds, I think even Andrew found the humor in it. Calmly but with more assertion, he said, "We don't stand a chance against these HoMs by ourselves. Especially if we bump into more of the ones armed with zombie-killers. They'll dead-dead us and kill her too. Either way, she's toast. At least if we meet up with Jackson, we've got a chance of getting out of here. If she dies, no one would blame you, Marco."

He was right – no one would blame me. I tried to save her but failed. Most of the zombies I knew might even thank me for letting her die. Batoltech Global, for one, would shed no tears. Jackson and his crew, and Tizzy too, would be thrilled, on their guaranteed way to the fabled Morgue Horde. Jackson may even be so grateful that he might graciously decide not to dead-dead Ash, Andrew, and me. Everyone's a winner.

Everyone apart from Senator Sadie Mitchell – zombie-hater extraordinaire.

"Okay," I said, nodding but keeping my gaze fixed firmly on the floor at my feet. I plugged my earpiece back in and pressed the button on my radio. "Red Six, this is Red Two. We are coming to you. Where are you? Over."

An uneasy moment of silence followed. Then Jackson's voice crackled in my ear. It was cold and emotionless. "Second floor, near the entrance to the central building. Over."

We returned to the office next door and were met with expectant gazes from Sadie, Qinyang and Doctor Liang.

"We're going to rendezvous with the rest of our team," I said reluctantly. "It's the best way to ensure your safety." *Liar,* my brain screamed. *It's the best way to save your own sorry ass.*

I spoke without making eye contact, "Follow us. Keep low and move fast."

I carefully opened the office door and peered outside. Still clear. Moving fast but cautiously, we headed down the hall towards the stairwell. We reached the fire-escape door at the bottom of it, and I gingerly pushed it open, with my rifle aimed in front of me.

Apart from an emergency exit light that made a slight clicking sound as it flickered on and off, there was complete silence in the stairwell. I took one more look up the gap between the flights of stairs just to be sure. No one peered over the railing down at me. No grenades were tossed from the top floor to bounce off metal and concrete on their way down to where we were standing.

Confident the coast was clear, I beckoned to the others to follow me. After ascending a couple of steps, Ash took point and Andrew moved up next to me. After a few more steps I paused, and turned to face our living companions.

"Listen up," I whispered. "There are a lot of places we could get ambushed on the way to our rendezvous. If that happens, stay behind us. We can take the hits; you can't."

"And if they are armed with zombie-killers?" Sadie asked.

I grimaced. "Then run, as fast as you can and hide."

Sadie breathed in deeply, her shoulders trembling.

"You'll be ok," I lied. "You've been great so far."

She smiled, her eyes welling up. "Are you sure? I feel like I'm going to burst into tears at any moment. I really don't want to die."

Neither did I. I nodded. "Yeah, dying really sucks."

Everyone wins apart from Sadie Mithcell.

I turned to Andrew. With a slight shake of my head, I mouthed, "I can't."

I looked up at Ash, who was a couple of steps in front of us. He nodded and locked eyes with Andrew.

Andrew ground his teeth for a moment. "Change of plans," he said. "We're going to take you to the roof. I've got a couple of flares somewhere in here," he pointed to his ribcage. "With any luck, you'll be able to draw someone's attention and get picked up. At the very least, we might be able to barricade the stairwell so no one can get to you."

Ash nodded approvingly.

To me, Andrew said, "Does that sound like a plan, Project 007?"

I smiled. "That sounds like a plan."

We crept up the stairs, pausing at each level to peer through the small round windows of the doors leading to the offices beyond.

Both the first and second floor were clear, and as we approached the third our pace quickened, for fear of what may be coming up behind us.

I looked back at our living companions. Sweat poured from Doctor Liang's brow. Qinyang's eyes were darting left and right and tears trickled down her cheeks.

Sadie was chewing her bottom lip. The tang of fresh blood assailed my nostrils. I wanted to tell her to stop but instead I turned away so she could not see me salivating.

We reached the third floor and I looked over the railing,

down the central gap. No one was following us.

I motioned again for everyone to stop. Feeling more confident, I pushed my face against the glass hole in the door. On the other side, nobody. Just another ghostly quiet hallway with vacant offices.

"Okay," I whispered to the others. "We're almost home free."

"Just one more flight," Andrew concurred.

"With any luck no one will even think to look on the roof for you," I said smugly.

Sadie opened her mouth to say something, but stopped. Her eyes bulged. She gasped and pointed a trembling finger behind me.

I turned. There, filling the porthole window of the door, was a man's face. His eyes were wild. Scraggly brown hair jutted out in every direction and a curly, matted beard clung to his chin.

Behind me, Sadie screamed. Qinyang screamed. I screamed louder than either of them.

"Here!" the crazy-eyed man yelled and kicked open the door. Teeth gritted in fierce determination, he leveled his automatic rifle at my head, but then something miraculous happened: we beat him to the punch – just like *real* soldiers.

Andrew, Ash and I raised our guns and opened fire. We didn't actually hit the red-band wearing maniac, who was less than five feet from us, but we did force him to dive back into the hallway, where the door swung shut on him. That small victory alone felt good. But sadly, it was short-lived.

Ash knelt, fixed his rifle on the door and, without looking back, pointed frantically for us to run.

We raced up the final flight of stairs. The door to the roof was within sight. However, as we got about halfway up, the door was booted open. Standing in the open doorway, sporting a hipster-sized brown beard and wielding a heavy machine gun with both hands, was a hulking mercenary. The sleeves of his black combat fatigues were torn off, exposing trunk-sized biceps. And there, stretched over the impossibly large muscle of his right arm, was a blue armband.

It was at that moment I realized there was no dignified way of yelling, "Yikes!"

The merc grinned maniacally down at us. Even before he squeezed the trigger, I knew what kind of ammunition was loaded inside the tank-destroyer sized gun.

"Zombie-killers!" I screamed and pushed everyone back down the stairs. The mercenary howled in triumph and unleashed a storm of bullets down on us. They ripped up the concrete steps and tore through the walls as if they were made of cardboard.

As I fled down the stairs, I returned fire, but my bullets struck only wall and concrete, and with far less ferocity than our attacker's.

"Go, go, *go*!" I yelled at the others. We sprinted down, almost tripping over each other as we ran. Sadie stumbled forward. I caught her arm with one hand and fired upwards with the other, not even bothering to see if any of my bullets hit their mark.

We reached the third floor, in time to see Ash fire into the door that the crazy-eyed merc was testing with his boot.

"Time to go!" I screamed at Ash.

I dashed down the next flight, overtaking everyone else. I was reminded of a T-shirt I once saw, worn by a bomb disposal expert, which read, "If you see me running, try and keep up." Trust me, right now the zombies in World War Z had nothing on me. I was the Usain Bolt of the undead. I was taking those steps two and three at a time. Oh yes, Zack Synder zombies could kiss my ass.

I reached the floor below. The others clambered down the steps trying to keep up with me. Ash was taking up the rear, shooting the occasional burst upwards as cover fire. I grabbed for the emergency exit door and tore it open, not bothering to look through its porthole window first.

Charging down the corridor in our direction were three more armed mercenaries - one with a blue armband and two with red.

Yup, that ain't happening. I slammed the door shut, cursing Jackson. *So much for clearing the second floor.*

Another burst of fire from the colossal mercenary chasing us down the stairs, destroyed concrete and tore holes through walls.

I turned, almost colliding with Sadie and Qinyang. I grabbed Sadie by the arm and shouted, "C'mon!" as I sprinted down the final flight of stairs.

At the bottom I could hear that the mercs from the floor

above had joined Conan the Bearded-Hairy-One in his pursuit of us. With nowhere else to go, I kicked open the fire escape door and prayed for the best.

I charged into the corridor beyond. "Follow me!" I screamed, with no idea where I was heading. All I knew was, we needed to get away.

I sprinted down the hallway, but now I was more mindful that I had civilians in tow and slowed my pace as much as I dared. Ash caught up with me and we ran side by side, weapons at the ready. Behind us ran Sadie, Qinyang and Doctor Liang, with Andrew taking up the rear position and doing his best to run backward.

The corridor took a sharp turn left. As we approached it, Andrew let out a panicked yell and fired a long burst from his gun. There was a pained cry.

"Got one!" he exclaimed. I didn't turn to see which one.

The Mercenaries returned fire before diving for cover, and a couple of bullets whizzed above my head.

We darted left. I sped down corridors at random at every crossroads or T-junction. At every turn, the HoMs seemed to be just behind us, as the sound of gunfire exploded, microseconds before we could dart left or right out of the line of sight.

Ahead, the corridor forked to the right and widened out.

"This way," I yelled and dashed toward it. I skidded right as I reached the fork. This corridor was short, only five yards long, and it ended in a pair of white double-doors with frosted glass built into them. I couldn't make out what was on the other side, but doubted it was another corridor judging from the amount of light pouring through them.

Ash and I shoulder-barged the doors open and had already charged through before we realized where we were. Which was about neck-high in crap.

Bad to the Bone

We burst into a huge, double story, diamond-shaped atrium. The floors were polished fake-marble and the walls clad in grey stone slabs. Large paintings of Chinese landscapes and portraits of royalty past and present, adorned the walls.

To our left, a glass revolving-door led out to the Embassy's white stone courtyard. Red wires, leading to a couple of bricks of C4, crisscrossed the door.

Sunlight flooded the room from three diamond-shaped skylights, similarly shaped windows towards the room's upper level, and through the glass door. This light, bouncing off the pale stonework and tiles, gave the impression of being outdoors.

Towards the revolving door was a half-moon shaped, marble fronted desk with a glass top. Two empty chairs stood behind the desk.

To the rear of the desk and central to the room was a wide, metal staircase, carpeted in light grey. This led to a floating walkway that ran the room's width, connecting the east and west wings of this building. Chrome topped, glass railings ran the length of the walkway and down each side of the staircase.

I had to admit, this was a spectacular room. The only thing that ruined it for me were the twenty or so armed mercenaries who opened fire on us the second we entered.

The room exploded in panicked gunfire from all directions. Obviously taken off-guard, the mercenaries seemed to be laying down cover fire rather than taking aim shots. That did not stop me from getting clipped by at least four bullets as I darted for cover, keeping Sadie behind me. One bullet grazed my jawline, ripping off a straight line of flesh, adding yet another scar to my collection.

As we ran, Ash and I returned fire, me at the mercs on the ground level, he at the ones on the walkway. Glass from the shattered railing showered down on us. The mercs ahead of me darted for cover behind the staircase. Others ran towards the double doors on the opposite side of the room.

Ash hit one of the bad guys on the walkway, and in true Hollywood style, he cried out, collapsed over the railing and fell to the floor below. This caused the others to duck. As if the glass-fronted barriers would offer them any protection.

Andrew also shot back at the mercenaries. However, having failed to reload his rifle after the last encounter, the only thing to come from his gun was an ominous *click, click, click.* And so, midway in our dash for safety, Andrew substituted bullets for sound effects.

"Bang, bang, bang, bang!" he shouted as he aimed at the startled mercs. Miraculously, this seemed to do the trick. Bad guys dived left and right to avoid Andrew's imaginary bullets. For the first time, I thought I understood his philosophy on life – it really didn't matter if all you were shooting were blanks, so long as people believed you were packing something big.

We all dove for the safety of the large visitors' desk and ducked in front of it. Ash and I risked popping our heads over the top to return fire. At the same time, Andrew manically fumbled inside the pocket of his tactical vest for a fresh clip.

"Goddamit!" someone bellowed. "Stop shooting. Liang is with them."

Instantly, the firing stopped. The only sound in the great room was the tinkle of glass shards as they fell to the stone floor.

Andrew and I exchanged glances. He briefly peeked over the desk and up at the walkway. A second later, when he ducked back down, his eyes were large as marbles.

"Holy crap," he whispered, "it's Travis Black."

Ash's mouth gaped. He shot a sneaky glance over the desk and then slumped back down, nodding grimly.

I had heard of Travis Black. We all had. I knew that name even before I died. He was on the FBI's top ten most wanted list. Notorious gun-for-hire, linked to kidnappings, murder, terror attacks, weapons and drug smuggling, arson, extortion; you name it, he's done it. Simultaneously he was the most feared and hated person in America.

"All we want," he shouted down from the walkway, "is Doctor Liang. He has something we want. Hand him over and you can sit this out with the rest of the hostages in the canteen.

Hell, I wouldn't even mind if you nibbled on a couple of them."

Sniggers and chuckles broke out amongst his men.

"What d'ya say, Net-Heads?" he continued.

I stood up, causing a chorus of gasps from my side of the desk.

Travis was standing proud on the walkway. He wore a black tactical combat outfit that looked tailor-made, probably by the same guy who makes Bruce Wayne's Batsuits. Hanging casually by his side was a black MP5 submachine gun. As soon as I stood up, a smirk spread across his square jaw. He ran a hand through his spikey black hair, taking time to caress it.

To his right were three goons wearing blue armbands. Four more had taken up position on the stairs, adorned with the same color armband. On the same level as us were another dozen or so mercenaries, all but four wearing red armbands.

Crouched by the far door were another two mercs, one wearing blue, the other red.

The double doors we had run through just moments before, swung open to reveal the bearded behemoth with five of his buddies.

Twenty mercenaries, my ass! By my calculations, there must be, well, at least three hundred in here, give or take a few.

"I may not be the smartest zombie...," I said.

"I can see that," Black said matter-of-factly, raising yet more giggles from his minions.

"But even I know you'll kill us the moment we hand over the doctor."

Out of the corner of my eye, I saw Jackson on the walkway. He had entered the room by the doorway leading to the west wing's second floor, close to where we had last seen him. With his rifle fixed straight ahead of him, he stalked Travis. Close behind him, crouched behind the human roadblock, were Tizzy, Loomis, and Word. For the first time ever, I was glad to see them.

Neither Travis nor any of his men had noticed the zombies creeping towards them. All eyes were focused on me. I just had to keep it that way.

I said as confidently as I could, "You may as well give it up, Black, Mr. Black, erm, Travis. There's no way out."

"Oh *no*!" he said, opening his eyes and comically planting a hand over his open mouth.

Jackson inched closer, like a ninja, if ninjas came in rhino size.

Seemingly amused at his own performance, Travis smiled and said, "Actually...we do have an escape route. It seems storm drains run directly underneath the building."

"Aha!" I exclaimed triumphantly. "I knew it. There is no way you would have told us that if you didn't plan on killing us all."

Travis nodded apologetically, and it dawned on me that my jubilance at being right was probably ill-advised.

"What can I say?" he said, "you got me."

"Wrong, *I've* got ya," Jackson said and pressed the muzzle of his automatic rifle against Travis's skull.

Suddenly, I was no longer the focus of attention. All guns and eyes were trained on Jackson. Tizzy pointed her weapon at the goons on the stairs while Loomis and Word covered the blue-bands standing next to Travis.

"Aha, in your face" I yelled at Travis and did a little victory dance.

Ash and Andrew stood up and pointed their guns at the mercs on our level. Ash nudged me to do the same. So, now feeling somewhat confident, I opted to aim my rifle at the bearded gorilla.

Travis raised a hand and motioned for his men to lower their weapons, which they did without question.

"Marco," Jackson shouted to me, not taking his eyes off Travis. "Is Senator Sadie Mitchell down there with you?"

I paused. "Hmm, what does she look like again?"

Before I could stop her, Sadie rose nervously to her feet. "Yes, I'm here."

Doctor Liang stood up, with Qinyang holding on tightly to the back of his suit jacket.

"Hail, hail, the gang's all here," said Travis with a smirk.

"Not everyone. We bagged four of your crew," Andrew said, cockily.

"Four?" Travis questioned and shot a glance over at the bearded mercenary.

"Three from red squad, one from blue," the merc grunted, sounding like his vocal cords had been made from a recycled tuba.

Without moving his head, Travis pivoted his eyes in Jackson's direction. "And you?" he asked.

Keeping one hand on his rifle, he reached into his pocket and pulled out the blue and red armband.

Travis eyed them. "Well, that is disappointing, Sergeant Cole."

"Shut up," Jackson growled. "Marco, come up here and bring the hostages with you."

He didn't need to ask me twice. Standing alongside the more experienced members of our squad, and covering these buttwipes from an elevated position, sounded like a fine plan to me.

We left the safety of the desk in a huddle.

With any luck, this would all be over in a few minutes. That would wipe the smug look off Travis Black's face. The idiot didn't even know that when you become a zombie, you lose any military rank you had. That being said, I was feeling so positive towards that mountainous beauty right now, I would call Jackson anything he wanted. Hell, I'd call him General Cole if he asked.

Somewhere in my mind, I saw a penny drop. It landed edge down into a squishy toasted marshmallow. I froze.

"What's the hold-up, Net-Head?" Jackson barked, his gun still flush with the back of Travis's skull.

"How did he know you were a sergeant?" I asked, pointing at Travis. "More to the point, how does he know *your* name?"

An insidious grin spread across Travis's face. "He's smarter than he looks," he said.

"He isn't but you're dumber than you look," hissed Jackson. He then moved his automatic rifle from Travis's head and pointed it in my direction. "Just bring them up here, numbnuts."

Tizzy's mouth was agape. "What the hell…?" she mouthed.

Loomis lowered her weapon and said quietly to her, "Follow our lead. It's all good."

"You're working with him?" I screamed at Jackson. "You traitor!"

"I-am-no-traitor," Jackson roared back, slamming a fist into his chest as each word came out of his mouth.

"And to be fair," Travis said casually, moving away from Jackson towards the stairs, "he doesn't work for me either. We just happen to find ourselves similarly aligned. You see, we both want the same thing."

"And what's that?" I asked.

Travis took the first two steps leading down. "More zombies," he said as if the answer were obvious.

He unclipped a black metal rod from the left leg of his combat pants and held it up. On the business end of the rod were two prongs. He pressed a button, and bright blue electricity arced between the prongs. He then touched it to the metal railing and it crackled furiously.

One of the blue-band mercs on the stairs, whose elbow had been touching the railing, let out a pained, "Aargh!" and involuntarily squeezed the trigger of his automatic weapon.

Shots rang out, causing everyone to duck. Regaining control of his motor functions, the merc rubbed his elbow furiously. He stopped the moment he realized all eyes were on him, even Travis's.

"S-sorry," he stammered. "It was the thing," he pointed to the cattleprod, "when you t-touched..."

Travis glared flaming daggers at him.

The merc grimaced. "Sorry. Sorry everyone," he said, even including us in his apology.

"Totally get it," Andrew said reassuringly. "No harm done."

"You know," I said, pointing at the cattleprod, "you really should be more careful with that thing."

"Marco!" Jackson roared so loudly I was scared he'd set off the explosives attached to the windows and revolving door. "Shut up!"

More calmly, Travis said, "If we're all quite finished, may I continue."

"Oh yeah," I said. "Sorry, bad guy speech. Go for it."

"Much obliged," Travis nodded to me, taking another step towards us, his cattle prod sparking against the metal railing. This caused every single person on the stairs and walkway to simultaneously move away from the railing.

If Travis noticed, he said nothing. "So, I'll take Doctor Liang off your hands. Then he'll tell me where he has hidden his laptop and how to get into it."

"Never!" Doctor Liang spat.

Travis puckered his lips and stopped right next to one of

the blue-band-wearing mercs. "If you don't, I'll kill the hostages one by one until you do."

Qinyang gasped. She looked at Doctor Lian, but he stared ahead bravely.

"Tell him!" she cried. Doctor Liang shook his head.

She turned to Travis and blurted, "He's hidden it in the ambassador's office."

"Aha!" Travis cheered. "Why, thank you. What's your name, beautiful?"

Her lip quivered. "Qinyang," she replied.

Travis clipped the cattleprod back to his combat pants. With one hand, he motioned enthusiastically for Qinyang to join him. "You've earned a spot right next to me here on these stairs. Come on up, Qinyang."

She smiled weakly, hesitated, then approached him.

"No," Sadie whispered and grabbed her by the wrist. Qinyang looked at her for a moment. She then pried Sadie's hand from her wrist and climbed the stairs to where Travis was standing.

"You see," Travis said, "with a little co-operation, we're already fifty percent of the way there. Now, Doctor Liang, why don't you start being a team player?"

"I will not tell you my password," Doctor Liang said defiantly.

Travis shook his head and leaned in close to Qinyang. "I don't think he believed me when I said I'd start killing hostages."

He raised his MP5 and shot Qinyang three times in the

back. She collapsed like a marionette puppet with its strings cut, and slid down the stairs

"Nooo!" Sadie screamed.

"You swine!" Doctor Liang yelled.

I raised my rifle to shoot Travis. I no longer cared if I got mowed down and made dead-dead. So long as I got to take this asshole with me, it would be a win.

Jackson fired a second before I could. Bullets slammed into my rifle, tearing it from my hand, along with the little finger from my left hand. Both it and the rifle skidded along the ground towards the revolving door.

"Don't," Jackson ordered, and trained his weapon on Ash and Andrew.

Tizzy stared at Travis in wide-eyed disbelief. She was no longer aiming her gun. Instead, she held it limply by her side. She glared at Word and Loomis, who shook her head slowly. "All's good," she said calmly. "Trust me."

Travis, seeming utterly unphased by the events that had just unfolded, said. "Once I've got what I want, we'll be out of your hair."

My eyes narrowed. "What about us?"

He smiled. "Well, after an epic gunfight that will sadly result in the termination of a few members of his team, Jackson will take out the bad guys and save all the hostages… most of them, at least," he said, looking with mock sympathy at Sadie. "He and his crew will return as heroes, thus building support for Batoltech Global's zombie initiative. In the meantime, I will sell the good Doctor's nanotechnology and buy myself an island somewhere." Travis pointed a finger at me. "Doesn't that sound like a great plan to you?"

"It sounds like a stupid plan to me," Andrew scoffed. "How's anyone going to believe that he," he nodded towards Jackson, "killed all the bad guys, if you've all escaped?"

Travis winced theatrically and sucked air in through pursed lips. "Gee, I hadn't thought about that." He patted the merc standing next to him on the shoulder.

The side of the man's mouth curled up into a grin. His grip tightened on his submachine gun. "Fire!"

The room erupted in a storm of bullets from all directions. All the mercenaries wearing blue armbands opened up fire on those wearing red, and us.

The huge bearded merc spun on the five men next to him, shoulder-barging them into each other. He then mowed them down with his heavy machine gun.

The terrified red bands, those that were still standing and had the wherewithal to react, returned fire, but their position was hopeless. They were now outnumbered and outgunned. Mercenaries, joined by Jackson, Loomis and Word, shot down on them from their elevated position.

Travis leaped down the last few steps of the staircase. Midflight, he raised his boot and caught me in the chest with a swift kick. I flew backward and slammed into the hard floor on the flat of my back.

Word vaulted the railing, dropping twelve feet to the ground below. As soon as he landed, he sprung to his feet and sliced a red band merc across his throat with his blade. He then turned his attention to Andrew and charged at him.

I rolled onto my stomach. Lying about five yards away was my rifle. I scrambled towards it, my feet failing to find traction on the slick floor. I half crawled and half slid toward it. Shards of stone exploded from the ground as bullets slammed into it, less than a foot to my right. I turned to see where they were coming from. Jackson had abandoned his attack on the mercenaries and was now focusing on me.

I dove to the left as more bullets hit the floor. Travis launched himself at Doctor Liang, striking him in the face with a headbutt. The Doctor cried out, blood spurting from his nose. Travis then lifted his MP5 and aimed it right at me. Bullets streaked out of the gun, fire igniting behind them like tiny comets. They hit the stone floor, just inches from me as I rolled desperately out of the way. However, unlike Jackson's bullets, these did not explode as they hit stones, flattening out and smashing the hard floor. These pierced it, sending up virtually no debris but creating perfectly clean holes from which tiny plumes of smoke arose. *Zombie-Killers. Oh, nuts.*

Screw my weapon. I needed to get out of here *now*. We all did. I planted my hands on the ground to steady myself, jumped to my feet and broke into a sprint. Ahead of me, Sadie was taking cover in front of the visitors' desk.

Word was charging Andrew, his sword arm raised high above his head. Andrew yelled in horror and unloaded the rest of his clip back at Word. Most of the bullets missed wildly. A couple ricocheted off Word's blade. Only two found their mark, hitting Word in the chest, causing him to stumble momentarily.

On the walkway, Loomis was shooting at anyone with a red armband. Her eyes were unblinking and with each kill, she licked her grinning lips.

Tizzy stood next to her, mesmerized with horror, watching events unfolding around her. Her assault rifle was readied but she didn't fire until the glass railing beside her exploded, causing her to angrily return fire on the mercenary who'd tried to end her.

Regaining his footing, Word lunged at Andrew, swinging his blade down in a wide arc. Andrew screamed and tried to parry it with his rifle, stock in one hand, barrel in the other. Word's sword cleaved it in half as easily as butter.

Andrew stumbled backward and fell onto his back, screaming in terror. Word darted forward and stood astride him. He lifted his blade like a praying mantis and prepared to bring it down on Andrew's skull.

Travis grabbed Doctor Liang by his shirt and wrenched him into the arms of one of his mercs. "Take him," he ordered, then ducked as one of the surviving red band mercenaries took a wild shot at him. With Travis's focus now on saving his own neck, I was able to skid along the floor towards the cover of the visitors' desk. But I was not close enough to rescue Andrew. Nor was I close enough to save Doctor Liang, who was being dragged up the stairs, with Travis fleeing past them for his life.

Word brought the wickedly sharp blade down on Andrew. Just inches from his face, the blade-arm came to a halt. Ash had grabbed it with one hand. Word looked at him in surprise. Then, executing a move he had learned during his days as a wrestler, Ash's other hand grabbed Word by the ankle and hauled him off his feet. Using his body as a counterweight, Ash spun him around four or five times and flung the diminutive marine through the air and straight at the bearded mercenary. Word slammed hard into him and both collapsed to the ground.

I reached Andrew and Ash in time to see Word bounce to his feet, ready to launch another deadly attack. The enormous merc hauled himself up, looking unsteady and confused. Word lifted his bladed arm. As he did so, he noticed a thick coating of blood that covered the upper five inches of the blade and trickled like syrup down its edge.

Word, mesmerized by the sticky, crimson fluid coating his weapon, suddenly forgot all about us. He brought the blade close to his face and his tongue snaked out to lick the blood. But he stopped short of tasting it. Instead, his eyes narrowed and his lip curled up. He spun around to face the bearded merc who was now standing straight up and towering over him.

All color had drained from the merc's face. He dropped his heavy machine gun with a clatter and clamped his hand to his stomach. Blood gushed between his fingers and he gawked at Word in confused horror. Word looked at the tip of his blade and then at the wound in the merc's stomach. He then stared the merc straight in the face, and I think they both knew what was about to happen, a micro-second before it did.

"*No!*" was all the bearded merc was able to say before Word lunged at him in a savage flurry of teeth and blade. We stood still, unable to tear our eyes from the horror unfolding before us. It was one thing to succumb to the primal urge all zombies have to consume flesh, but to see it unleashed with such savagery, filled me with disgust and self-loathing.

Three bullets, smashing into the side of Ash's skull, broke us from our trance. He collapsed to the floor.

"Nooo!" I screamed, reaching down to him while scanning for the origin of the bullets. I looked up and saw Jackson glaring down at us with demented glee, the muzzle of his assault rifle still smoking.

Between a Zombie and a Hard Case

Regular bullets, my mind screamed. *Hopefully*. I turned my attention back to Ash; he raised one hand and gently pushed me away. He got to his knees and plunged his hands through his shirt. He ripped apart the zip in his abdomen, shoved both hands inside his chest and pulled free one flashbang grenade and one smoke grenade.

We all shared the briefest of glances, a silent, almost psychic exchange.

Ash pulled both pins with his teeth. He hurled the flashbang over the desk and the smoke grenade toward the door where Word was brutally devouring the giant mercenary as if he were a bearded Big Mac.

I dove for Sadie and shouted, "Close your eyes and cover your ears."

The flashbang exploded in a thunderous roar of blinding light. Simultaneously, thick smoke erupted from the smoke grenade, filling the west half of the room.

The flashbang had exploded just as a mortally wounded red band merc threw a grenade at Travis. The intense light from the flashbang caused his throw to go wild so, instead of landing at the top of the stairs by Travis's feet, it landed midway, rolled down two steps, then fell through a gap in the stairs. It exploded, obliterating the lower half of the staircase in a storm of glass and metal that showered the room. The explosion instantly killed two of the blue band mercs standing on the stairs.

Everyone still with a pulse was temporarily lost to the chaos around them. They reeled, deafened and blinded by the flashbang. Others coughed uncontrollably as smoke choked their lungs. More dived for cover, seeking refuge from shrapnel raining through the air.

This was all the distraction we needed. I pulled Sadie to her feet and dragged her across the room, back toward the double doors we had entered by moments earlier. Ash and Andrew sprinted after us.

"Hold your breath," I warned Sadie as we approached the doors and wall of noxious smoke. I pulled her into the cloud.

At the last moment I saw Word, mostly obscured by the grey smoke that billowed around him. He sat astride the bearded mercenary, his face buried in his neck, gnawing at flesh like a wild animal. I jumped aside and yanked Sadie away, praying she had not witnessed the carnage.

We all burst through the double doors. Behind me, I heard Jackson roar, "Loomis, Ortiz, get them!"

Ash grabbed me by the shoulder. He pulled me in the

direction he was heading, which happened to be the same corridor we had run a few minutes earlier, fleeing from the mercenaries.

As we ran, I looked back to see if anyone was following us. There was no one, but it would only be a matter of time. In the main hall, the firefight was now nothing more than the occasional double-tap of blue-band mercs executing any of the red-bands that were still breathing.

It occurred to me that not one of us was still in possession of a primary weapon. I felt for the holster on my hip. My pistol was there, which was kind of a mixed blessing because I was a worse shot with that weapon than I was with my assault rifle.

"*Hmmm*, stay behind me, like at all times," I said to Sadie, and then to Andrew: "Do you still have a sidearm?"

He shot me a knowing wink and pulled his pistol from his holster. Ash automatically did the same. We cautiously turned the corner and, about a third of the way down the corridor, came to a door with a white sign. Below the Chinese characters, the translation read: 'No Entry. Authorized Personnel Only'.

Ash pointed to it, then mimed with two fingers, someone walking downstairs.

"Got it," I turned to Andrew and Sadie. "This must lead down to the basement where Travis Black said there was a way out. Come on."

Ash, pistol aimed, opened the door. Sure enough, on the other side, were concrete steps leading down. Ash crept forward, and we followed in his considerable wake, peering around him every now and then to get a look at what was ahead.

White plastered walls did little to brighten the dim stairwell or the corridor beyond that. Thick metal pipes ran along the ceiling, and a low, droning hum reverberated down them. The passage opened into a narrow room filled with large airconditioning units that rattled and spat out ice particles.

Sadie hugged her arms across her chest, and I saw goosebumps pucker her flesh.

Beyond this room, a short corridor led onward. Not out of bravery, I took the lead ahead of Ash; being behind him reminded me of being stuck behind a truck on the freeway, frustrated that I couldn't see what was ahead of it.

Pistol aimed, I stalked ahead. The gloomy corridor continued for about five more yards and ended in a T- junction. Just as we approached the corner, something heavy and metallic hit the concrete floor to the right, followed by a man's angry cursing. Both nearly made me jump out of my skin, which admittedly is easier to do when said skin is already in the process of decay.

We all froze. I turned slowly to the others and pressed a finger to my lips. I inched forward to the junction, hugging the right wall.

As I got to the corner, I peered first to the left. The short corridor in that direction ended in a metal door with a card reader attached to the wall next to it. Judging by how cool it was down here, I guessed beyond that door was the server room.

I then risked poking my head around the corner to look down the right-hand side of the corridor. They say that when a person loses an arm or leg, they can suffer phantom pains for years to come, as if the limb was still there. I could well believe that because, as I looked in the direction of the noise, my non-existent heart was pounding in my chest.

The corridor to the right was about eight yards long. Midway along, to the left and the right were doorways. At the far end, a round hole gaped in the wall, about three feet in diameter. Only the dimmest of lights filtered from the other side, but I could hear rushing water. I had no doubt it was coming from the storm drain on the other side.

Standing in front of the hole, with an assault rifle slung over his shoulder and wielding a sledgehammer, was a sweaty and dirty-looking mercenary. He had stripped down to a vest, but a blue armband was still strapped around his bulging bicep. He took another swing at the wall, and another chunk of masonry broke away and crashed to the floor.

Flat against the right wall were two metal storage cupboards. Next to the opening, on the floor, was a heavy-duty bag filled with rubble and another that looked about half full. Leaning against the cupboard was a broom and a dustpan and brush.

For a moment, I wondered if and why they intended to clean up after themselves, but then it occurred to me. For Travis's ruse to work, no one must know he and some of his crew had escaped. They must have planned to sweep up all the mess created by smashing a hole in the wall and then maneuver the metal cupboards back into place so that no one could find their escape route.

Confident that the sounds of rushing water and noisily pounding airconditioning units would mask the sound of my voice, I turned to the others and whispered: "That's their way out."

Ash, Andrew and Sadie all took turns to glance around the corner.

"Just one bad guy," I said. "We take him out, and you…" I pointed to Sadie, "get the hell out of here."

"What about you?" she asked quietly.

I shook my head, "We can't leave without rescuing the other hostages." I didn't feel the need to tell her that the explosives in our heads would detonate if we left the mission zone. So we were screwed either way. At least going back for the hostages gave us a chance to go out as heroes.

I looked at Ash and Andrew and whispered, "Ready."

They nodded.

I mouthed, "One…two…three."

We burst around the corner. Five or six shots were fired before the mercenary even knew he was under attack, by which time it was too late. His face contorted with pain; he dropped the sledgehammer and spun around. He reached for the AK47 slung over his shoulder, squeezing the trigger as he collapsed to the ground. The short burst of rifle fire punctured pipes in the ceiling, and steam billowed out of the holes. Then his weapon fell from his hand and the merc was still.

We paused for a moment, looking down at the body. I suspected Ash and Andrew were wondering the same thing as me - which one of us had ended this man's life?

Suddenly a figure appeared on the other side of the hole in the wall - a bald man wearing combat fatigues. He roared and opened up with an AK47. Ash dove forward, landing on the flat of his stomach. With his pistol pointed out in front of him with both hands, he returned fire.

Andrew and I darted back around the corner as bullets from the AK47 tore into the wall. I pointed my pistol around the corner and returned fire. The man ducked behind the wall and I could hear him loading a fresh clip into his weapon.

Ash jumped to his knees, crawled forward a few more feet, and took aim. I crouched, using the wall as cover, and pointed my gun at the hole in the wall. Andrew stood up, leaned above me, and did the same thing.

Without looking back, I motioned with my other hand for Sadie to move back towards the room with the airconditioning units.

A fine jet of steam from a burst pipe in the ceiling forced Ash to move even closer to the hole.

For a terrifying moment, nothing happened. No one moved. Our pistols posed, ready to shoot anything that popped back up through the hole. Absurdly, I found myself trying to hold my breath, even though I had not breathed in months.

Ash lowered his gun, then cautiously reached into the hole in his stomach. After a couple of seconds, he produced a hand grenade and shot me a wicked grin. He pulled the pin and threw it in the direction of the hole in the wall.

Then, the most ridiculous synchronicity I had ever witnessed occurred. At the same time as Ash's grenade sailed through the air, the merc on the other side of the hole tossed one of his own through the opening.

"Crap!" the merc exclaimed, as I'm sure Ash would have if he could.

Without time to seek cover, Ash grabbed a metal cabinet and pulled it in front of him in an effort to shield the blast.

I dove backward, propelling Andrew back at the same time.

The explosion was deafening. The whole building seemed to rock. Metal and concrete collapsed from the ceiling. Rubble and dust billowed around the corner where Andrew and I lay on the ground.

Ash, cupboard and all, was propelled back by the explosion. They shot past the T-Junction and were slammed against the metal door, followed by an avalanche of rubble, metal and dust.

Ash! I pushed myself off Andrew and darted back toward the blasted corridor. I turned the corner and was confronted with the devastation the explosion had caused. Thick pipes that seconds before had lined the ceiling, were now hanging down like a barricade of metal tendrils. Concrete and rubble were piled as high as my waist. The metal cupboard that Ash had not used as a shield, had been blasted against the wall of debris, making the corridor even more impassable.

I turned in the direction of Ash. Now twisted and buckled, the metal cupboard was wedged fast at a forty-five-degree angle between the walls, sandwiching Ash against the door. A small mountain of rubble covered the cupboard and almost all of Ash's limbs that protruded from underneath it.

"Ash!" I yelled out.

Ash's hand pushed up through the shattered bricks and gave a thumbs up.

"Ash," I cried again, this time with relief. For the first time, I dared to believe we could survive this.

No one heard the blast, I willed the universe. *No one will come down to the basement, and no one will stop us from clearing this rubble nor stop us from getting Sadie to safety.*

We were just a few yards from the way out.

We can do this! I thought.

Just then, the universe replied, *Guess again, loser.*

A Dead Reckoning

Sadie screamed, "Marco!"

I spun around to see Tizzy and Loomis charging down the corridor towards us. Instinctively I ran forward to protect Sadie.

Andrew was scrambling on the floor for his sidearm, which he must have dropped when I bumped into him. He grabbed it and sprang to his feet, just as I barrelled past him.

Loomis entered the section of corridor that opened out, a second or two before Tizzy. Without breaking stride, she punched Sadie in the face, sending her smashing against an airconditioning unit, and lunged for Andrew. He pointed his weapon at her. Loomis swatted it out of his hand. It clattered along the floor and under one of the units.

Before I could react, Tizzy slammed into me with such force that I was catapulted back towards the blasted corridor.

I hit the ground, dazed. Being dazed as a zombie is different from when you are alive. It's like someone turning off the lights for a second. My lights came back on just in time to see Andrew get hurled against a wall by Loomis.

By the time I'd jumped to my feet, Tizzy was already in the short corridor with me. She shook her head and raised her automatic rifle in line with mine. Resin hardened bones or not, taking a full clip at this range was going to take me out for sure.

Sadie was now on her feet. She charged forward, let out a banshee-like warcry and leaped onto Tizzy's back. She wrapped one arm around her neck and grabbed her assault rifle with the other.

Tizzy flailed around, trying to dislodge the battle-crazed Senator.

I looked down at my hand to check that I was still holding my pistol. I was. I aimed it at Tizzy, but she was thrashing around so much, I could not take the very real risk of shooting Sadie.

Andrew was stumbling to his feet as Loomis pressed her onslaught. She punched him twice in the face and followed this up with an elbow to his jaw. Andrew cried out, reeling backward and placing his arm on one of the air conditioning units to steady himself. Loomis's unblinking eyes glistened. Snarling gleefully, she whipped out a knife from a sheath on her hip and skewered Andrew's forearm to the unit, the blade grinding as it pierced the metal casing.

Andrew looked in horror at the blade sticking through his arm. He tried to pull away. The blade sliced a long slit down his forearm, eventually hitting bone, and he could pull no further.

Loomis grabbed Andrew's face, gripping his jaw so tightly that her fingernails tore into his flesh.

"Open up, creep," she sneered and forced his mouth open. With her free hand, she drew her pistol. "What was it you said to me? Oh yeah, I'd like to give you something to swallow." She rammed the gun into his open mouth.

Andrew's eyes bulged in terror and he gurgled something undecipherable.

I turned from Tizzy to Loomis and squeezed the trigger, four times in rapid succession, walking closer to her as I did so. There were three cracks and one click, announcing the clip was now empty. Two of the bullets had only hit the wall, but one connected with Loomis on the side of her forehead, gouging away a thick strip of flesh.

She staggered away from Andrew, yanking the gun from his mouth, feeling with her fingers the patch of exposed bone on her forehead.

She glared at me, her face contorting with fury. "Look what you've done, you asshole."

She turned the gun on me and fired the entire clip. As bullets forced me back, slamming into my chest, gut and shoulders, more gunfire erupted to my right.

Sadie was clinging to Tizzy's back like a bull rider at the Rodeo World Championships. They grappled with the rifle. Tizzy's finger squeezed the trigger in the struggle and the clip emptied into the floor and ceiling.

Her gun now empty, Loomis leaped the last yard or so between us, headbutting me. The sound of hardened bone on bone made a hollow 'thunk.' She growled in frustration and grabbed me by the shoulder straps of my tactical vest. She spun me around and pushed me into Andrew. I collided with him and we both fell against the air-conditioning unit.

Tizzy finally managed to rip Sadie off her back. She fell straight onto her butt, looked at us desperately, turned and tried to crawl over to us on her hands and knees. She got about halfway when Loomis reached down, grabbed a handful of Sadie's hair and yanked her backward. Sadie cried out in pain, trying to grab Loomis's hand to tear it free.

"Oh no, bitch," Loomis snarled. "You're coming with us."

Andrew screamed and wrenched the blade out of his arm. Like me, he prepared to charge, but then Tizzy dropped her assault rifle and drew the pistol with the zombie-killer bullet she had taken from the dead mercenary. She pointed it at us. We froze, daring not to move an inch.

"Let me go," Sadie shouted, still struggling against the grip Loomis had on her hair.

"Not a chance, Senator," Loomis replied. "Oh, I know all about *you*."

Some of the fight seemed to leave Sadie. More calmly, she asked, "Are you going to eat me?"

Loomis shook her and scoffed, "Hell, no! We need to make it look like hostiles killed you. Wouldn't do our cause much good if you were eaten, would it?"

Loomis gave Andrew and me an icy stare and chewed her lower lip in anticipation. "Go on, Ortiz, do it."

Tizzy pointed the gun first at my head and then at Andrew.

Her lips puckered and her brow furrowed.

"Tiz…er, Angelique, don't do this," I pleaded. "This isn't right. We're soldiers. We're supposed to protect people. If you need to dead-dead us, fine. But don't let them kill this lady."

"She'd see us all dead-dead," Tizzy said cooly.

I shrugged. "Maybe we should be. Especially if we have forgotten how precious life is."

"Do it, Ortiz," Loomis goaded. "This time next week, we'll be sitting pretty with The Morgue Horde."

Still, Tizzy did not squeeze the trigger.

Loomis secured her grip on Sadie's hair, leaned a little closer to Tizzy and said softly: "Be more than your beginnings."

A flash of anger shot across Tizzy's face and she glanced at Loomis for a second. Maybe this truth was a little too close to home, or perhaps she believed she had something to prove to Loomis and the others. Maybe she needed to prove she was just as good as them. Whatever the reason, she gripped the gun with more commitment.

She pointed it menacingly at me and then at Andrew, and back again.

"What are you waiting for?" Loomis asked.

Through gritted teeth, Tizzy confessed, "There's only one zombie-killer bullet left in this gun."

Loomis chuckled. "Then shoot the one that pisses you off the most."

Tizzy nodded. "Good call." With that, she turned and blew Loomis's brains out.

Her knees buckled, she released her grip on Sadie's hair and collapsed to the ground.

"Be more than your beginnings?" Tizzy spat. "Condescending bitch."

Sadie looked down at Loomis's lifeless body and then at Tizzy. "Thank you," she said softly.

"Don't get too comfortable," Tizzy pointed a finger at her, "I may kill you yet."

Then Ash appeared, taking us all by surprise. He was covered from head to toe in dust and grease and brandishing a blood-covered AK47. He pointed it at Tizzy's head.

"Woah!" Andrew and I yelled in unison. Ash looked from Tizzy to us. "She's on our side."

"Don't get ahead of yourself," Tizzy said, shaking her head. She pointed at Sadie. "I can't believe we're contemplating helping this zombie-hater."

Sadie winced. "Is that what you think of me?"

We all nodded, but I was the only one to say, "Yeah, kinda."

Sadie sighed, and her eyes reddened. She walked right up to me. "I don't hate zombies, Marco. I don't hate you. I don't hate any of you."

"So why are you trying to get us all destroyed?" Tizzy asked.

"Because I hate what they are doing to you," she said. Tears filled her eyes. "To say that a person can be owned, be forced to submit to the will of another, to be traded like objects. I mean, for Christ's sake, you are identified by numbers tattooed on your skin. Do you know what happened the last time people did this to other people?"

I genuinely didn't, but I figured it didn't end well based on her increasingly distressed tone.

She wiped the tears from her face with the back of her hand. "To deny a person of their fundamental human rights is wrong on every level. Thousands have died over the years, have sacrificed everything to fight this injustice. I cannot sit back and let it happen again. I don't hate zombies. I just don't want anyone else to be subjected to the things you have been subjected to. I want those already created to be released from this *life*, and be allowed to move on. I cannot live in a world where a human being is again allowed to be owned by another."

I remained dead silent. I no longer felt worried about my fate - only Sadie's. The odds may be stacked against us in this building full of trained killers, but the battle ahead of her seemed impossible.

"But we're not human," I said. "Not anymore, at least. We are zombies, and legally, zombies have no rights."

Sadie put her hand gently to my cheek. "Oh, Marco. Don't you get it? There's a difference between what is legally right and what is morally right."

"I get it," Tizzy said, her voice quavering. Ash moved up behind Tizzy and nodded solemnly.

"Your name is Angelique, right?" Sadie asked.

Tizzy nodded. "Yeah, but my friends, like these idiots," she said with a wry smile, pointing at Andrew and me, "call me Tizzy."

Sadie smiled a genuinely warm smile. "So, what's the plan, Tizzy."

"To keep you safe," she replied. "I get why they want *you* dead, but I don't get what they want with that doctor."

"He has created nanobots," I said, "that can make a whole bunch more nanobots without having sex. And they can make Dead-Heads, even without an NPC pod. Apparently, it'd be worth billions on the black market if the mercs got their hands on it."

"Forget the HoMs," Tizzy said, looking concerned. "What would happen if Batoltech Global got their hands on those nanobots?"

Sadie thought about it for a while. "They'd be able to create millions of zombies that only they would have the technology to control."

I slumped against the table.

Andrew gulped. "You don't think the mercs are on Batoltech's payroll, do you?"

"It wouldn't surprise me," Tizzy said. She straightened up as if standing to attention. "Right, we need to get you," she pointed at Sadie, "and the rest of the hostages to safety. More importantly, we need to rescue Liang before he spills his guts."

"Hmmm, guts," I said without thinking. Everyone paused to look at me. Quickly, I said, "Okay, what are we waiting for?"

"Hold on there, Brainiac." Tizzy held up a hand. "You ain't

going to be able to fluke your way through this one. Between us, the doctor and the hostages, are about twenty highly trained HoMs armed with zombie-killers. Not to mention their psycho leader and two pissed off and dangerous zombies. To be honest, I think the chances of any of us getting out of this alive is, like, zero."

"So why risk it?" Sadie asked.

Tizzy chewed her lip. "Because I'm sick of living, or not living, like this. But if I'm going out, it's gonna be swinging. What about you, guys?" she asked the rest of us. "Are you with me?"

Now that's how you deliver a Clint Eastwood speech.

"I'm in," I said. "Better dead than undead."

A grin spread across Andrew's face. "Better dead than dickless."

Ash patted Tizzy on the shoulder and gave her a thumbs-up.

Tizzy smiled. "Alright." She pointed at Sadie, "You, hide in here. Do not move until we come back for you. The rest of you, let's save the freaking day or get dead-dead trying."

Yippee Ki Yay

On the second floor, we took turns peering down the corridor where two bad guys, armed with MP5s, guarded the double doors leading from the west wing into the main entrance hall.

I was the last one to scope them out. All the confidence I had filled myself with earlier, slid out of my butthole. I had a side-arm with one full clip. Ash still had his pistol and bloodied AK47, and Andrew had taken no small amount of satisfaction from commandeering Loomis's automatic rifle. Tizzy was armed with, well, a Tizzy. Even so, we seemed desperately outnumbered and outgunned.

The idea of charging headlong into the hall where we had barely managed to escape the carnage of mere minutes earlier, seemed like utter madness.

"Alright," Tizzy whispered, "here's how it's going to go down."

We all listened intently. I, in particular, was hoping she would unveil a plan that did not involve a suicidal dash into a merc-filled hall.

"I'm going to take out those two sentries," she said, "and then we're going to bust into that room, gun blazing."

Oh well.

"I'll deal with all the HoMs in the main hall," she continued.

Now we're talking.

"Andrew and Ash," she said, "while I'm drawing their fire, you head to the canteen at the rear, eliminate any hostiles along the way, and rescue the hostages. When you've secured them, lead them out by the hole leading to the storm drain. With any luck, Sadie will have the path cleared by the time you get there."

Solid plan.

"Marco…" She looked at me. "You head straight to the east wing, take out Travis Black and anyone with him, and rescue Doctor Liang."

Hmm, say what now? "Er, shouldn't we stick together? Or at least you and I stick together?"

Tizzy shook her head. "No. I'm the diversion. Got it?"

Without waiting for a response, Tizzy reached into her abdomen and pulled out a hand-grenade. She shot me a little grin, pulled the pin, and tossed the grenade in the direction of the mercs.

I heard one of them utter, "Uh-oh," a fraction of a second before it exploded. The debris had not even had a chance to settle before Tizzy was sprinting towards what remained of the double doors. One was hanging away from the frame, attached by a single twisted hinge. The other had been completely blown off its hinges and had skidded along the walkway overlooking the main hall, coming to a halt beside the staircase.

The remnants of the two mercs were dripping from the ceiling, smeared up the walls and pooling on the carpet. I'm pretty sure I imagined the rumbling of the clear plastic bag that now acted as my stomach.

As Tizzy approached the visceral carnage, she dropped to her knees, skidding along the floor. For a moment, I thought she was going to grab a quick bite. It turned she was collecting the dropped MP5s.

Two more mercs on the walkway, who had obviously been hit by the flying door, were struggling to get to their feet. Armed with a blazing MP5 in each hand, Tizzy gunned them down before they succeeded.

We charged after her. I ignored all the fresh meat under my feet, hoping the gradually mounting hunger would keep me short-tempered and violent. Traits I needed to help keep me alive right now.

By the time we'd reached the shattered doors, Tizzy was charging across the walkway, ferociously roaring as she did so. Below, mercs were shooting up at her from all directions. I could tell from the way the bullets ripped through the walkway and the ceiling that now they were firing nothing but zombie-killers.

As soon as my foot hit the walkway, I fired frantically down on the enemy. I didn't bother to aim or check if I was even close to hitting anyone. I dared only poke my hand over the railing and fire what remained of my clip. Andrew similarly fired blindly downwards from the other side of the walkway. Only Ash took the time to send a couple of well-aimed and considered shots into the main hall below.

Tizzy reached the blasted door lying by the stairs. Instead of charging down, she flipped mid-air onto her back, landing on the door. Then, using both feet, she kicked the glass and steel railing, propelling herself and the door down the stairs like a sled.

As the door shot downwards, Tizzy held out an MP5 in each hand and unleashed a lead hurricane in all directions. Bullets shattered the glass railings, tearing into mercs standing on either side of the staircase.

She screamed, "Die, you mother f…" Before she could finish the sentence, the door reached the section of the stairs that had been destroyed by a hand-grenade in the previous confrontation. The metal here was bent upward. Suddenly, Tizzy and the door were airborne. The door whirled mid-flight like a frisbee and crashed-landed on the stone floor. All the time, Tizzy was creating a 360-degree zone of death, shooting anything that moved as she spun around and around.

I have to say, it was the most impressive thing I'd ever seen. It took a moment for me to realize I had stopped shooting myself to admire the spectacle below. And another moment to notice that Andrew and Ash had also paused their attack to watch the show.

"I told you, didn't I," Andrew said, nudging me, "she's tougher than piranha nipples."

"Guys!" she shouted up, snapping us out of our collective trance.

The mercs beneath us had started to regroup and were now returning fire. Tizzy rolled off the door and scooted for the cover of the visitors' desk.

Ash looked over the walkway towards a large door at the rear of the room. As we had been advised, it led to the canteen full of hostages. For Ash and Andrew to reach them, they needed to get off the walkway to where Tizzy was in a pitched battle against the HoMs.

Ash frowned as he looked at the destroyed stairs, a wreck of twisted and spiky metal. It seemed to beg for someone to try to navigate it so they could fall and be impaled. After apparently giving it some thought, he turned to Andrew and winced apologetically.

"Huh? What?" Andrew asked, confused. Then before he could say anything more, Ash grabbed him by his crotch and tactical vest and pitched him over the railing.

"You schmuck!" Andrew cried out as he fell to the ground.

Ash pointed urgently for me to run to the double doors on the far end of the walkway, then vaulted over the railing himself.

Not wasting another second, I dashed along the walkway, chancing glances over both sides. To the front of the room, Tizzy was taking heavy gunfire. However, some of the mercs now focused their attention on Ash and Andrew, who had entered the fray on the other side of the room.

I could see no sign of either Jackson or Word. This made my

redundant sphincter pucker, like a sea anemone being poked with a stick. If they weren't here, they were somewhere else in the embassy, and I could be running headlong toward them.

Only when I had burst through the double doors did it dawn on me that my only weapon was out of ammo. I was about to turn back and grab one of the automatic guns on the walkway when I heard an agonized scream somewhere ahead of me.

Directly on the other side of the doors was a short corridor that ended in a T-Junction. The carpet running the length of it was a deep red. On either side were office doors, dark mahogany in color. Gold nameplates adorned each one, and I suspected you needed an important title to get an office in this wing.

Directly to my left was a staircase leading both up and down. Another cry of pain echoed down the stairs. I abandoned any idea of getting a replacement weapon and charged upward.

When I reached a door leading to the third floor, there was another bloodcurdling scream. Now I could also hear the unmistakable sound of Travis Black chuckling.

I cautiously opened the door to a corridor identical to the one on the floor below.

Travis's voice came from a room on my right. "If I were you," he was saying, "I would start talking. Or else, I'm going to continue to crank this sucker up until you do, or until I fry your heart."

I crept forward, thankful for the thick carpet beneath my feet. The door was slightly ajar, and I peeked through the gap.

The room looked less like an office and more like a Doctor's examination room. A few framed paintings hung on the walls. The room was tastefully furnished, with books neatly arranged in a small floating bookcase, a desk towards the far end with a chair on either side, two closed oak cabinets and a metal filing cabinet tucked away in the corner.

To the right of the room was a black leather reclining bed, to which Doctor Liang was strapped. Blood trickled from his nose over his cut lip; his left eye was bruised and swollen shut. Blood spatters now accompanied the dirt and oil stains on his white shirt. His feet were bare, and the soles looked bright red and raw. Standing over him was Travis, holding a pair of defibrillator paddles connected by curly wires to an open black bag sitting on a small table next to the bed. The bag looked more like a laptop case than something that could house a defibrillator.

Travis was grinning sadistically at Doctor Liang. "I'm doing you a favor. My man Paxon over there, wanted to cut strips off you and make you watch as he ate them."

I tried to get a better look inside the room, but a third of it was beyond my field of vision. Word had to be standing by the near wall.

"So why don't you play ball," Travis continued, "and tell me how to access the nanobot files?"

"Never," Doctor Liang spluttered, coughing up blood.

Travis sighed, "You do know that eventually, we'll be able to hack your encryption without you, right?"

"Then…argh…do it," Doctor Liang coughed.

Travis moved closer to Doctor Liang's feet and rubbed the defibrillator paddles together. "Ok, this is gonna hurt."

Dammit! I needed to save him, but how? Travis had an MP5 filled with zombie-killers, a cattle prod most likely charged to 1.21 gigawatts, and a defibrillator that I swear I could hear humming. And let's not forget Word, lurking in the shadows with a head-cleaving sword.

What did I have? A bad case of rot-breath and an empty pistol. Not great odds.

Wait a second. They don't know it's out of ammo.

I kicked open the door, taking Travis by surprise. He jumped back, away from Doctor Liang. I quickly moved to the side of the room where I hoped Word was least likely to be standing. Sure enough, he was standing next to the wall by the door.

Before either could react, I pointed my pistol at Travis's head. "Anyone moves, and I'll shoot you in the head with this fully-loaded gun."

Word remained motionless, only tilting his head to one side when I spoke.

Travis raised his hands but still looked a little too confident for my liking. The corner of his mouth curled upward slightly.

"Put those down." I pointed with my pistol to the paddles Travis was holding.

"Ok." He slowly placed them back into position on the defibrillator.

"There, done. Now let's not do anything stupid."

"You might be asking too much there," Word muttered.

Travis raised his eyebrows and turned his head in Word's direction. "Is this the one you said was dumber than a lobotomized goldfish?"

I shot Word a scathing look. "That was unnecessarily mean."

Word ignored me and nodded to Travis. "Gun's probably not even loaded."

"It is too!" I said, sounding nowhere near as confident as I'd have liked.

Travis's brow wrinkled. He pointed to the ceiling. "Then perhaps you'd like to give us a warning shot? It is customary, after all."

"Err," my brain stalled. Not for time; it literally stalled. I had nothing.

"Told you," Word said, taking a step closer and lifting his bladed arm like a duellist's salute.

"Wait!" I shouted. "I don't want to give a warning shot because…" I wondered if they could hear the static bouncing around the inside of my skull.

Word took another step closer and Travis reached for his MP5.

Aha! my brain screamed. I pointed the gun with more vigor at Travis's head, firmly placing my finger on the trigger to show I meant business.

"I don't want to give you a warning shot," I said, and they paused, "because I don't want to waste a bullet, and I don't want to damage public property."

They exchanged glances.

"There!" I yelled triumphantly. "In your face!"

Click.

Oh, dear God, please tell me I didn't just accidentally pull the trigger.

Travis laughed out loud. "What kind of idiot charges into a hostile situation with an unloaded gun?"

"That kind of idiot," Word answered flatly, pointing at me.

"Hmm," Travis nodded in agreement, reaching for his MP5. At the same time, Word charged forward.

"Uh-oh," seemed like the most appropriate thing to say at this moment. I hurled my pistol at Travis. It spun in the air and smacked him right in the middle of his forehead with a painful *thunk*.

"Ow!" He dropped his MP5 and clasped both hands to his face.

Word lunged at me, bringing his sword down in a wide arc. I jumped back, but not quickly enough. His blade sliced through my tactical vest, deep into my flesh, and glanced off of my ribs, causing my entire body to judder.

It stumbled back into the open door. Word brought the blade up high, aiming it at my skull, and thrust it forward, throwing all his weight behind it. I moved my head at the last second. The blade cut into my right cheek, gouging out a chunk of the bone, then embedded itself deep into the mahogany door.

A flash of panic crossed Word's face. He tugged on the blade but it was stuck fast. Word braced a foot against the door, grabbed his left arm with his right hand and started to tug with both.

I was not about to let him pull it free. I jumped high into the air and smashed my elbow down on the part of Word's arm where the blade was grafted to bone and flesh. A horrid snap and tearing sound followed and Word's upper arm was ripped free. He tumbled backward to the floor while the blade remained immovably skewered into the door. For an instant I wanted to flick the free end of it, to see if it would make a comical *boing* sound as they do in cartoons. I might have too, if not for the fact that the end of this one had no hilt but was, instead, covered in torn flesh, bone and sinew. Besides, I could see Travis scrambling to retrieve his MP5.

I ran and bolted down the corridor. About midway, it dawned on me I was running further away from anyone who could help, such as Tizzy, Ash, and, at a push, Andrew. I turned to see Word hurtling straight for me, his face contorted in rage.

I knew right away he was too fast for me to outrun. However, due to his small frame and the fact that his arm was missing, I was pretty sure I could take him. That misguided confidence vanished when he leaped into the air and roundhouse kicked me in the face, causing my head to bounce off the wall.

While I was still reeling from that attack, he spun around again, kicking me in the gut. I heard a tearing sound as the zip in my abdomen tore apart.

I hit the ground and skidded back three or four feet. I looked up in time to see Word jump high into the air and plunge toward me, knee first. I rolled out of the way just in time. Instead of his bony knee smashing into my nose, it slammed into the carpeted floor. He thrust out his right arm to steady himself. Without thinking, I swatted his arm as hard as I could. It flicked out from underneath him and he fell flat on his face.

I jumped to my feet and ran as fast as I could, back in the direction of Liang. I desperately hoped that Travis had not found his MP5, or if he had, I could wrestle it from him and waste him and Word at the same time.

Behind me, I heard Word gaining, and fast. I reached the open door and skidded to a halt. Inside, Travis had indeed managed to find his automatic weapon. A small trickle of blood rolled down from a pistol-butt-shaped lump on his forehead.

He stood next to the bed to which the doctor was strapped. He saw me, smiled, and raised his gun.

I reached in and grabbed the door handle. I knew the door would not stop the bullets, but if he could not see me when he took aim, I stood a chance. I slammed the door shut in time to see Word charging toward me at what seemed like a hundred miles per hour.

I fell backward in terror. I will never know if Word saw it at the last moment, or if his scalpel-sharp sword, which was still stuck in the door at a ninety-degree angle at just about neck height, had gone unnoticed. Either way, when Word launched himself at me, his body collapsed on my chest and his head rolled along the carpet until it came to a stop by the stairwell door.

I pushed his headless corpse off me in disgust. At the same time, bullets from Travis's MP5 turned the door into Swiss cheese. Had I not been lying prone on the ground, I would have been toast. Travis continued to riddle the door and wall with bullets until there were none left in his gun.

I heard him curse. This was my chance. I sprung to my feet, flung open the door, and rushed at him as he was searching his pockets for a fresh clip.

As Word had done to me seconds earlier, I launched myself at Travis. He sidestepped me effortlessly, like a champion bullfighter. I slammed face-first into one of the wooden cabinets.

I turned in time to see Travis bearing down on me, cattle prod in hand. I rolled to the left and the pointed end of his weapon, crackling with sparks of electricity, missed me by mere inches and hit the cabinet instead.

I tried to sweep the legs out from under him, but he jumped back as if expecting the attack. While I hadn't managed to trip him, the added gap between us allowed me to scramble to my feet.

He thrust the cattle prod at me again and I ducked to the right. However, as I did so, he brought his left elbow up and smashed it into my jaw. I heard a crack and felt a couple of back teeth come loose on my tongue.

I threw a punch at him but he blocked it, got my arm in a lock and battered my face repeatedly against the desk. Each time he did so, the lights would go out for a micro-second. By the time he'd spun me back around, I had no idea where or who I was.

He had me pinned against the desk by my throat. I grabbed his wrist, trying to pry it free, but he was simply too strong.

I looked in the direction of Doctor Liang. I had let him down as well as my friends. I wanted to say sorry, but the words would not come.

Travis glared down at me and smiled. "You've got heart, kid, but you're just no match for a guy who doesn't have one."

Somewhere in the back of my mind, I could hear Mr. Marshmallow say, "You're not done yet, my boy."

I gritted my teeth and struggled against his grip with all my might. "Garrr!" I roared in frustration.

"Oh, quit your bellyaching," Travis said. "At least this will be quick. Your friends, on the other hand," he leaned in closer, fixing me with a cold stare, "I intend on taking them apart piece by piece to see how much punishment they can really take."

"Nooo!" I screamed, frantically clawing at his immovable hold on my throat.

He raised his cattleprod high above my head. It arced with intense blue light.

I was still tightly gripping Travis's wrist when I felt something crawl down my arm. Travis raised the cattleprod an inch or two higher, lining it up with my right eye.

The cuff of my sleeve bulged for a moment, then Eric scuttled out from underneath it and up my hand. He then plunged his stinger into the back of Travis's hand.

Travis screamed in agony. He simultaneously let go of both my neck and the cattleprod and clasped his wrist in agony.

I sat upright, caught the cattleprod mid-flight, rammed it into Travis's open mouth and down the bastard's throat. He gurgled and collapsed to his knees. He looked up at me, his eyes bulging.

I pressed the button on the cattleprod. Travis's body went rigid. I could hear the electricity sparking from the spokes of the prod, deep inside his throat. Smoke erupted from his mouth, along with the pleasant odor of barbecuing flesh. I kept my finger pressed down hard on the button until the skin around his neck turned black and the cattleprod fell silent.

Travis finally collapsed to the floor. The cattle prod slid out of his throat, covered in crispy blood and bile.

I tried the button one more time, but it was as dead as its owner. I let it fall to the floor and stared at Travis. The smell of cooked flesh was intoxicating. Salivating, I bared my teeth and prepared to fall upon Travis's motionless body and take a chunk out of his deliciously seared neck.

"What are you doing?" gasped Doctor Liang.

"Well I was about to…erm…" I stamped my foot. "Oh, come on! I only eat bad guys."

Doctor Liang looked mortified.

"Oh, fine. Whatever," I huffed and stomped over to him. "Just don't blame me if I get hungry enough to take a bite out of you later."

I freed him from his restraints.

"Thank you," he said weakly.

"Can you stand?" I asked.

“I don’t know,” he said. He gingerly sat upright and placed his feet on the floor, wincing in pain. “My feet,” he moaned.

“I know,” I said. “I’m sorry but I have to get you out of here.”

“Why were your friends helping Black?” he asked, placing an arm limply over my shoulder.

“They weren’t *my* friends,” I said. “My friends are currently trying to save you and everyone else in this building.”

I hoped they were ok. “It looks like Travis already found a buyer for your technology - Batoltech Global. Did you ever stop to think about what would happen if they got hold of your little creations?”

What little color remained in Doctor Liang’s face, drained away. “They could create an army of undead.”

I nodded. “That’s why we need to make sure no one gets hold of your technology. Where’s your laptop?”

He pointed towards the desk. And there it was, on the far end, close to where Travis had pinned me down.

I thought for a moment. And then another. Static returned to my clueless mind. If we left it here, someone could find it. If we took it with us, someone could take it from us.

A scent of marshmallows floated in the air, and simultaneously an idea popped into my head.

Last Zombie Standing

"Will this work?" Doctor Liang asked.

"Honestly?" I said, "I doubt it."

I slung the bag over my shoulder and helped the doctor stand. With my arm around his waist, we slowly made our way back to the building's central section.

I was feeling naked. Travis's MP5 was utterly out of ammo, as was my gun, so it was pointless taking either. The cattleprod was spent and I couldn't dislodge Word's sword from the door, not that I would have been able to use it if I had. Probably end up cutting off one of my own limbs instead of someone else's. I also had to take off my tactical vest that Word had sliced in two.

Only my shirt covered the gaping hole in my sternum in which Eric was now wriggling. I thought about how he saved my life. *Damn, I owe that guy a giant bug.*

"What are you humming?" Doctor Liang asked when we reached the stairs.

"Huh?" *Was I humming?* I thought for a moment and smiled.

"It's an old song. It goes, 'I know an old lady who swallowed a fly, I don't know why she swallowed a fly, perhaps she'll die.' It just reminded me of my pet scorpion, who is currently scrounging around where I think my spleen used to be."

"Oh," he said.

Yeah, I wouldn't know what to say to that either.

With each step, Doctor Liang grunted in pain. This was going to be a long haul, but the only way out was through the storm drain, which felt like a bubillion miles away.

We reached the second floor and the double doors leading to the walkway of the central building. As I pushed open the door, Doctor Liang cried out in pain and stumbled. I supported him as best I could and used my hip to shove the door the rest of the way open. Focused as I was on him, we had already taken a few steps onto the walkway before I noticed Jackson.

He was standing beyond the ruined staircase and about fifteen feet from the blasted double doors leading to the west wing.

Just in front of him, looking petrified, was Sadie Mitchell. Her eyes were red, and even from here I could see her trembling. One of Jackson's mighty hands was clasped around her throat. The other held a pistol, trained in our direction.

His eyes narrowed and his lips parted, displaying gritted teeth. He asked, though I suspected he already knew the answer: "Travis and Word?"

I grinned. "Dead and dead-dead."

He looked away briefly, up toward the heavens, shaking his head in disbelief.

"Oh, well," he said with a sigh. "Plan B."

He pulled the trigger. Sadie screamed. For an instant I thought he had shot me. Then Doctor Liang slumped from my arms to the ground. Blood slowly seeped across his shirt from a single bullet hole in his chest. He stared up at me with lifeless eyes.

"*Why*?" I roared at Jackson.

Jackson shook his head. "He was no longer needed, but his laptop is," he said, pointing to the bag on my shoulder. He nodded towards Sadie. "Give it to me or I'll put a bullet in her skull."

I was about to say, "You're going to kill us both anyway," but figured that might prompt him to come to his senses and do just that. For now I was happy to play along to buy us some time.

I took a couple of cautious steps closer to him.

Sadie sniffed, her eyes pleading and filled with tears. She looked at me, shook her head and mouthed: "No. Run."

"It's ok," I said softly.

"Do it!" Jackson barked, his grip tightening around Sadie's neck.

Suddenly I spied something moving behind Jackson, creeping down the corridor towards the open doorway and the walkway. It was Tizzy.

Jackson hadn't noticed her, and I needed to keep it that way.

I walked toward him, more boldly now. I unslung the bag from my shoulder and held it up at arm's length.

"Let her go," I said.

"When I get the laptop," Jackson said. *Yeah, right,* I thought. Never mind, we were both bluffing now.

Tizzy stealthfully approached the doorway. I could see her favorite knife, gripped in her hand. I was a little disappointed it wasn't a gun loaded with zombie-killer bullets, but I guess she must have run out of ammo at some point. Still, if anyone could slice Jackson to pieces with a foot-long knife, it'd be Tizzy.

When I was within a couple of yards of Jackson, I tossed the bag forward. It landed by his feet. He looked down, his brows furrowing, and roughly shoved Sadie toward me.

With his gun still pointing in our general direction, he knelt and unzipped the bag with his free hand.

Tizzy silently crossed the threshold and stalked toward Jackson.

"What the hell is this?" he said, staring at the defibrillator machine inside the bag.

Grinning from ear to ear, I said, "It's what I used to fry Liang's laptop."

"What?" he roared. "You stupid sonofabitch!"

He sprang to his feet and aimed his weapon at us. I grabbed Sadie and pulled her behind me. Before he could pull the trigger, Tizzy screamed, drawing his attention. He turned, just as she brought her knife down on his arm. The blade severed his hand clean off at the wrist. It, and the gun it was holding, fell to the floor.

Jackson stared, in utter horror, at the stump where his hand had once been. He glared at Tizzy and his expression turned to one of hatred.

Tizzy unleashed a flurry of attacks on Jackson, her blade slashing deep into his arms as he blocked each assault. However, each cut seemed to do nothing more than infuriate him further.

Tizzy took a half-step back, then lurched forward, plunging her knife into Jackson's stomach. With his left hand, he grabbed her by the collar of her tactical vest, lifted her clean off the ground and headbutted her. Tizzy's eyes rolled backward. He tossed her to the side and, before she even hit the ground, gave her a sidekick to the ribs. The impact was so hard, not only did it send Tizzy flying backward a good couple of yards, I swore I heard at least one of her resin-hardened ribs snap.

Not sure what I was hoping to achieve, I ran at Jackson and punched him square in the jaw. He turned and looked at me with contempt. He grabbed my face with his left hand and swung his right elbow at it. It was like being hit by a freight train. My whole body seemed to rattle. For an instant, everything went blank as I'm sure the NPC pod in my skull - and all the nanobots coursing through my body - let out a collective, "WTF?"

By the time my vision returned, I was already on the ground, my face only inches away from the open defibrillator case. Jackson reached down and grabbed me by the small of my back and hauled me up. As he did so, I reached down and turned the voltage dial on the machine to the max and hit the charge button. A red light blinked on, and a digital display read, CHARGING.

Jackson lifted me high into the air like a ragdoll. "You are worthless," he barked. "You don't deserve this gift."

"Gift?" I yelled back. "Are you kidding me? I've had socks for Christmas I've appreciated more than this. You can't take your stinking gift and shove it."

Tizzy screamed. She was back on her feet and charging once more at Jackson. He turned and hurled me at her. I hit her square in the chest and we collapsed in a heap on the floor.

Jackson pulled the knife from his gut and hurtled towards us. Each time one of his feet hit the floor, the entire walkway seemed to shake. He raised the blade and the massive muscles in his arm tensed. He stabbed down, throwing his full weight behind the attack. At the last second, Tizzy shoved me out of the way. Instead of the knife splitting my skull in two, it sunk deep into her ribcage.

She screamed furiously, struggling against Jackson. He smiled and pressed down harder. The remainder of the blade disappeared into her chest; the hilt compressed her ribs. I heard a squeaking sound as the tip of the knife exited her back and embedded itself into the wooden floor.

Jackson knelt astride Tizzy and smacked his huge hand onto her forehead, clasping it tightly. He turned to me and said coldly, "You think I could twist her head clean off with one hand?"

Underneath Jackson's palm, I heard Tizzy's muffled cry.

"No, you asshole," I roared. I rolled toward him but he slammed the stump of his right arm into my chest, sending me skidding backward toward the railing.

His eyes glistened insanely. Tizzy thrashed underneath him and gripped his wrist with both hands as he started to twist with his. I could hear sinew and muscle begin to tear.

"No!" I screamed. I climbed to my feet and made to leap on him. Before I could, I was deafened by the sounds of BLAM! BLAM! BLAM! BLAM!

Bullets blasted into Jackson's back. He instantly released his grip on Tizzy and twisted around to see where the attack was coming from. Three more shots hit his skull, knocking his head back like it was taking jabs from a heavyweight boxer.

Gunfire rang out one more time, its bullet going wild, before the unmistakable click sound of an empty clip.

Standing no more than six feet away was Sadie. In her outstretched hands, with smoke still wafting from its muzzle, was Jackson's pistol.

Jackson raised himself from the ground and felt his forehead. The skin where the bullets had hit was hanging in tatters. He pinched some of it between his thumb and forefinger and tore it free, admiring the fleshy chunks for a moment before casually tossing them to the ground.

"Damn, bitch," Jackson chirped. "I almost forgot about you.

You could have run right out of here. Blew that chance, didn't you?"

I glanced at Tizzy. Her head hung at a slightly odd angle, but she was not dead-dead. She was tugging frantically at the knife that pinned her to the floor.

As I went to help her, she hissed, "No. Get him!"

Easier said than done, lady.

Jackson marched towards Sadie, who was matching each of his steps forward with a step backward. The only difference was that hers were not sending tremors along the walkway.

"Now," he said without emotion, "I'm going to have to kill your zombie-hating ass."

I screamed and charged at him, just as he turned. With one mighty swipe of his right forearm, he swatted me away like a fly. I flew into the metal handrail, bouncing off it and falling on my back.

I shouted, struggling to my feet: "Dammit, Jackson, she doesn't hate zombies!"

He turned to me. "Huh?"

I stood up straight, my bones cracking back into position. "Sadie's not trying to destroy us - she's trying to free us."

Jackson scrunched up his face, causing more skin to peel away from his wrinkled brow.

"Jesus, don't you get it?" I said, and moved closer to him. "We're not assets to be owned. We may be dead, but we're still human beings. We still have feelings. We can still think. We still have dreams and hopes.

But as zombies, we're treated as nothing more than slaves."

Jackson bellowed in fury. "I am not a slave!" he screamed, pounding his chest with the stump of his right arm.

In a flash, he was on me again. He lifted me into the air with one hand and slammed me onto the ground. I lay there for a moment, chest pressed against the floor, my face arched up and looking in Tizzy's direction. She was yanking the knife in her chest back and forth, trying to pry it free.

Hurry up, Tizzy. I need your help.

Again I was hoisted into the air until my face was level with Jackson's.

"I am a patriot!" he roared and lobbed me at the railing. I hit it so hard, not only did the glass explode on impact, but the upper half of my body hung over the edge. I had to grab the metal to stop myself from crashing to the ground floor.

Jackson grabbed me by an ankle, spun me around and hurled me like a shotput. My body skipped across the floor, arms and legs flailing.

"I take orders because that's what Marines do," he shouted, "and I am a Marine."

I had barely come to a halt when Jackson pulled me off the ground by my shoulder and slammed my head against the metal handrail twice, buckling it. He tossed me backward, and I fell to the ground once more on my chest.

I lifted my head. Just a couple of inches from my nose was the defibrillator. The digital display read: CHARGED.

"I am no one's slave," Jackson said, more calmly. "I do what

I do for our country and for our future."

He grabbed me by my back and effortlessly lifted me off the ground, but not before I was able to do what I needed to do.

He dropped me to my feet and spun me around. He glared down at me, his eyes cold and dead. "And I am the future," he growled. "Clear?"

I feigned a cough and motioned down with my eyes. Jackson looked down at the two defibrillator paddles pressed against his massive chest. His gaze returned to me. I smiled broadly.

"Clear," I said with a wink, and pressed the buttons on the paddles. More than a thousand volts of electricity surged through Jackson's body. Propelled backward, he smashed into the railing where his spine snapped on impact. He slumped, his arms hanging over the metal bar.

From seemingly nowhere, Tizzy appeared by my side. She grabbed Jackson's head and yanked it back, exposing his throat.

"You're not the future," she said through clenched teeth. "You're fucking history."

With blinding speed, she brought her knife down on his neck, decapitating him with one clean stroke.

She held his lifeless head aloft for a moment, then let it fall to the floor below. She looked at me and said, "What?"

I sighed, "You couldn't let me have that one cool line, could you? No, you had to swoop in and say something even cooler."

"Oh, shut up," she scoffed as she grabbed her jaw with one

hand and her hair with the other and clicked her tilted head back into place.

She walked over to Sadie. "Are you ok?"

Sadie nodded and smiled weakly. "Thank you. Both of you."

Tizzy shrugged, "Yeah, well, let's see where that thanks gets us."

Sadie gently grabbed her arm and said, "I promise that, if I can get the Stockton bill overturned, I will find a way to free the zombies already created, so you can…live…in peace."

Tizzy nodded but seemed unconvinced. "Okay."

Sadie walked up to me and said, smiling: "You really are far more special than you give yourself credit for."

I shrugged, "I'm just a zombie."

She put her arms around me and hugged me tightly. "Not to me, you're not. Not to me."

I may have mentioned before that, as a zombie, you don't feel much. But I could feel that hug.

And boy, it felt good.

EPILOGUE

I lay on my plastic covered bunk in the Blue Room and stared up at the ceiling. The last twenty-four hours played over and over in my mind.

Sure, I had acquired a whole bunch of new cuts, holes and scrapes that would never heal. But somewhere out there, Sadie Mitchell was still alive.

I'm sure I had made some powerful enemies over the last day. But I had also made a couple of new friends. And, let's be honest, Sadie Mitchell is alive because of me. Not too shabby for a burger flipper, even if I say so myself.

Had I doomed all zombies by saving her? I wasn't sure. Maybe I had just saved a lot of people from the fate that Tizzy, Ash, Andrew and I, and every other zombie, have to endure. So perhaps that's not a bad thing.

I was reasonably sure that Emily Aiken would 'dismantle' me tomorrow and discover I was the zombie carrying the 'rogue' NPC pod. But I'm ok with that because Sadie Mitchell is alive. With any luck, she will bring down Batoltech Global.

I hope, if she succeeds, my friends will make it to The

Pastures. That would be nice.

Sure, I would have liked to keep on living, but boy, I've lived a lot since I died.

I remembered Erik. I let him out and he ran across my chest. Tomorrow, before I get summoned to Dr. Aiken for dismantling, I think I'll ask Ash to look after him. He'd like a pet, I guess.

For now, there was only one thing left to do. I closed my eyes and let the blue take on darker and darker hues until there was nothing but black. It did not take long for trees and a welcoming campfire to materialize.

"You did well, son," Mr. Marshmallow said as he stepped out of the shadows.

I smiled. "Y'know what? I think I did."

He nodded.

"You got any marshmallows for me?" I asked

He smiled, "I certainly do."

I sat on a log beside him, and he handed me a long straight stick with four oversized, fluffy marshmallows skewered on it, two pink and two white.

I started to toast them over the warm flames, not wanting this moment to end but knowing full well that it would. The topmost marshmallow ignited in orange flames and plumes of black smoke. I blew it out and stared at the charred, sugary treat. For a moment, I wondered why we subjected marshmallows to the flames. Weren't they perfect just the way they were?

"Emily is going to kill me tomorrow, isn't she?" I asked, not taking my focus off the marshmallows.

"I'm afraid so," said Mr. Marshmallow. "I've learned that you're the first scheduled for dismantling, followed by Andrew Johnson, Ashley King and Angelique Ortiz."

"Tizzy," I said softly. "Her friends call her Tizzy."

"Tizzy," Mr. Marshmallow repeated.

I really wished I wasn't holding a stick full of melting treats. They were the last thing in the world I wanted now.

"Well, maybe once they find out their missing NPC pod is in my head, they'll spare them," I said.

"I'm afraid not," he replied mournfully. "Batoltech will want to silence you all now."

Nuts! "Because we know too much?" I asked.

He nodded. "And not enough."

"What do you mean, 'not enough? And even if I knew more, what could I do about it now?"

"You can't give up, Marco," said Mr. Marshmallow. "You and your friends have to escape."

"How?" I said, throwing my stick into the flames and standing up. "We all have Top-Poppers in our heads, remember. The moment we take one step outside of the base, Dr. Aiken will be scooping up her NPC pod with a dustpan and brush. We can't escape. It's over."

Mr. Marshmallow stood up too, his treat-laden stick still firmly grasped in his hand.

He looked both sad and desperate. I placed my hands on his

shoulders. "I only came here to say goodbye and to say thanks for giving my death meaning."

"You still have a reason to live," he said.

"You mean, un-live?" I said with a slight smile. "Maybe, but not enough to keep going. I'm done, but now I think I'm ok with that."

"I'm sorry, my boy," Mr. Marshmallow said, "but I'm not."

He plucked a chunky pink marshmallow off the end of his stick, looked at it for a second. It was steaming, on the point of melting and turning into a gooey mass. He then did the last thing I ever expected him to do with it.

He stuck it straight in the middle of my forehead.

"Aargh!" I screamed. *Oh my God, it burns!* It did not feel like a toasted marshmallow, but rather a red hot lump of coal searing into my skull. I tore at it with my hands, but it was stuck fast.

Then it hit me like a freight train. My arms shot to my side and my entire body went rigid. Images flashed through my brain, like someone assailing it with a flipbook.

And there it was. Within a couple of seconds, my brain was flooding with the memories of my last tweleve hours as a living, breathing human being. What was once Dead Air was now burnt into my mind, in 4K ultra-high-definition, with Dolby surround sound.

Holy shit! I sat bolt-upright in my bunk. My mouth gaped open so wide that I barely noticed the fly that swooped in. Eric clambered up my neck, across my cheek, reached into my mouth with a claw and plucked it out.

He then ran back down my chest to munch on his winged snack.

I sat there, unable to move, as the enormity of what I had recalled, as vividly as if it had just happened, sank in.

My death was no accident. I was murdered. Murdered by Batoltech Global so they could fulfill some stupid quota.

Batoltech may have killed me once, but I'll be damned if I was going to let them kill me again.

I grabbed Eric and leaped off my bunk. "C'mon. We're getting the hell outta here."

THE END

...LIKE HELL IT IS!

About The Author

Martin John was born in Birmingham, England in 1972. At the age of 10, he moved to South Africa. There, he developed a love for campfire tales of ghosts and goblins but absolutely no love of camping.

He spent most of his childhood and teens with his head buried in books written by the masters of horror: Stephen King, Dean Koontz, and James Herbert. Although some children would have been mentally scarred by reading these books at such an early age, Martin's therapist assured him he was messed up long before then.

In his twenties, Martin flitted between countries, before finally settling down in England. There, he pursued a career in sales and business development, quickly becoming a slave to the luxuries this lifestyle afforded him… such as food, electricity, and on occasion, warm water.

Recently, he walked away from the rat-race to write full-time. The Chronicles of Marco the Zombie, is his second novel which combines his love of zombies, action, and comedy.

Martin lives in the countryside with his family and three dogs.

To discover more about Martin and his books, please visit his website:

www.hopesend.co.uk

You can also connect with him via the following social media:

www.instagram.com/authormartinjohn

www.twitter.com/martinjohn_e

Also by Martin John

Hope's End

Available in paperback, on Kindle and on Audible from Amazon.

Printed in Great Britain
by Amazon

61252001R00196